Just as the light disappeared, the kitchen door imploded, the heavy brass doorknob bouncing off the wall behind it. A black form came at me out of the darkness, blocking out all light behind it. Something caught me in the chest, threw me backward. I felt myself airborne for a split second. Then I slammed down on the kitchen floor and lay there helpless.

Then there was weight on me and I couldn't move my arms, an oppressive, awful heaviness that was crushing my chest, pinning me to the floor, with the world going blacker around me by the second.

In what I was afraid was going to be my last coherent thought, I realized I couldn't breathe anymore. . . .

By Steven Womack:

The Harry James Denton Books
DEAD FOLKS' BLUES*
TORCH TOWN BOOGIE*
WAY PAST DEAD*
CHAIN OF FOOLS*

The Jack Lynch Trilogy
MURPHY'S FAULT
SMASH CUT
THE SOFTWARE BOMB

*Published by Ballantine Books

DEAD FOLKS' BLUES

Steven Womack

BALLANTINE BOOKS • NEW YORK

Copyright © 1992 by Steven Womack

All rights reserved under International and Pan-American Copyright Conventions. Published in the United States by Ballantine Books, a division of Random House, Inc., New York, and simultaneously in Canada by Random House of Canada Limited, Toronto.

Library of Congress Catalog Card Number: 92-97042

ISBN 0-345-37674-9

Manufactured in the United States of America

First Edition: January 1993

15 14 13 12 11 10 9 8

Acknowledgments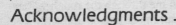

I'm deeply indebted to a number of people who helped me out with advice, guidance, inspiration, and an insider's point of view of many things I was unfamiliar with. Here are just a few:

Roberta Rosser, C.M.A.,—better known as Bert—of Nashville's T.E. Simpkins Forensic Science Center—better known as The Morgue—was tremendously helpful in explaining how autopsies are done, how coroners work, and the unique perspective one can't help but gain in that line of work.

Lieutenant Tommy Jacobs, head of the Metropolitan Nashville-Davidson County Police Department Homicide Division, gave me great insights into a homicide investigator's work, how witnesses are interrogated, and a sense of the unusual mindset that police work calls for. He also lent me a copy of Dr. LeMoyne Snyder's *Homicide Investigation*, which I'd advise against reading on a full stomach.

I know just enough about guns to get hurt by one. That's why when I needed to know more about weapons, I went to Ed Mason, owner of Madison, Tennessee's Gun Mart. He's smart, helpful, and heavily armed. He knows his work. I'm grateful to him.

Jeff and Amy Morland, of DB Locators, Inc., in Nashville (I'll let you guess what the *DB* stands for) gave me deep and wonderful insights into the business of skip tracing and the art of repo'ing. Writers make it up; these guys do it for real. In the midst of it all, Amy finds time to write. And well, at that.

As always, Jeris Bragan and Woody Eargle, two long-time attendees of my writing workshop at the Tennessee State Penitentiary, contributed more than I can explain here. Their support and friendship means a lot.

Carole Abel, my agent, mother-confessor, and confidante, has patiently and serenely seen me through the rough waters of publishing. In fact, she's kept me in this business the last few years. The jury's still out on whether this is a boon to humanity, but *I'm* grateful as hell.

Joe Blades, whose editorial guidance and friendship is a wonderful gift, continues to amaze me. It's hard to get used to an editor who finds time to be a good friend as well as an inspired editor. I'm having a great time making the adjustment, though.

Jean Yarbrough, my mother-in-law, a voracious reader and super copy editor, was understanding enough (or foolish enough, depending on one's perspective) to let her daughter marry a writer. She helped me a lot in preparing this manuscript. You'll hear no mother-in-law jokes in this house.

My wife, Dr. Cathryn Yarbrough, insisted on editing this manuscript while awaiting treatment for mugging injuries in the Vanderbilt Hospital emergency room. Talk about grit. See why I married this woman? At the risk of repeating myself, all writers should fall in love with a psychologist. After that, they should marry one.

Finally, I'm grateful for all the things that make Nashville such a fascinating place to live. No kidding. It's a writer's gold mine.

DEAD FOLKS'
BLUES

Chapter 1

All right, I'll tell you. But you have to promise not to laugh, okay? I'm a private investigator. In Nashville, Tennessee.

Stop snickering.

No, I do not wear a trench coat, or a double-breasted suit, or a homburg. I don't smoke cigarettes or drink straight Scotch out of the desk drawer in my office, and I don't smack women around.

These days, they hit back. Hard.

Neither do I sing country music, nor write country music, nor even listen to country music. My tastes run to jazz, and I did not just fall off the turnip truck. I was born here, but I went to school in Boston, spent my junior year abroad in France, and wear shoes almost every day. I can lay on a country accent as thick as molasses on a frosty morning, if I have to. But I can also throw in enough Newport, Rhode Island, to make Tom Wicker sound like a hick.

I can hear you now: *But a private detective, in Nashville, Tennessee? Give me a break. . . .*

Well, let me tell you, friend, we've got a million people in this city now. And any city that'll elect as mayor a guy who plays harmonica on *Donahue* and explains how it's okay for him to be engaged to his fourth wife while still married to his third, is a city that's got character. I've been to some interesting and corrupt locales in my time: New Orleans, New York City, all of Texas. And believe me, they've got nothing on this place.

After all, how many cities elect a sheriff named Fate, a

man who winds up in a federal penitentiary for corruption and gets visits from his buddy Waylon Jennings? Speaking of sheriffs, I think this state holds the national record for the most ex-sheriffs now doing time behind bars.

Freaking Greek tragedy, that's what it is. I love this city. It cracks me up.

So I'm a detective. I didn't say I was a competent detective. I didn't even say I'd been doing it very long. In fact, I just opened my office about two months ago, a couple of weeks after I got fired from the paper.

I was a newspaper reporter, and I like to think I was a good one. In fact, I was too good. The publisher of the newspaper had a brother who was a lobbyist, and he got involved with this group of *amusement* operators; you know, guys who run video game parlors and stuff like that. These operators—to coin a phrase—had a pretty strong lobby working to pass a law that allowed video poker machines to pay off. I mean, it's not like pinball machines and video games hadn't been paying off for years anyway. It's just that these guys were trying to get it legal so they could stop paying protection money to the small-town cops.

Anyway, the publisher's brother was handing out hundred dollar bills like business cards on Legislative Plaza. Most people knew that it was standard operating procedure on the Hill. But this guy started getting cocky, because his brother owned the local paper and they were all well-connected. Blatant as hell he was, so I wrote a story about his contributions that were papering the legislative halls in green.

I knew the city editor would never sanction the story, but I decided to throw it in the queue just to get a rise out of the desk. Only problem was, we had this new guy on the night staff. We'd hired him from Oklahoma, and he really didn't know his way around yet. He released the story.

The exposé ran page one, below the fold.

Nobody was more surprised than I was. The early edition hit the newsstand, and the publisher hit the ceiling. Went completely ballistic. He had the story pulled and loose copies collected from the newsstands.

By noon, the story was gone and so was I.

So here I am, thirty-five years old, living from paycheck to paycheck, and with a name that's, professionally speaking, Mud. But what the hell, I was getting bored anyway. I remembered reading somewhere that in this state the only prerequisite for a detective's license is a background check. I had a hard time believing it was that slack, so I called a buddy in the D.A.'s office. He said the law was changing in January; after the first of the year, you'd actually have to have credentials to be licensed.

So with six weeks to spare, I rushed downtown, paid my $75.00, had my picture taken, passed a quick computer check, and became a private investigator.

I sunk the last of my meager savings into setting up an office down on Seventh Avenue, near Church Street, in a dumpy building nestled between a tiny restaurant and a three-story parking lot. I was on the top floor, one room only, with a dirty, greasy window that looked out on an alley strewn with broken bottles of Night Train and Wild Irish Rose. But it was only $200.00 a month, utilities included. Factor in a hundred bucks or so to get the phone started up, a couple hundred for stationery and business cards, and another hundred for an old wooden desk and a filing cabinet, and voilà: instant office.

I was almost proud that day, when the sign painter finished stenciling HARRY JAMES DENTON—PRIVATE INVESTIGATIONS on my door. I just hope to hell my parents don't find out.

I figured my skills as a reporter would easily transfer to my new field, and I hoped my hanging around the courthouse for the better part of ten years would get me jobs.

Wrong.

I went from instant office to instant poverty. I called every lawyer I knew, every politician, every well-connected crony I could find.

I couldn't get arrested.

A month after I opened up, I had to give up my expensive apartment in Green Hills and move across the river to East Nashville, to the funky part of town, to the neighborhood where Archie Bunker would've lived if he'd been born in Music City and driven a truck for a living. I found a little old retired lady who'd had her attic converted into an apartment. She knocked ten bucks a month off the rent if I'd cut the grass in the summertime. I took it.

Finally, I called Lonnie Smith, a buddy I'd met back when I was doing a story about repo men. Lonnie came to Nashville to make it big in the Grand Ole Opry and wound up repossessing cars. He's been doing it about twenty years now. And he hates the movie *Repo Man*.

"That picture sucked," he said, in his rapid-fire, high-pitched voice. "Repo'ing ain't nothing like that. Most of the time the job is downright boring."

He was trying to talk me into going to work for him, repossessing cars and tracking down deadbeats.

"Business's been good lately," he peppered. "And it ain't anywhere near as dangerous as people think. I've repossessed ten, maybe fifteen thousand cars in my life. And I only been beat up about a dozen times."

Thanks, Lonnie. I'm real reassured.

Times being what they were, though, I took the job. Our first gig together was grabbing some guy's pickup out by the lake. We drove out I-40, got off at Stewart's Ferry Pike, and cut left to drive across Percy Priest Dam. It was a cold day, windy, one of the last before the summer's heat settled in. In this part of the country, you don't get much spring; one day you're freezing, the next you're sweating. The whitecaps on the lake jumped, as sharp and white as teeth. We drove on a mile or so past the lake and pulled into an apartment complex.

"I know the guy lives here, but I don't know which apartment."

"So let's ask at the office," I offered.

Lonnie turned to me in the cab of his dirty pickup and grinned. "How long you been in the real world?"

"They won't tell you, huh?"

"Violation of privacy. But there're ways."

We walked into the office where a creamy redhead in a flowered dress sat behind a typewriter.

"Excuse me, ma'am," Lonnie drawled, switching into his good-ole-boy voice. Nobody would ever have guessed Lonnie'd moved down here from Brooklyn. "But I lost my buddy, Joey Richards. I was over here helping him move in a month or so ago, and I know it was over this way—" Lonnie pointed off in some vague direction past her head. "But for the life of me, darlin', I can't remember which building it was. Can you help me here?"

She eyed us cautiously. Lonnie'd warned me this might be dirty work, so I was in an old flannel shirt and jeans. Red stared at us a second, then decided we were too dumb to be anything but what we looked like.

"I'm not really supposed to give out that information," she said.

"Aw, Joey ain't gonna mind. He's waiting for us right now. We're gonna go fishing."

Lonnie was as slick as Elvis's pomade. Red didn't have a chance. She pulled a computer printout off her desk and scanned the list.

"Okay, he's down in C Building. Apartment nine."

Lonnie grinned at her. She smiled back, hoping, I guess, that he wasn't going to hit on her or anything.

"First we find his truck and block it in," Lonnie explained back out in the cold wind, "then we knock on his door. See if he'll give us the keys."

"You think he might do that?"

"Sometimes they do. People usually know when they're about to get repo'd. Hell, the finance companies give 'em every chance they can. What the hell's a finance company going to do with a bunch of repossessed cars? They don't want vehicles; they want their money. Yeah," Lonnie continued, spitting out the left side of his mouth, "he knows we're coming."

I climbed back in the cab of Lonnie's truck and picked up the Xeroxed paperwork. Guy had an '84 Ford Ranger, red, license number DTB 042. "So we just drive around, huh?"

"Yeah, I called the warehouse where the guy works. Today's his day off. He ought to be here somewhere."

We cruised the parking lot slowly. There was no red Ford pickup in front of C Building.

"Maybe the guy's not here," I said.

"Nah, he's here. Sucker knows we're after him. He's got the truck hid somewhere."

We drove on around. In the back of the complex, there was an area roped off for people to park boats and trailers, to keep them out of the way of the regular traffic. Behind that parking area, partially up on the grass, sat a red Ford Ranger backed in, nose out, so you couldn't see the license plate.

"Boogie-woogie," Lonnie sang. My heart started beating faster. Lonnie wheeled his three-quarter ton Chevy around the boats, then pulled up in front of the Ranger and parked T-bone style. The woods were behind the truck, us in front.

Lonnie hopped out on his side and went around to the back of the Ford.

"Got him," he said. "Plates check out."

I tried the door to the truck. "Locked."

"Okay," Lonnie instructed, "let's go knock on the guy's door."

We trotted around the complex to C Building and up a flight. Lonnie turned to me, grinned, and knocked on the door three times.

We heard a shuffling inside, and the low drone of a television. But no answer to our knock. Lonnie pounded on the door again, this time a little harder.

"Mr. Richards, can we talk to you, sir?" he shouted.

There was only silence from inside, not even the television now.

"Mr. Richards," Lonnie called, banging the door one last time.

"What do we do now?" I asked. Lonnie stood there a moment, glaring at the door.

"Guy wants to be an asshole, 'sokay by me. Let's go get his truck."

"You going to hot wire it?"

Lonnie grinned at me again. "You are new at this. Nobody hot wires cars, anymore, son. It's too much trouble. Besides, you damage a repo'd car, you gotta pay for it. If I ain't got a key what fits it, we'll just call a wrecker."

We walked back to the trucks. Lonnie reached under the seat and extracted a ring of keys as big around as a Frisbee. Then he pulled out a thin hacksaw blade with a notch cut in one end. I'd never seen anybody slim jim a car open before. I watched in admiration as Lonnie slipped the blade inside the door, past the rotting black-rubber seal, and swished it around for a couple of seconds. Then he seemed to latch on to something, pull just a hair, and I saw the door lock inside the cab of the Ranger pop up.

"Damn, man," I said, "I'm impressed."

Lonnie smiled. "Nothing to it. Beats punching a time clock."

He climbed inside the truck and fiddled with the keys, trying to find the match for the Ranger's ignition lock. I was beginning to think maybe this car repossessing stuff wasn't too shabby a way to make a living . . . when I heard footsteps pounding up the asphalt behind us.

I turned just as this balding, unshaved guy in a T-shirt, belly hanging over his belt like a sack of flour, came charging straight at us with an ax handle raised over his head. My eyes popped wide open as the guy let out a lunatic banshee scream.

"Lonnie!" I yelled. Lonnie glanced up just as Fatty brought down the ax handle on the hood of the Chevy. The three-quarter ton was built like a tank and beat all to hell anyway, so it's not like it did any actual damage to it. But it pissed Lonnie off real bad.

"Hey!" he yelled. "Cut that out!"

I was away from the guy, both trucks between us. And I was determined to keep it that way. He was swinging his ax handle like a Louisville slugger, connecting with anything that got in his way. Lonnie hopped down from the Ranger and ran around in front of the guy, then stopped just beyond swinging range.

"Put it down, fella," he warned. "We have to call the cops out here, you're going to spend a weekend in jail."

Fatty growled. I mean, really growled, like a dog or something, then raised the handle over his head and came straight at Lonnie like a bull.

Lonnie sidestepped him, ducked, and stuck out a leg. The guy caught the instep of Lonnie's right foot with his right ankle and lost his footing. The ax handle flailed helplessly in midair before the guy completely lost his balance, slipped over a concrete curb, and wound up facedown in the dirt.

Lonnie was over him in a second, yanking the guy's face up by a handful of hair. Then he jerked a small aerosol can out of his rear pocket and sprayed the guy's face. Liberally. Next thing you know, the guy's choking and heaving and blowing chunks all over the side of his pickup.

"Mace?" I asked, as Lonnie walked around to the front of the Chevy.

"That guy fuck up my truck?" he demanded. I stepped around front next to him.

"Looks like he dinged the hood a few times," I commented. "Didn't get the headlights, though. You going to swear out a warrant?"

Lonnie looked over at Fatty, who by now was up on all fours, gasping for breath, the worst of his convulsions passing.

"The hell with it," Lonnie spat. "It'll take too long for Metro to get here. I ain't got the time. Let's go."

Lonnie tossed me the keys to the Chevy. I started the motor, then sat in the cab with the truck idling until Lonnie got the Ford running. Then I pulled out of his way and let him go first. I trailed him to make sure our newfound friend didn't try anything else. As we turned left around one of the apartment buildings, I checked in the rearview mirror. Fatty was pulling himself up to his feet now, shaking, trying to get his balance back.

I felt sorry for the guy. If you're a hot-shot land developer and you file bankruptcy owing the banks a couple hundred million, you get your picture in the paper. But fall behind on a two-hundred-a-month loan payment, then two goons come steal your truck and spray Mace all over you on your day off. I began to wonder if I could get my job at the paper back.

Chapter 2

Lonnie was giving me forty bucks a car on repo work, and we were getting in six to ten a week. So I was making it, barely. But I was having a good time with my new life. I unloaded the expensive Honda with the four-hundred-a-month car note and bought a repo'd '85 Escort from a finance company. What the hell; it wasn't pretty, but it ran. And it was paid for.

I also started skip tracing for Lonnie, using the phone in my office. Skip tracing's not quite as risky, but it's about as intense. Somebody falls behind on a loan payment, the bank sends them a letter, and it gets returned NOT AT THIS ADDRESS. So some silly-assed bank officer calls the number in the file folder and explains that he's trying to locate the person who's fallen behind in his payments.

They usually don't have much luck, which should come as no surprise. Not many people are willing to cooperate with a bank on the trail of a deadbeat. And the suits at the bank, being all but completely bereft of imagination, don't know what else to do, so they turn the account over to a skip tracer.

Lonnie's got a terminal in his office that runs off credit reports. It's scary the stuff that comes in off these computers. Nobody has any secrets these days. Frightening. Anyway, Lonnie runs a credit bureau report, sticks it in a file with the bank's paperwork, then hands it over to me. I get twenty bucks for each verified address and phone number, with an extra five thrown in for verifying employment. It was pretty rough at first, but after a few days' practice, I got to where I

10

could scam about six or eight a day, when I'd make myself
work at it.

A couple months go by, and things are cruising along. I
still haven't got a case yet, but I'm bringing in a few bucks
now and then subcontracting for Lonnie. The two guys down
the hall are songwriters and publishers: Slim and Ray. They
told me their last names, but I've never been able to remember them. They rent another one-room office and write songs
all day and listen to tapes from other starving songwriters. I
don't really know how it all works; it just seems like everybody I've ever met in the music business is hungry. Like the
old joke you hear down on Music Row: Know what they call
a Nashville musician without a girlfriend? Homeless.

Occasionally, at the end of the day, I'll stop by Slim and
Ray's office and have a beer with them. Cocktail hour for
these two starts around four. The singing gets a little louder.
People drop by with guitars. The place turns into a regular
little party, and they're playing all this moaning and groaning, crying in your beer stuff. But some of it's pretty good,
and I can't really knock it.

One Wednesday afternoon, I was sitting in my office with
a stack of folders in front of me. I opened the top one; a
Linda Wolford at 2545 Forest Avenue had defaulted on an
unsecured personal note. The bank couldn't even go after
this lady's car. They sent her a half-dozen notices. All were
returned. Somebody from the bank called. A female voice
claiming to be a roommate said Linda Wolford moved away.
Sorry, no forwarding address. No phone number.

I figure if I call this lady up and say "Hey, I need to verify
your identity and address so the bank can nail your ass," I'm
probably not going to get very far. I decided to run the UPS
scam on her, then picked up the phone and dialed the number.

"Hello."

"Yeah, I'm trying to reach Linda Wolford at 2454 Forest
Drive."

"Ugh, who wants to know?"

"This is Carter over at UPS Customer Service. We had a

package to deliver for a Ms. Wolford that came back as undeliverable. We're just trying to find the right address so we don't have to send the package back.''

''What's in the package?''

''I don't know that, ma'am, but it's insured for two hundred dollars and it's prepaid, so you don't owe anything on it. Must be a gift or something.''

''And what address was that?''

''2454 Forest Drive, ma'am.''

You usually get a chuckle or a sigh of anticipation at this point. This time, it came right on schedule.

''Oh, that's it, Mr. Carter. I'm Linda Wolford, but my address is 2545 Forest Drive.''

''I'm grinning now.'' *Bang, got her.* ''Let me see, you're Linda Wolford at 2545 Forest Drive, correct?''

''Yes, sir.''

''Great, Ms. Wolford. Sorry for the inconvenience. You'll be hearing from us in a few days.'' *Yeah, and give my regards to the bankruptcy judge.*

''Thanks for going to the trouble to find me.''

''All part of the service, ma'am. All part of the service.''

So after twelve years of private school and four years of private university, I'm making a living by lying to people. Which puts me up there with some of the top biz school graduates in the country.

For a guy who got canned and had to move into a dumpy little apartment in a neighborhood filled with old Buicks on concrete blocks in the front yards, I'm doing okay. I'm having a swell time. I'm getting by. I'm nailing deadbeats. Life is sweet.

I close the folder in front of me, then look up from my desk just as the door opens. Rachel Fletcher is standing in my doorway.

Damn.

She was Rachel Todd when I first met her, back when we were undergraduates at Boston U. in the Seventies. Maybe it's my own dysfunction, but spending my adolescence at a boy's school kind of skewed my early perceptions of women. In fact, when I met this woman freshman year, at some dumb mixer on campus, it was like being run over by a truck, just as powerful and marginally less painful. Her blond hair was longer then, her face a little fuller, with the last traces of teenage baby fat still hanging on. But she was gorgeous, drop-dead-leave-your-tongue-in-the-dirt gorgeous. And somehow I got her to date me. A couple of weeks later, I got her to sleep with me, only we didn't sleep very much. Three years later, she left me and married some dweeb named Fletcher, a rich prick who went on to become a doctor.

What the hell! I made peace with it a long time ago. So unlike some other relationships I've wound up in, I don't carry too much baggage from this one. But seeing her looking down on me that day was, for a long moment, akin to getting hit by that truck again.

She opened the door without knocking. I guess she figured she'd be walking in on a secretary and a waiting room and all the other normal business fixtures. She looked surprised to see me, as if she wasn't really sure I was who she thought I was. Then she turned and stared at the black lettering on the frosted glass. She shook her head almost imperceptibly, then stepped in, closing the door behind her.

"Hi, Harry. How've you been?"

By this time, I was standing behind my desk without even realizing I'd gotten up. I looked her over, trying not to gape. You have to understand, I hadn't exactly—well, I think the euphemism is *been*—with anybody in quite some time. Kind of a long dry spell, you see, but at least partly by choice. So when I found myself alone in a closed office with a lovely blonde, and not just any lovely blonde, damn it, but *this* blonde, I had to remember not to drool out loud. And remembering she was a natural blonde didn't help.

"Hi, Rachel," I said, hoping like hell my voice held up. "How are you?"

"I'm fine, Harry. How are you?"

I stood there a second, awkward and tight, then finally managed to activate my tongue.

"Nervous, actually. You're the last person I expected to walk into my office."

"Don't be nervous, Harry. I'm not a process server."

"Good. I got nothing worth suing for. Have a seat."

She was dressed in a black silk blouse, white pants with a sheen bright enough to hurt your eyes and a crease sharp enough to pick your teeth with. I hoped my chair wouldn't get her dirty. She'd lost the weight in her face, leaving the outline of high cheekbones visible just underneath her skin. I always suspected there was great bone structure buried there someplace. Her skin was as alabaster as always, as clear as unpolluted snow. Her hands were thinner as well, and the soft blue of her veins gave a tinge of color to them.

Or maybe it was because they were knotted tighter than a dick's hatband. Whatever the hell a dick's hatband is; I've been hearing that expression for years now and it's always struck me as just this side of vulgar. In any case, Rachel Fletcher's face may have been calm and smiling, but her hands were knotted together like a rugby scrum.

"Can I get you anything? Coffee? There's a soda machine down the hall."

"No, thanks, Harry. I'm fine." Her hands continued squirming. She noticed me looking, then self-consciously pulled them apart and uncomfortably put one on each arm-rest of the chair. It was as if her arms had become two foreign objects hanging off her, and she didn't know what to do with them.

"It's good to see you, Harry. How long's it been now?"

I thought back. "Maybe ten years ago. The benefit for Children's Hospital."

"That's right. What happened to that woman you were seeing then? The tall one, with the dark hair pulled back tight."

Who was that? I thought. *Was that—* "Oh, yeah, that was before I got married. Debbie, I think her name was. Long time ago."

"Right," she said.

"How about you, Rachel? You and what's-his-name still—?"

"Conrad," she said, "and yes, we're still married. In name, anyway."

Her focus dropped to the floor. I decided to sit and wait for her to continue. Finally, she did. "Harry, I know things haven't always been that easy for us."

"No worries." I grinned at her as I spoke. "I've always prided myself on being a gracious loser."

She looked up quickly. "You weren't a loser, Harry. You've never been a loser. I never thought you were." Her head drifted to the right, her sadness a weight pulling her down. "I've just made some mistakes in my life."

I suddenly felt sorry for her, the first time in years I'd felt anything at all for her. And I was surprised to see it was that. But there was something about her, despite the great looks, the obvious wealth and health, and all the other accoutrements, that was downright pitiable. I wanted to reach across the desk and touch her, but knew that was probably the worst thing I could do.

"What is it, Rachel? Why are you here?"

She opened her bag, a small silver clutch, and withdrew a pack of cigarettes, the long, skinny kind with blue and red flowers intertwined on the paper. Her hand shook as she took out a disposable butane lighter in a gold case and lit the cigarette.

"It's Connie," she began, after taking a good long pull on the smoke. "He's gotten himself into some trouble. I'm terribly worried about him."

"When'd you start those?" I gathered from her glare that she considered the question inappropriate.

"What kind of trouble?" I asked, trying to extricate myself.

She hesitated, self-consciously lifting her hand to take another drag off the cigarette. "He's been gambling again. Heavily, I'm afraid. Apparently he's into somebody for a lot of money. He's getting threatening phone calls, letters."

I fought the urge to smile. I remembered Dr. Conrad

Fletcher as a smug, conceited, privileged jerk. Somehow, seeing him up to his keister in bookie reptiles was at the very least amusing, at the very most downright pleasurable.

"I tried to call you at the paper," she continued. "Just to see if you had any advice. They told me you were no longer employed there."

"Diplomats. Actually, Rachel, I was fired. Booted out on my ass."

"I'm sorry."

"I'm not."

"Anyway, someone on the desk gave me your phone number and address. I had no idea you'd become a—"

"Private investigator?" I said, grinning. "Yeah, sounds a little goofy to me, too."

Rachel smiled back, the first real one she'd cracked since she sat down. "I decided to come see you in a professional capacity, rather than just an old friend asking for advice."

"What kind of letters and phone calls are we talking about here?"

She opened up the purse again, took out a torn-open envelope. Cheap paper, available at any drugstore, electric typewriter, no return address, mailed from a downtown zip code. The note inside read:

Fletcher:
Your account is seriously overdue. You're going to settle up within 24 hours or we're going to turn you over to our collections staff. You won't find that very pleasant.

Simple, straightforward, to the point. I'd written some articles in my time that had generated unhappy letters, a few of them threatening. The rule around the newspaper office was that the ones that ranted and raved and threatened to cut your gonads off were the ones you could laugh about over a beer. The calm, serious, understated ones were the ones you kept and reread over and over in your dreams, the ones that make you wake up in a cold sweat.

This one was definitely a keeper.

"The letter came in yesterday's mail. I opened it by accident; Connie gets furious when I open his mail, but I just wasn't paying attention."

"Have you shown it to him?"

Her eyes rolled. "Oh, God, no. He'd throw a fit. He's got a terrible temper, you know."

"And the phone calls?"

"Just two. One about a week ago. One this morning."

"What did they say?"

"The first time, a voice asked to speak to Connie, and he wasn't home. I asked who it was. The man wouldn't say. He just hung up. The second time was yesterday. Same voice. He asked to speak to Connie, and when I said he wasn't home, the man asked if Connie had gotten the letter."

"What'd you do?"

"I panicked, I guess. I asked who it was and he said 'never mind,' that Dr. Fletcher would know who he was and he'd goddamn better take the note seriously."

She looked me directly in the eyes, the clear blue of hers shimmering in my office light. "That's when I started looking for you."

I shifted uneasily in the chair. I wasn't at all sure this was something I wanted to take on. To begin with, I didn't much care for the s.o.b., and on top of that, I had a feeling that if I started getting involved with Rachel Fletcher again, I might want to get involved with Rachel Fletcher again.

The office suddenly seemed very stuffy. "Have you talked to Conrad about this? Does he know you're here?"

"Heavens, no. If he did, he'd blow a fuse. Things haven't been going so well with us these past few years. What with his work and all. We don't spend much time with each other. And when he's not working, he's always off somewhere else. Gambling, apparently."

"This isn't an easy question, Rachel, but I've got to ask it. Is there another woman in here anywhere?"

She looked as if her face had just gone numb and she was afraid to raise her hand to her cheek, afraid she wouldn't be able to feel anything, afraid she wouldn't be there anymore.

"I don't think so," she whispered. "I don't know."

"So what do you want me to do, Rachel?"

She hesitated, fumbling with her still-lit cigarette butt, wondering what to do with it.

"Just mash it on the floor," I suggested. "I'm afraid I don't have an ashtray. Sorry."

She dropped the cigarette. I watched her right knee swivel back and forth as she ground the butt out.

"Could you find out who he owes the money to? And how much?" There was a pleading tone to her voice, a tone more vulnerable than any I'd heard out of her. "Whatever it is, I'll see that it's paid. I don't want anything to happen to him."

"I may have to talk to Conrad," I said.

"No, please. At least don't tell him we've spoken. If you have to talk to him, make it look like some other reason. I can't have him finding out that I know what's going on with him."

"If he truly has a gambling problem, he's going to need some help."

"I'll deal with that after this is over. For now, I just don't want him to get hurt. Please help me get through this, Harry. Then we'll work on getting Connie straightened out."

"You're going to protect him, right? You're going to fix things for him. The twelve-steppers would call you the Enabler."

She flared. "I'm hiring you in a professional capacity, Harry, but not as a therapist. That's something else we can deal with when the time's right. For now, do you want to help or not?"

"Rachel, I—"

"Of course, I'm going to pay your standard rate." She reached into her purse again, this time drawing forth an expensive leather wallet with some kind of designer medallion on it. I didn't recognize the brand; out of my league. She pulled out a fanfold of hundred dollar bills.

"Rachel, that's not—"

"Don't be silly. Are you going to tell me you can afford to work for free? What's your rate?"

I'll give her this much; she'd become a lot tougher since we used to date in college. I guess life with a doctor'll do that to you.

"Two-fifty a day, plus expenses."

She counted off a stack of green, leafy bills. "Here's enough for a week, with an extra fifty thrown in to cover extras. We'll settle up when you find out who these bastards are."

"Rachel, are you sure you wouldn't be better off going to the police?"

She leaned across the desk and dropped the money on my desk calendar. Then she stood up, a hardness in her face that I hadn't seen before.

"I want this taken care of. Discreetly. And I want you to do it. Do we have a deal?"

I raised my head and eyed her, my lips tightening involuntarily, my mouth suddenly dry.

I never could say no to her.

Chapter 3

Then there was the money. There's always the money, and there never seems to be enough since I said goodbye to the paper. Having the chance to bank five days' worth of fees was something that, from a strictly business sense, I couldn't pass up.

Of course, if I had any business sense in the first place, I wouldn't be caught in this squeeze. After Rachel left my office, I pocketed the $1,300.00 and walked down Seventh Avenue to the parking garage where I kept the Ford. I was a month behind on my contract and would've given the space up, but parking in downtown Nashville is about like parking in downtown Manhattan. Believe me, I've tried both.

I gave the attendant one of the hundreds, then waited while he brought me my receipt and change. Now I was not only current, I was a month ahead. And if I wasn't careful, I was going to wind up paying more to park the Ford than I paid for the car itself.

I checked my watch as I pulled out into the line of cars moving, at four miles an hour, toward Broadway. I had just enough time to swing by the bank and deposit the other twelve hundred before my four o'clock racquetball game with Walter. Maybe I should have plunged immediately into Rachel's case, but I needed a few hours to figure out a game plan. Her clock could start running tomorrow.

Walter Quinlan and I have known each other since we both went to the same boarding school over twenty years ago. We're buddies in the way that men who've known each other a long time are buddies, but I can't say that we've ever been really close. For one thing, Walter's an attorney, and I was a newspaper reporter, two occupations not exactly designed to foster trust and intimacy between individuals.

But we play racquetball once a week and occasionally grab lunch together downtown when he's not in court. Beyond that, we rarely see each other. Walter runs in different circles. While my circle of friends is gravitating more and more toward people who sit on their porches and drink beer in their boxer shorts, Walter's runs toward the Belle Meade types who spend more in tennis club fees than most people pay in income taxes.

Walter's friends drive BMWs and Jaguars. Mine tune up their Dodges in the front yard.

Walter was already in the court warming up when I opened the heavy wooden door and slipped in five minutes late. Walter's one of those people who always look like they just had their hair cut. He wears workout clothes that cost as much as the last suit I bought, and he regularly beats the stew out of me with a $200.00 Ektelon racquet (an instrument I would personally like to drop in a trash compactor). The guy's a holdover yuppie, up for partner this year at the law firm of Potter & Bell. He was divorced last year from some Belle Meade socialite with an IQ of 135 and nothing to do with it.

I pushed the door shut behind me. "Hey, guy, what's happening?"

Walter fired one from the serve line. It hit the wall maybe an inch off the floor and came screaming out in a black streak. Walter's killer serve had been the death of me more than once. I wondered why I kept playing with him. More than anything else in the world, Walter Quinlan hated to lose. On the rare occasions when I beat him, he did not take it well.

"You're late," he said.

"Traffic's terrible. Couldn't find a parking space."

"If you'd pay for a space in the lot," he said, bouncing another black ball off the floor, "you wouldn't have that trouble."

"I already pay for one parking space a month," I said, my voice echoing off the cavernous walls of the racquetball court. "I can't afford another."

I leaned against the wall, hands out, racquet dangling from my right wrist, and did calf stretches. Walter walked over, rested his back against the wall, then slid down in a squat.

"I got turned down for partner last Friday," he said quietly.

It took a moment for his words to penetrate. I pushed myself off the wall and sank, cross-legged, to the floor in front of him.

"Get the hell out of here," I said, aghast.

Walter snickered. "That's basically what they said."

"What the—? Did they give you a reason?"

His eyes darted back and forth. They were darker, filled with more intensity than I'd ever seen before. There were even traces of purplish circles under his eye sockets, marring an otherwise too-perfect preppie face.

"They never give a reason. In fact, they didn't actually tell me I wasn't going to make the cut. It's my year, though, and when the list came out, I wasn't on it.

"It's weird, man," he continued after a moment. "It's like nobody'll discuss it. And there's no appeal. Six years I spent working for these guys."

"What are you going to do?"

"Well, I can stay on as an associate another year or two. It's not as if they actually lock you out of the office. I'll need to get out as quickly as possible, though. Move on to something else."

"Do you have any idea why they passed you over?" I wanted to put my hand on his shoulder or something, but guys don't do that stuff.

He rubbed his hands on his forehead. "I've got the sneakiest little suspicion it's related to my divorcing Madelyn. Her father's in the Belle Meade Country Club with Sam Potter. They golf together."

"But, man, I thought the divorce was her idea."

"It was," he sighed, "but only after she found out I was

boinking one of her girlfriends. What was I supposed to do, though? Bitch hit on me. It wasn't my fault. I didn't do anything."

Yeah, I thought, *nothing but not keep it in your pants*.

"Aw, jeez, buddy, I'm really sorry. I know how tough it is, man. Listen, we don't have to be here. You can't be in the mood for this today. Why don't we go get a beer?"

He tapped his racquet on the hard wooden floor. "Actually, I'm kind of up for this. Want to go for it?"

I dropped my head down, stared at the floor between my legs. "Oh, hell. I think I'm in trouble today."

I looked up to see Walter's glistening white teeth, as regular as the kernels on an ear of corn, lined up behind a malicious smile.

"I'll give you first serve," he said.

It was the only way I'd have a chance at him, the killer frame of mind he was in. He was tense, poised on the balls of his feet. Taking up position behind me, he danced around gingerly as if I was going to turn around and open up on him with a shotgun—and he wanted to be sure he could get out of the way. A lock of hair dropped down on his forehead, centered perfectly above his eyes. Even in sweaty disarray, this guy looked like something out of *GQ*.

I bounced the ball a few times, trying to get my timing right. Then I cocked my arm and let one fly. It wasn't a bad serve, at least not for me, but I should have opened with a lob instead of a power serve. Walter was locked and loaded in the pissed-off position, just waiting for me to zing one by him.

He jumped to his right, sent the ball flying to the upper-left-hand corner. It took a slow bounce off the roof, then came straight down at me. There was no time to prepare; I raised my racquet and let the ball bounce off it. It landed fair, then dribbled back off the floor. Walter was there as fast as a rat, his racquet under the ball, flipping it expertly off the corner away from me. I lunged for it and wound up on the floor. The ball bounced lazily past me.

"Oh, hell," I said again, pulling myself up.

I didn't score a point for the next twenty minutes. I did manage to return a few serves, a couple of times even got into a volley, but that's about all. Walter usually beat me, but this time he was slaughtering me. He played not with skill, but with a controlled fury, as if each shot off his racquet was a bullet aimed at the head of one of the suits who'd turned him down.

I was sweating like a linebacker in a summer workout, my gray YMCA sweatshirt several shades darker and heavier. The score was now 12–3 in the second game. I'd finally figured out that the only chance I had was to fake power serves and then give him slow lobs off the ceiling. The truth was, I was too tired to fire missiles at him anyway.

My serve went high, but I must have laid some heavy English on it, because it went off the back wall, zipped crazily to my right, onto the side wall, and then back toward the front wall. Walter ran like hell for it, but he was slightly off target and too far back. His racquet went across his body in a blur, whooshing as it missed its target. I was behind him, already raising my arms to celebrate getting one by him, when he slammed into the front wall and screamed like a kamikaze pilot.

He whipped around, sweat flying off him in all directions, and roared again. There was a look in his eyes of raw, uncontrollable rage, and for the tiniest part of a second, I thought he was going to come after me.

I dropped my arms, victory celebration over. "Hey, bro, chill out. Just a game, man."

He tightened his arms around him, as if by pulling in on himself he could regain control.

"Sorry, man, guess I'm a little tense today."

"Want to take a break?"

He pushed wet, straight hair off his forehead, spreading it back greaseball-style, and raised his racquet. "After this game."

I stepped to the line again, wondering if his performance was just an attempt to psych me.

"What the hell," I whispered to myself at the serving line, "I can take this guy."

I put everything I had behind it. The ball hit the front wall to my left, a few inches off the floor. It was easily the best and hardest serve that ever came out of me. The ball zipped past my left shoulder in a blur. I didn't even look behind, just dropped to a half squat, my legs cocked, ready to go after his return.

Only problem was, I never saw it. All I did was hear it. There was a loud pinging sound, then an echoing ring as the ball went past me unseen, like a Hollywood sound effect of a ricocheting bullet. The ball boomeranged past me and was gone before I could even figure out which direction it came from.

I looked around. Walter was behind me, relaxed now, grinning. I spread my arms, the outstretched racquet in my right hand like a frying pan.

"Where did it go?"

He pointed with his racquet. I turned; the ball had come to rest on the floor in the right-hand corner.

"Isn't there a rule against breaking Mach I?" I asked. Walter laughed as he came to the serving line.

The game was over in about two minutes.

"Let's take a break," I panted. I stumbled over to the left wall and settled down in a puddle of my own sweat. Walter walked around in circles, nervously bouncing the ball, waiting for another chance to maul me.

"So what are you up to?" he asked.

I thought for a second. Client confidentiality was a big one with me. "You still my lawyer?" I asked.

He looked at me. "Of course, I'm still your lawyer. Any reason I shouldn't be?"

"No, it's just that I got my first client today."

"No bull, man, that's great! About freaking time."

"Yeah, well, you know her."

"I do?"

"Rachel. Rachel Fletcher."

He dropped down in front of me, balanced on the balls of his feet, his racquet in front of him for balance.

"Rachel Fletcher?"

I smiled. Walter once had the hots for Rachel as well, but she had broken up with me and was already seeing Connie by the time they met.

"Yeah, Rachel."

"She's not divorcing that bastard she's married to, is she?"

I smiled. "What, Walter, you waiting for your shot?"

"No, jerk off, just curious. That's all. If anybody's waiting for a shot at her, it's probably you."

"Maybe," I said. "Maybe not. And no, she's not divorcing him. But he's into some bookies, and they're starting to make threatening noises."

"What for? I mean, what's his game? Ponies? Football?"

"You know, I forgot to ask."

He spewed out something that sounded like disgust. "Some detective."

"Hey, give me a break, I just talked to her this afternoon. Haven't had a chance to formulate my strategy."

"Well, I hope you come up with a better strategy for him than you do racquetball."

"Okay, buddy, that's it," I said. "I've taken as much of this as I'm going to take. Prepare to eat rubber."

He laughed, stood up, turned his back on me. "Loser serves?"

I bounced the ball a few times, cocked my elbow, and let one fly. It wasn't a bad serve, but Walter had no trouble getting to it. His return was a little weaker, though. Maybe he was getting tired, too. I made it to the ball just as it was waist high, then cross-armed it hard. It hit the left wall, bounced into the back wall, then headed toward the floor. I dodged as Walter streaked by me and, with a loud grunt, caught the ball and sent it flying toward the ceiling.

I caught it on the return and managed to send it back to him. We had a pretty good volley going, the best one of the day. A thought flashed through my head that this was fun, and that I was going to hate to see it end no matter who got that point.

My right foot hit a puddle of sweat just as I was lunging toward the right wall. Something in my ankle gave way; pain shot up the outside of my right leg all the way to my hip. I felt myself becoming airborne, and the next thing I knew, I slammed into the hard wooden floor, facing the ceiling, wondering which way was up.

Walter's face appeared above me, an apparently genuine look of concern on his face. "You okay?"

I tried to focus on him and take a mental inventory of my physical state at the same time. My head took a nasty bang, but I figured it was more or less intact. The ankle, though, was another story. If I were lucky, it was only sprained.

"Nothing a heart transplant won't cure."

Walter grinned, reached out a hand to me. "Hell, boy, you can't replace what you haven't got."

I let Walter pull me up until I was firmly on my rump. I could see the ankle was swollen through my jock sock. I gingerly pulled down the thick cotton.

Maybe it wasn't too bad. A little red, swollen, but no exposed bone splinters, no streaking, not too much purple and yellow. And the pain was beginning to throb down to a gentle agony.

"Help me up, man. I need to get some ice." I grabbed his hand, and he pulled me up on my good leg.

I threw my arm around his shoulder—guys can do that when they're physically wounded—and let him help me into the locker room. One of the attendants got me a high-tech, chemical ice bag, and I sat on a bench, sweat still cascading off me, nursing the leg.

Walter stripped down for his shower, then wrapped a towel around his waist and sat next to me.

"That's going to be sore tomorrow."

"You asshole, it's sore *now*."

"You going to be okay?"

"Yeah," I said, moving the bag around a bit. "You know, it's funny. I was wondering how I could approach Fletcher

without his suspecting why I was really there. Now I've got
a reason.''

Walter looked at me strangely. His expression was one I
couldn't come anywhere near reading.

"Yeah," he agreed. "Maybe you need to go have that
looked at.''

By seven that evening, I knew I was going to have to have the leg X-rayed. The pain wasn't severe, but the swelling remained, and the ankle was stiffening up. I'd broken an ankle playing soccer in high school, so I had an idea of what might be going down.

I was only kidding when I told Walter that now I had an excuse to see Fletcher. But the more I thought of it, the better the idea seemed. Besides, if I went to the emergency room at the university medical center, my insurance would cover it. If I went to the local doc-in-a-box, it came out of my own pocket.

It's tough driving a straight shift car with a bum right leg. By now the ankle wouldn't bend at all, so pressing the accelerator meant doing it all with hip and knee. The usual traffic out 21st Avenue didn't help either. The university was still in session. It was a cool, clear night, and the streets were filled with freshly scrubbed little rich kids out for a stroll.

The university area was one of my favorite parts of town, though. In a city full of automobiles, with lousy mass transit and few sidewalks, it was a delight to see strollers out enjoying the weather. It had turned into a beautiful evening.

For once, my parking karma improved, and I was able to find a spot off 21st, barely a block from the emergency room. I limped up onto the walk and inched down to the huge glass doors, which slid open as I approached as if the building were hungry for another one. I checked in at the desk, described my problem, filled out paperwork for twenty minutes, then sat in a chair.

Thank God I didn't have a sucking chest wound.

By nine o'clock, somebody deigned to see me. It was another hour before a doctor walked in and handed me the verdict. "Mr. Denton, we think you're going to live," he said.

Typical E.R. humor. "Your X rays are fine. Nothing broken. I think it's a bad sprain, maybe a pulled ligament. Nothing to take you down in the lower forty and shoot you over."

The doctor was young, fresh-faced, clean-cut, cheerful, with a white lab coat that had his name stenciled over the left pocket in green thread. He was obviously early enough in his shift that he could still put together a coherent sentence.

"That's great," I said. "So what do I do with it?"

"I'm going to wrap it for you," he announced, pulling a chrome stool over to the foot of the table where I sat, bum leg dangling over the side. "Keep it elevated. Stay off it a few days. If the swelling hasn't abated considerably in twenty-four hours, see your own doctor. Fair enough?"

"Fair enough," I said. The doctor unwrapped a flesh-colored elastic bandage—one the insurance company would probably be billed about a hundred bucks for—and started gently wrapping the softball attached to the end of my leg.

"Say, Doc, I got a friend here in the hospital. He's on staff and the med school faculty both. Conrad Fletcher."

I yelped as the gentle healing hand jerked my ankle about sixty degrees to the right.

"Sorry," the doctor said. "Hand slipped. Fletcher, you say?"

"Yeah, Dr. Conrad Fletcher." I couldn't fail to notice that he was winding the bandage progressively tighter.

"Yes, I know him. I did my surgical residency under him."

"Great. You wouldn't happen to know if he's around the hospital tonight, would you? I'd like to say hi."

The young doctor looked up at me, any trace of warmth gone from his face. "Check with the nurses' station on the fourth floor. If he's around anywhere, they'll know."

He pushed two silver clips onto the bandage to secure it.

He stood up, handed me some papers, and then was gone. A nurse came in after him with another set of papers for my signature. Then, thank heavens, my interface with the health-care system was over.

I asked for directions to the fourth floor nurses' station.

"East or west?" the blond, teenage candy striper asked. Again, I tried not to drool too loudly.

"I don't know. Whatever's closest."

"Follow the yellow line down that hall. It'll go left, then down another hall to a bunch of elevators. Grab one to the fourth floor and the nurses' station should be right there."

"Great." I limped away, following the yellow line down the hard linoleum as it ran parallel to, intersected with, and melded with other lines. All I needed was Toto hoofing along beside me.

Hospitals late at night are weird places. The lights seem turned down low, but they're probably not. The air is heavier, stuffier, as if the crowds of people who parade back and forth in the halls during the day had sucked all the oxygen out. On this night the people who passed looked more drawn, more tired, than the daytime people. The place was quieter, slower, creepier.

I was the only one on the huge elevator creaking its way to the fourth floor. The doors pulled apart in front of me. Visiting hours were over; the lights were dimmer than ever. I hobbled down the hall, more from stiffness than pain. The hall dead-ended into a T. I stood for a second at the intersec-tion, my head bobbing first one way, then the other, and did a mental coin flip.

I turned right and walked maybe ten feet. So far, I hadn't seen anybody or anything besides a few stainless-steel carts loaded down with medical gear. The place was a freaking ghost town, and if I didn't find Fletcher quickly, I was going home to catch my nightly rerun of *Green Acres* on cable. I was tired, sore, and there was a cold one in the refrigerator with my name on it.

I saw light and headed toward it. The hall intersected with another one again, and off to the left was a glass-enclosed nurses' station. There were no nurses around, or at least nobody who resembled a nurse. But a woman with her back to me, in a well-tailored red dress, sat at a computer terminal. The phosphorescent green of the VDT bathed her dark hair in an eerie glow.

I leaned on the counter, in a break between the high glass walls of Fort Nurse. "Excuse me, miss."

No answer. Maybe she considered the *miss* a pejorative. I cleared my throat, leaned in a little farther.

"Excuse me, *Ms*. . . ."

The wheels of the chair spun on the floor as she pivoted. The woman stared at me through glasses that looked stern on her. Her face was professional, just a little this side of tense, very pretty. Sharp nose, hair pulled back, with a green halo around her head: a high-tech angel with a clamped-shut sphincter.

"Visiting hours are over, sir." Voice clear, crisp, professional. Cold.

"I know," I said, as warmly as I could muster. "I'm looking for Dr. Fletcher. I was told he might be up here."

Her eyes flicked, checking for a staff I.D. badge.

"I'm a friend," I explained. "I was in the emergency room for a bum ankle. Thought as long as I was here—"

"He's awfully busy," she said, even colder. Everybody got frosty when I claimed to be Fletcher's friend.

"He won't mind. Trust me."

A tiny snort fled the sharply defined nose. She'd heard that line before. "He was on the floor about twenty minutes ago. Head down that hall to your right. You should catch him coming back."

I smiled at her, not that it would cut any ice. "Thanks. I appreciate it."

Before the words escaped my mouth, she turned and was back on the monitor. I followed her directions. A long hall was in front of me, the walls converging to a point down where the light got so dim it was only a pale yellow, with the shimmering red of an exit sign over a door to the left. I got a faint whiff of antiseptic as my heels clicked slowly on the hard floor. A door opened ahead of me, to the right, and a nurse with a clipboard and a B.P. cuff exited, made a few notes on the clipboard, then glanced past me and went into the next room.

I could hear faint television sounds coming from one of those little hospital-bed pillow speakers. The door to my right now was partially open; I glanced inside to see the flickering images of a television bouncing off the glossy wall paint, and a wrapped leg in the air at a 45 degree angle, held suspended by metal framework and a series of wires.

Still no sign of Conrad Fletcher. I was nearing the end of the hall now, a window in front of me shutting out the city's nighttime parade. Not only was there no sign of Fletcher, there wasn't much evidence of anything else: patients, nurses, orderlies. I gave up, turned around, and headed back down the hall toward the elevator, almost relieved that I hadn't found the guy.

I heard a swishing noise behind me and glanced over my left shoulder. The door at the end of the hall, perhaps a dozen rooms away on the right, opened and a nurse stepped out. I thought it curious that her hands were free. No clipboard, no sphyg, no medication tray, no gear of any kind. She stepped out into the hall, stopped, and gaped at me. I got the feeling she was nervous about something. I kept walking, but tilted my head and shifted a little so I could catch her out of the corner of my eye.

She was still standing there, frozen. Then she reached up and fastened the top button of her nurse's dress. She was smoothing down the front of her uniform when I lost sight of her for a second. She was too far away, and the light too dim, for me to get a decent look at her. I walked on a few more steps, then gave a casual glance backward to see what she was up to now.

She was gone.

I came to a full stop, turned. Yeah, she was gone. Screw it, I thought. There were a half-dozen doors she could have gone into, as well as another hallway off to my left. No big deal. I turned around. Again I heard the swishing, airy sound of a door closing behind me, all the way at the end of the hall.

What the hell?

Something wasn't right here, so I turned and limped back down the hall, a little faster this time, headed toward that last door down the hall on my right. From way behind me at the nurse's station, I heard the low murmur of voices and thought to myself that if I wasn't careful, I was going to get in trouble. That's all I needed, to get hassled by hospital security and escorted out of the building. Talk about blowing my credibility.

I was two doors away, surrounded in the hot red light of the exit sign, when I heard a sound—a rustling maybe—coming from inside the last room. And a voice saying something I couldn't understand. A strained voice—that much I could tell—and only one person speaking. I walked farther down and I heard a rustling noise, then a squeaking like a weight being dropped on rollers.

The door was in front of me now. I reached out and grabbed the handle. Then I hesitated. What if there was a patient in there getting, like, an enema or something? My mind ran in a million different directions, thinking of all the potential medical procedures that I didn't want to see, when suddenly I noticed—

It's quiet.

Not a sound, not a whisper of breath, not the crunch of a disposable needle being stuffed in a Sharp's container. No sound of hands being washed, relieved groans, drugged sighs. Nothing. Dead silence.

The handle of the door was cold in my grip. I pushed it open, just a crack. No light escaped. If there was somebody in there, they were either asleep or they liked the dark. I pushed the door open, figuring I could always act embarrassed, apologize, and get the hell out.

The light in the hall flooded the darkened room. My eyes adjusted—and I saw someone on the bed. Only his legs were dangling off the side. He was wearing street shoes and dress pants.

And a doctor's white lab coat.

I stepped over to the bed quickly, straining to see the face across the bed. The door closed behind me, throwing the room into complete darkness. I fumbled at the head of the bed for the cord that would fire up the fluorescent light. I found the cord, but it kept dancing off my hand; it was as if I was trying to swat an insect at midnight. Finally I grabbed and pulled. The light flickered, then filled the room with a mellow blue-white light.

And there was Conrad Fletcher, sprawled out on the bed with his arms outstretched. My heart suddenly went into power stroke. I could feel the sucker pounding in my chest like a bilge pump gone wild.

I leaned over the bed, touched his face. He was cold, but shock-cold, not dead-cold. He was sweating like a wrestler, flushed. His breathing was shallow. I pulled an eyelid open, not that I knew what the hell I was doing. I'd just seen it done that way on television. His eyes were unfocused, staring ahead, pupils dilating fast. I let the eyelid snap shut and felt for a pulse in his neck. There was one, but I wouldn't have bet the rent money on it.

"Oh, boy," I whispered, wondering what to do next.

When out of nowhere, the sky in front of me exploded into a kagillion-bazillion sparkling lights, and I was weightless, floating high above the bed, then falling down a long dark tunnel. Just like in the movies.

The last thing I remembered was feeling myself fall forward onto Fletcher, his weight under me like an exhausted lover.

Chapter 5 ⎯⎯⎯⎯⎯⎯⎯

A murder squad detective once told me that most of the stuff you see in movies and read in books is complete crap.

Like this business of getting knocked out by somebody. That's bull. It just don't happen like that. Somebody taps you on the back of the head, you're going to be dazed. You might stagger, maybe fall down. But this movie nonsense where somebody wallops the daylights out of you and you gently nod off, then some luscious babe waves smelling salts under your nose and you come to and go "oh, what happened"—that's a load. Somebody hits you hard enough to do that, you're either comatose for a month or you're dead.

Fortunately, I hadn't been hit that hard.

Everything went black, and I saw sparkles behind my eyelids for a few moments. I felt I was going under. But just when I lost all sense of being in the world, I came right back to it. Like diving into a black pool, then coming straight to the surface.

It was dark in the room again. Whoever decided to play thumper on my skull had yanked the pull chain on the fluorescent light. There was a rustling behind me, then a burst of hot light as the hospital door swung open. Then darkness again, and silence. I fought to turn, to get a glimpse of something, anything, as I lay there tangled and dazed on Fletcher's body. But my brain was sending out signals my body was still ignoring.

Whoever it was got away. At that moment, I realized two important things: first, I was in a helluva mess; second, my head hurt so bad I almost forgot my ankle.

After a few seconds, it occurred to me that if I didn't start moving, I was going to roll right off Fletcher. I couldn't feel him moving—or breathing. I knew I had to do something, so I argued with my extremities until I felt something respond to a *twitch* command. I slid off him and stood up, unsteady, shaky, frightened, hoping there wasn't a second person hanging around with a slapjack. I fought off vertigo in the blackness of the room, then turned and limped toward the faint crack of light emanating beneath the door.

The hallway was empty again, and even the dimmed night-shift lights were blazingly painful. My eyes scrunched to slits. I put my left hand out to steady myself against the wall and brought my right hand up behind my shoulder to probe for the knot I knew would be there.

Bad idea. It was like getting slapped on the back of the head by Edward Scissorhands. I yelped an obscenity, then followed it with a few appropriate self-criticisms.

I brought my right hand up in front of my face. The hand was slick, wet with the coppery freshness of new blood. Great. I'd never been hit like that before. The movies could use a dose of reality. Only who'd pay to see Mel Gibson get clobbered and go silly for a few hours?

I still wasn't thinking clearly; not yet, anyway. So when the door opened a few rooms up and to the left, my first thought was that whoever popped me was coming back to finish the job. I started to turn away and slipped, falling against the cold shiny wallpaper. My footing gave way and I slid down until I was planted firmly on my butt. The young blond nurse with the clipboard and sphyg looked at me, her eyes wide as jar tops. I closed my eyes for a bit, then felt her next to me. If she was going to finish me off, there wasn't a whole lot I could do about it.

"Are you all right?" A soft hand with a firm grip settled on my shoulder. Felt good; first time in a while.

I opened my eyes. Her chest was in my face now as she stretched over me, examining the back of my head. It was a nice chest, but I was too goofy to enjoy the moment.

"What'd you do?" she asked, her voice sweet, soothing. "Trip and fall?"

I raised my head. Her fingers were still touching my scalp six inches or so above my collar. She had a gentle touch. I looked into her eyes; in my fog I tried to determine what color they were. Hazel, probably. Then it came back to me.

"Dr. Fletcher's in that room down there," I said, my right hand flopping around in some vaguely accurate direction. "I think he's dead."

A crack of a gasp came out of her, then a second set of white-panted legs appeared next to us. I looked up. An older woman, starched white cap on her head, glared down at us.

"What happ—" she said.

"Get security," the nurse beside me interrupted. She stood, her torso rising smoothly, silently.

"And watch him," she ordered, pointing down at me.

I heard the soft padding of her nurse sneakers as she moved away. I settled back against the hard wall, glad to have somebody else in charge.

Damn if I didn't get to make a second trip to the emergency room. This time, though, I didn't have to wait out front with the peasants. I was taken directly downstairs to a cubicle and plopped on an examining table, with a blue-uniformed hospital security cop standing wordlessly at attention beside me.

I was beginning to get my wits back, those that weren't beyond recovery. I knew the cops would arrive soon, and that I would have to figure out what to tell them. The problem was that I wasn't exactly a veteran at this detective stuff. Maybe it would have helped if I'd had some training first. But how was I to know my first case was going to be a front-page felony?

High-powered surgeon/compulsive gambler murdered in hospital room! Private detective hired by wife to shadow husband discovers body! I visualized my parents seeing their son's picture in a tabloid every time they went through the express lane.

The same young doctor who torqued my ankle came in to work on my head.

"Haven't I seen you somewhere before?" he asked. After a moment, I realized he was serious. I pulled up my pant leg, showing off the elastic bandage.

"Oh, yeah," he said. "You're the . . ."

"Friend of Fletcher's?"

"Hey, is it true? Fletcher really dead?" The resident's face brightened at the prospect.

"News travels fast," I commented.

"It would probably be better if you gentlemen didn't discuss that," the uniform said. I looked over at him. OFFICER REED, his nameplate read. "The Metro police will want to question you first."

The doctor's eyes darkened. My experience is that doctors—even beginners—don't appreciate civilians telling them what to do.

"You can step outside," he said to the officer.

"No can do, Doc. My orders are to stick with this guy."

"I can't really talk now," I said, hoping to bring peace to the world. "Don't worry, though, Doctor. All your wishes will come true."

The doctor stood on tiptoe and pulled my head around to examine it. "Any dizziness?" he asked.

"A touch at first. But it went away."

"Nausea? Shakiness?"

"Only at first. Better now."

I grimaced as he pried apart the edges of the cut.

"You've got quite a knot here," he observed.

"For this, you went to medical school?"

He pulled out a penlight, then shone it in my eyes one at a time. I blinked. I couldn't help it; it hurt like the devil.

"Pupils are responding," he said. "That's good. Everything looks okay. If you've got a concussion, it's a mild one. I'll sign you in for twenty-four hours' observation, if you want. But I think you'll be okay."

The only thing I wanted to do was escape from that place. "I'll pass. Thankfully, I've got a thick skull."

"I'll have a nurse dress the wound," he recited as he scribbled notes on a pad. "We'll give you a skin local, probably have to shave off about a quarter's worth of hair. No stitches, but a couple of butterflies. Go home, get some rest. Keep Neosporin on it. You'll be solid in a day or two."

"Great."

"You start getting dizzy, seeing spots before your eyes, any similar reaction, then see your own doctor or get back in here. Okay?"

"Yeah, I got you."

"You can go as soon as the nurse finishes with you."

I looked over at the campus cop. We made eye contact; I knew I wasn't going anywhere.

By then, it was sometime after midnight. I was fried and getting more fried by the minute. My ankle ached, and the spray-on yellow goop they promised would numb my head while the nurse worked on it failed miserably. This middle-aged angel of mercy clipped my hair back away from the cut. Then she pressed the edges of the cut together with a pair of vise grips and taped it shut with duct tape—or so I imagined. I'll probably get an aneurysm when I pull it off.

Then came the inevitable waiting. The campus cop pulled up a chair. I lay on the examining table, found that putting my head back even on a pillow was like slamming into a brick wall, then rolled onto my side. About an hour later, I was drifting off when I began to hear voices that didn't sound like medical people. The curtain to the cubicle slid back. A hefty, middle-aged man in a brown suit, carrying a loose-leaf notebook, stepped in. He motioned to the campus cop, and the guy disappeared in about half a second.

Cop body language, I guess.

I sat up on the edge of the table, the dry white paper cover crinkling beneath me. My sense of smell was coming back; I realized I was ravenous. Somebody outside was drinking coffee; it smelled marvelous.

"I'm Sergeant Spellman, Metro Homicide," he said. Up close, he had pockmarked skin, the last residue of teenage acne, and his hair was graying. I recognized him. We'd met a year or two earlier when I was reporting the murder of a country music star's head roadie. Turned out the guy supplemented his income with ventures into the pharmaceutical import-export business, and wound up taking a header off the I-265 bridge over the Cumberland. Occupational hazard, I hear.

"I'm Harry Denton," I said, offering him my hand. "We've met before."

He stared at me, questioning, as he shook my hand. "Oh, yeah. You're the newspaper reporter."

"Ex-newspaper reporter. I'm a private investigator now."

Spellman choked off a snort. "Sorry to keep you waiting so long, but we had to finish our on-scene upstairs. You know the routine."

Actually, I didn't know the routine, but I was willing to take his word. "So what's the program now?" I asked.

"Has the doctor released you?"

"Yeah. If I spend any more time in this hospital, I may not survive."

Spellman grinned. "I hate 'em, too. I'd rather take a horse whipping than see a doctor. You feel like answering some questions?"

I looked down at my watch: 1:20 A.M. "Right now?"

"We like to interview witnesses as quickly as possible," he said. "You get a good night's sleep, big breakfast tomorrow morning, get back to business, I guarantee you won't remember what you're remembering now."

"Am I under arrest?"

Spellman grinned again. "You do anything to get arrested for?"

"No, definitely not."

"Then this is only a request."

I brought up my hand and rubbed my eyes, stretching the skin on my face to try to bring some feeling back into it. The only feeling, though, was the searing pain in the back of my head.

"You work this late all the time?" I asked.

"Just like being a doctor. Some nights you're on call, some nights you're not."

"The press pick up on this yet?"

"If they haven't, they will soon."

"You notified the decedent's next-of-kin?"

"Why don't you let me ask the questions, Mr. Denton."

"I just thought she ought to be called."

"What's it to you?"

I looked up at him. There were dark circles under his eyes as well. Guess everybody looks like hell in the middle of the night.

"That's who I'm working for," I said, at least savvy enough to know that in this state, client privilege doesn't extend to P.I.s. "Fletcher's wife hired me to get him out of a jam."

Sergeant Spellman's eyes flicked from his notebook to me, then back down. "Yeah," he said. "We need to talk."

Which is how I found myself on the way to the Metropolitan Nashville/Davidson County Criminal Justice Center at just shy of two o'clock in the freaking morning.

Chapter 6

Spellman offered to give me a ride downtown; I was too tired to argue otherwise. We pulled out of the med center parking lot onto 21st Avenue. The white and fluorescent blues of the emergency room faded quickly into the dark oranges of the city streetlights and the neon rainbows of restaurant signs, retail shops, all-night pancake houses. At two in the morning, Nashville's a strange compound of insomniac music types, graveyard-shift workers, and people looking for love or trouble and not caring very much which one they find first.

I sat in the unmarked Ford Crown Victoria and rested my head against the back of the seat. Every time we hit a pothole my head felt like it was coming apart. But I was too tired to sit up straight.

"What happens next?" I asked.

"We just want a statement from you. That's all." Spellman navigated expertly through the thick traffic on Broadway. I thought of the line from some twenty-five-year-old Rolling Stones lament: *Don't people ever want to go to bed. . . .*

"There's not much to say, I just came across the guy—"

"Not now," Spellman said. "Wait till we get downtown."

I settled back as we crossed over I-40 and drove past Union Station. My uncle, the one I'm named after, worked the L & N railroad for decades before he died, back before the automobile makers conspired to screw the trains into obliv-

43

ion. Now only freight trains came through the station, and it's mostly home for pigeons.

Ten minutes later, I followed Spellman into the police station, down the earth-tone carpeted halls to an interview room. It was quiet there in the middle of the night, a cold kind of quiet.

I sat at a table in front of a portable tape recorder. Spellman sat across from me and opened his notebook. Then he leaned across and fiddled with the tape recorder.

"Want anything? Coffee, a Coke maybe?"

"Cup of coffee'd be great," I answered. "Milk, half a sugar."

He stood back up, left the room for a minute. There was a mirror on the wall behind me. I wondered who was watching from the other side. Figured I'd better not pick my nose or scratch my crotch.

Spellman came in with a Styrofoam cup in each hand. Steam wafted off the coffee.

"Powdered's all we had. Can't keep milk around here. It starts stinking after awhile."

"No problem."

I sipped the coffee as Spellman jacked around with the tape recorder again, then pressed the RECORD button. He recited his title and name, the date and time, then asked me to state my full name and address into the mike.

So asked, so done. Then Spellman opened his notebook and scanned a page of notes. "Tell me what happened from the time you got to the medical center until you found Dr. Fletcher's body," he instructed.

I began the narrative. It felt strange trying to recollect, and recreate in my mind, an entire evening's events. Like most people, I go through life relatively oblivious to everything around me. There's so much stimulation, so much stress, these days, that if you paid attention to everything, you'd never get anything done and lose your sanity in the process. It's like some New Age fruitcake telling you to live every day as if it were your last; hell, that's impossible. You'd be so overloaded you'd explode, and it *would* be your last day.

It only took a few minutes to recite the tale. I tried to remember everything like a professional. It was impossible to tell from Spellman's face what he thought. He sat there in his tan shirt and brown flowered polyester necktie like a law enforcement sphinx, making a few notes here and there and watching the tape recorder spin.

Then his tone changed. Suddenly, we were into details.

"Where did you park your car?"

"Off 21st, a block or so from the hospital."

"Where off 21st?"

I thought for a moment. "I don't know the name of the street. I mean, this is Nashville, man. I saw a space, I grabbed it."

"You don't know where your car is?"

"Of course, I know where my car is. I just don't know the name of the street."

"Who else knew you were going to the hospital?"

"Nobody."

"You didn't call anybody?"

"I live alone, Lieutenant. My landlady was asleep."

"You didn't call a girlfriend? Maybe tell her you were meeting her later?"

"I'm not seeing anyone right now."

He raised an eyebrow. "No relationships with women, huh?"

I cocked an eyebrow right back at him. What the hell was going on here?

"I said not right now. I didn't mean never."

"Who's your client?"

I hesitated, then remembered he already knew. "Rachel Fletcher, Conrad Fletcher's wife."

He was firing questions like this was the freaking Double Jeopardy round: When did she hire you? Where? How much did she pay you?

"Why did you wait until ten at night to go to the emergency room?"

"My ankle didn't start hurting bad until then."

"Why did you go looking for Fletcher?"

I felt myself going dizzy again. "I don't know. Not really. I was thinking I ought to connect with the guy. Maybe talk to him. I was going to wing it, make it up as I went along. Maybe that wasn't such a good idea."

"Tell me again the sequence of events in the hallway."

"I heard a noise behind me. I turned. There was a nurse coming out of a room."

"Was it the room where Fletcher was?"

"Maybe," I said. "I'm not sure. It was dark. I was at the other end of the hall."

"Get a look at her?"

"I vaguely remember thinking it odd that she didn't have a clipboard or anything. She just stood there, staring at me."

"Then?"

"She seemed stiff, awkward. Then she reached up and kind of smoothed down her blouse. I turned away for a sec. When I turned back, she was gone. I don't know where. Maybe into another room. There's a stairwell exit down at that end of the hall, too. Anyway, I thought it was weird. That's when I headed down the hall and found him."

Then the clincher: "Why did Rachel Fletcher hire you?"

I hesitated, decided I'd had about enough. "Client privilege," I said. "That's personal information between me and my client."

Color rose in Spellman's face. Twenty-five years ago, he'd have brought in a couple of the boys with rubber hoses to work me over. But that was then, as they say, and this is now, and I've got to give Spellman credit: he kept his cool.

"Client privilege is not recognized in a private investigator-client relationship. We can either have you deposed by the district attorney, or we could stretch it and have you charged with interfering with a police investigation."

I thought I saw the faintest trace of a smile on his face. "What's it going to be?"

I smiled back at him. I had a feeling I'd lost this one; may as well flow with it. "She told me Fletcher was a compulsive gambler. Up to his ya-ya with some bookie. She didn't know who. Said they'd been threatening him, and she wanted me to find out what was going on. Arrange to pay off the guy quietly.''

"You believe that?" Spellman asked. "A top gun surgeon, med school faculty, into some street bookies?''

"I've seen weirder.'' And so had he.

Spellman leaned back in his chair. "Why'd she come to you? You just opened shop. You're not even in the yellow pages yet. How'd she find you?"

Again, I found myself hesitating. I knew that without realizing it, I'd compromised myself by taking the case in the first place. I'm a little slow on the uptake sometimes, but I did have sense enough to recognize that the worst reflex would be trying to shuck and jive my way out of this.

"Rachel and I were involved in college. Pretty seriously. Then along came this guy Fletcher, and the next thing I know, I'm looking at the world from inside the dumper. She and Fletcher got married, moved away to New York. I moved back here. Then Rachel and Conrad came back when he got his appointment at the hospital. I didn't see them socially. She saw my byline in the newspaper. When she got in trouble, she tracked me down.''

Spellman made a few notes, then reached up and stroked the rough side of his cheek. "So this guy Fletcher stole your girlfriend. Years later, the lady comes to you for help. Little more than twenty-four hours later, he's on his way to Forensics.'' He paused again, stared right through me. "Interesting,'' he observed.

My attitude problem erupted suddenly. "Oh, Jesus, Spellman, use your brain. Who'd be stupid enough to kill somebody, then get caught in the same room with the still-fresh corpse? What, you think I wasted Fletcher, then slammed my own head into the wall to cover it?''

Spellman snapped the notebook shut. "Actually, we already checked that out. Doctor says it would have been tough for you to give yourself that kind of injury, and there was nothing in the room that would have made it any easier for you.''

I shifted in the seat and must have put my weight down

the wrong way; this jolt went through my bum ankle, all the way up my leg, and into my rump. The back of my neck was stiffening up. I rotated my head and felt the bones grind and snap together like steel marbles in a box. What minuscule help that spray-on crap had given my pate was long gone. What a night.

"You're serious, aren't you? You think I murdered him?"

Spellman shook his head, held a palm out in front of him. "Whoa, fellow, I didn't say that. We just need everybody's story, that's all. We don't even know what killed him yet. That's going to have to wait for the medical examiner. The rest of it's just routine. But you've got to admit," he continued, "this all looks pretty flaky. What if the coroner comes back with a finding that Fletcher was, say, smothered with a pillow? And you the only one in the room."

"But I wasn't the only one in the room! Whoever dropped that dump truck on my head was in there, too!"

"But you didn't get a look at whoever it was. Nobody else saw anybody leave that room. Everybody else on the floor can account for his whereabouts the whole evening. So what happened to *this* person?"

I looked at him as coldly as I could muster. "My guess is that since he murdered Conrad Fletcher, he probably got the hell out of there."

I stood up. It came off as a gesture of defiance, but it was mostly that my legs were cramping. Either way, I didn't care anymore.

"I've answered about as many questions as I feel like answering tonight," I said. "If it's okay with you gents, I'm going to call a buddy for a ride back to my car."

"We're through, anyway," Spellman said. "I can have a uniform drive you back."

"No, thanks," I said. "I think I need a return to civilian life."

"No problem, fella," Walter cracked as we walked out the front door of the police station. His BMW was parked on the street, in a spot on the James Robertson Parkway right out front. "I enjoy waking up at three in the morning. Do it all the time."

It was pretty lousy of me to roust him so early, but I needed a friend to talk to and a lawyer as well. Walter was the only one who met both qualifications.

"How you feel?"

"Like death on a soda cracker," I answered truthfully.

"You don't look even that good."

"Thanks. I owe you one, buddy," I panted, trying to keep up with him on my bum leg. Walter went at everything like killing rats.

"I'll take it out on you when the ankle mends."

Walter unlocked the driver's door to the BMW and disabled the alarm. He reached down to flick a switch on the armrest and the passenger door lock button popped up. I climbed in to the smell of leather car seats. The night was still bright orange under the streetlights; even the usual middle of the night pedestrian parade of the homeless, the blistered, and the demented had diminished.

"Sun'll be up soon," I said.

"Harry," Walter said, his hand pausing before he twisted the ignition key. "You are through with this business, aren't you?"

"I don't know. Can you believe those idiots, thinking I offed Fletcher?"

Walter started the car, then put it into gear. The BMW took off as smooth as a blue point oyster sliding down a throat. "They mirandize you?"

"No."

"Then they don't really think you did it. They put a little pressure on, though. Ask you a lot of detailed questions. They want you to say a lot in your statement, even if it's irrelevant. That way, they can come back in a year or so and impugn your testimony if you do become a suspect."

"More to work with, huh?"

"You got it," he said. "You get a look at whoever bashed you?"

"If I had, I'd have told the cops. But no, not a glance."

"Don't worry. You're off the hook. Let it go."

I fumbled with a row of black switches on my armrest and lowered the window. A big whiff of the rendering plant filled the car. It was like sticking your head in a freshly opened bag of dry dog food. This is the only city I know that locates incinerators, rendering plants, thermal plants, anything that stinks, right downtown.

"I don't know," I said.

"Don't know what?"

"Whether or not I'm off the hook."

"Oh, no," he sighed. "I've seen that glint in your eye before. You're going to stay on this son of a bitch, aren't you?"

I turned to him. "Yeah. Think I will."

"Listen, bunghole, what makes you think Fletcher's killer won't do it again?"

"Maybe—"

"Harry, as your attorney, I advise you to go home, drink a quart of tequila, and get one of those cheap weekend deals to the Bahamas."

"I hate tequila."

"Whatever."

"Walter, this may not make any sense, but I'm staring middle age right in the face. I feel like a failure."

"Oh, c'mon," he said. "Give it a rest. You've been reading too many of those male sensitivity books."

"No, I mean it. You and I went to college together. Look at you: you drive a BMW; you're a successful lawyer. Even if you didn't make partner, you've got a future. I live in somebody's attic in East Nashville, drive a six-year-old Ford, and have an ex-wife who spreads dirt about me to anybody who'll listen."

"Harry, you've been feeling sorry for yourself ever since the paper canned you."

"It's not that, Walt. This is different." I stared out the window as we drove over the Church Street Viaduct. Below us, street people sleeping in the Gulch were stirring to life.

"I want to know I can do something well, even if it's just be a cheap, sleazy private investigator."

Walter laughed. "The sleazy part'll be easy. The rest, I don't know. One thing you need to keep in mind: the cops are going to assume right off that Rachel killed Conrad. You get involved, they'll figure you're in on it."

"Jesus, Walter," I sighed. "Not you, too."

"Are you sure you aren't just thinking with your pecker?"

I looked over at Walter. Sometimes he could be a real jerk.

Chapter 7 _____

Walter's two-bit psychoanalysis pissed me off at first, but the truth was I'd already considered it. Rachel Fletcher comes to me with this story about her husband being in trouble with bookies and can I help him out and all that good stuff. The next thing you know, he's dead. C'mon, give me a break. Something's stinko.

If I were a real detective, I'd have gone home, chugged a couple of shots of cheap bourbon, smoked a pack of unfiltered cigarettes, and grabbed a few hours' shut-eye. But bourbon gives me heartburn like the devil, and the one time I smoked a cigarette was when I was twelve—out behind my grandparents' garage. My father was going to spank me, until he decided that twenty minutes of projectile vomiting was punishment enough.

And I sure as hell needed more than a few hours of shut-eye. I hate to confess it, but if I don't get an unbroken eight hours of sleep every night, I'm not worth killing the next day. Just a wuss, I guess.

By the time I got back to East Nashville, it was nearly four in the morning. I decided to hide out for a while and regroup. I closed all the blinds, made myself a cup of hot chocolate, turned the ringer off on the phone, and crawled into bed. I drifted off to sleep as an all-night news program played out some hostage drama in the Mideast.

When I woke up, the soaps were on. Something about somebody being unfaithful to somebody else, or some such melodramatic twaddle. I was too dazed to know or care what

52

they were talking about. I fumbled for the remote control. The room sank back into blessed silence.

Only I couldn't sink back into sleep. I lay there awhile, but it just wasn't going to happen.

The answering machine light was blinking a fast red. I pushed the button; the synthesized voice on a chip said: "Hello, you have . . . two . . . messages."

Rachel's voice came next: "Harry, are you there? Harry? The police were here. They told me. . . . Oh, God, Harry—" There was a long silence, followed by a phlegmatic wet sob. "Call me."

Lonnie Smith, my repo buddy, was next: "Got one in Shelbyville, man, you interested? Trans Am, T-tops, should be a fun ride. I'll bring the truck back. You can drive the Pontiac. Call me, dude."

Great, I'm in the middle of a murder, and now Lonnie wants me to swipe a car as well.

There was a box on the front page of the morning paper, a short bulletin about Conrad's death. Apparently it all happened too late to get full treatment. I suspected the story would be all over the afternoon paper, though. I also figured my answering machine at work would be overloaded with reporter calls as well, which is why I decided to stay away from my office for a while.

I decided to take a chance and go see Dr. Marsha. I met Marsha Helms about five years ago, when I was covering a murder for the paper. I'd just been moved off the Lifestyles section onto Cityside, and it was my first real chance to get involved with the law enforcement bureaucracy in this town. Marsha helped me appreciably—gave me a lot of inside information, details I probably wasn't supposed to know.

Marsha's tall, maybe an inch or two taller than me, and striking. Jet-black hair, red-frame glasses, a nose as sharp and well defined as a wasp's sting. But not what you'd call classically beautiful. Attractive, though, and with a personality that could best—and diplomatically—be described as off the wall.

What else would you expect from a lady who cuts open dead bodies for a living?

I crossed over the river on the Memorial Bridge, through the dense lunchtime traffic, past the police station, then maneuvered my way around to First Avenue. The partly cobblestone street runs down behind all the old buildings on Second Avenue, the ones that were feed stores and blacksmith shops a hundred years ago, beautifully renovated restaurants, bars, and dance clubs now. Cities get gentrified all the time, but seldom with the class of this town. People flowed freely, happily. Tourists mixed in with suited business people, street singers, and city workers in a buzz saw of activity. I drove past the replica of Fort Nashborough, past Riverfront Park, on out First Avenue until it changes into Hermitage Avenue. One of the things that make this city so wonderful is that you can get lost forever if you don't grasp the concept of street names changing mid-block—and that Old Hickory Boulevard has no beginning and no end. It's just kind of everywhere.

Around the bend, just past the building that's a different Oriental restaurant, with a different owner every six weeks, is Metro General Hospital. It's a nineteenth-century facility overloaded with twenty-first century stresses: eleven-year-old girls pregnant by their fathers, their younger brothers, or cousins; junkies; alcoholics; AIDS patients who never heard of health insurance, even if they could afford it. The knifings, stabbings, car wrecks, plane crashes—they all go to General.

I made a left turn just past the main entrance of the hospital into an unidentified parking lot. Up a short hill, behind a rise that blocks the building from the road, sits the Forensic Science Center.

Strange place, the Nashville morgue. I don't know if morgues are like this all over, but this city's is more of a bunker than anything else. The doors are heavy, armorplated, and the few windows in the place are bulletproof. Inside, the staff's got the makings of a pretty good arsenal, and they all know where the bullets go.

Go figure. I mean, who'd want to blast their way into a morgue? God help anybody who tries, though.

Kay Delacorte sat at her desk, eyeing me through the thick glass. She made a face kind of like a kid biting into a sour ball and pushed a button on a wall next to her desk.

"What do *you* want?"

I looked at her through the glass, gave her my best lost boy look. "C'mon, Kay. Can I come in?"

She giggled, her laugh coming through the speaker as static. Kay's bright, funny, with a real *M*A*S*H* sense of humor. Guess that's what it takes. At forty something, she's the oldest staffer at the morgue, a combination earth mother-social director for the employees.

"What for?"

"I want to talk to Doc Marsha."

"She doesn't want to talk to you." Kay was messing with me now. All part of the game.

"C'mon, Kay, you're not careful here, you're going to make me think of my ex-wife."

"Oh, God forbid . . ." she yelled, laughing as she pushed another button. The door buzzer wailed. I grabbed the handle and pulled. The front door to the morgue is so heavy you've got to grasp it with both hands and plant your feet solid or you'll never make it.

The bunker door swung open, and I stepped into the heavily air-conditioned building. I shivered slightly after being outside in the hot sun. Every time I've ever been in this building, it's as cold as a meat locker. So to speak.

"You've got a lot of nerve, showing your face around here after all this time." Kay was teasing me now, or at least I hoped that's what she was doing. Tough to tell with her.

"I know it's been a long time, babe. But since I got canned at the paper, I don't have much chance to get down here."

She stood up, motioned for me. I stepped over to her desk and leaned in. She gave me a quick hug, a peck on the cheek.

"I saw your name in the paper," she said. "You okay?"

"Little tired. Little sore. Nothing heavy. I guess you know why I'm here."

"Yeah, and it's a good thing Dr. Henry's up in East Tennessee."

Dr. Henry Krohlmeyer, all the right credentials including Stanford Medical School, was the head meat cutter, the official city medical examiner. He also probably would've thrown me out, given the circumstances. My being here was most improper, and I knew it.

"He's out of town?" I asked, surprised.

"Seminar. Won't be back until tomorrow."

"So you guys haven't autopsied Fletcher yet?"

"Dr. Marsha did it. Dr. Henry'll sign off on it when he gets back."

"You think she'll talk to me?"

"I'll check, Harry. Best I can do."

Kay walked back to Marsha's office, which was one of two smaller offices occupied by the forensic pathologists. Off to another side was an office shared by the three forensic investigators.

Kay walked back in a moment, a wicked grin on her face. "Yeah, go on back there. But be prepared."

I had a feeling I knew what she was talking about. Time was when Marsha and I had done a fair amount of flirting, back before I got my divorce. Still under the delusion that I had a marriage, I backed off. Stupid me . . .

I smiled at Kay, thanked her, and limped on back.

"You know," she said behind me, "you need a vacation. You look like hell."

I turned to her. "People keep telling me that."

"You should listen."

Marsha sat behind her cluttered desk. Behind her, on a windowsill beneath another pane of bullet-proof glass, sat a dozen or so tiny pill bottles, each marked with a black felt tip pen, each holding a bullet that had been pulled out of one of her customers. Grim work, I thought, but these people seem to thrive on it. In fact, Marsha's office was filled with other souvenirs: a human skull, a large specimen bottle with a human fetus preserved in formaldehyde, framed color pictures of gruesome murder scenes.

"Who does your decorating?" I asked. "The Addams Family?"

She smiled at me, revealing a mouth full of perfect white teeth. Marsha Helms was even prettier than I'd remembered; maybe it was because I'd been in the middle of a long, dry spell. Maybe she just was, and it took me this long to notice.

"Hello, Harry." She stood up, and up, and up, and up. God, she was tall. She stuck out a hand, which I took gratefully and shook gently. "Good to see you, again."

"Good to see you, Marsh. How's it going?"

"Busy. Long hot summer. The murder rate's up fourteen percent this year over last, and we aren't even through the worst part of the summer yet."

And now I'd been a party, however inadvertently, to making it a notch worse.

"So I've heard." I sat in a scuffed, city-issue office chair across from her.

"You're limping," she said. "What happened?"

"Nothing much. Compound fracture. I just had 'em stuff the bone back in and wrap it."

"Heard you got bopped on the head. Stitches?"

"Coupla hundred. But it'll be okay."

We stared at each other for a moment, a thankfully non-pregnant pause. "Such a tough guy," she chided. "I guess it comes with being a private . . . dick."

"So you heard?"

"Yeah. What happened at the newspaper?" Marsha crossed her legs and leaned back in her office chair. She was wearing a long black skirt that peeked out beneath her white lab coat. Great legs, I thought, distracted for a moment. Sorry, can't help it.

"I hacked off the wrong people. Attitude problem, I guess."

"I'm surprised you lasted as long as you did. I heard about you and Lanie, too."

"Yeah," I said, uncomfortable. I don't like reopening old wounds—the new ones are bad enough. What the hell, it's all in the past, anyway. Letting go of things is tough, but hanging on's even tougher. "I'm glad it's over."

"Pretty rough?"

"In places."

She looked down at her desk. "You should've called me. Somebody to talk to. Shoulder to cry on, maybe."

I thought for a moment. This was encouraging news, especially for a person in my situation. Wonder if my landlady would mind my having company some evening? I'd never asked her; it simply hadn't occurred to me.

"Why don't I do that sometime?"

She looked back at me, smile gone from her face. "But that's not why you're here now?"

"No, Marsh. You did Fletcher, right?"

"I was there. I was the one who did the on-scene. You were already gone by then."

"They took me down to E.R."

"So what do you want to know?"

"What killed him, Marsh? What killed Conrad Fletcher?"

"You know how much trouble I'd get in for divulging that?"

I leaned forward in the chair, a self-conscious attempt to convey sincerity with body language. I'm never able to pull off that sort of thing, but I keep trying.

"Marsha, I just want to know because, well, I'm involved. It'll be a matter of public record eventually, anyway. Let me know what I'm up against. Whatever you tell me doesn't go any further than this office."

She stood up, thumbed through a stack of file folders, and pulled out one near the top. "C'mon. I'm only doing this because Dr. Henry's out of the office and Charlie's out running a D.O.A. car wreck."

She walked past me quickly, her lab coat brushing against my arm. I followed her out of the office, past Kay Delacorte's desk, and through the door into the autopsy room. Two tilting tables with bright overhead lights sat shiny, cold, and clean. Off to the left were the tool kits laid out on white towels, the brutal Stryker saw on its side, on a shelf by itself. Marsha's heels clicked sharply on the tile floor as we walked out of the autopsy room into the receiving room.

"We got him in here just after midnight. I grabbed a couple hours' sleep, then came in at five to do the autopsy. He's in the cooler now. The mortician's supposed to pick him up around two. You ready for this?"

"Who else you got in there?"

"Suicide, came in about five thirty this morning. We haven't even cleaned him up yet. But it's not too bad. Small caliber under the chin. He's in one piece." Her left eyebrow tilted up. "Mostly . . ."

Jesus, I thought, I hope I don't pass out on her.

"C'mon," she grinned. "At least this one hasn't got a steering column through his chest."

"Okay," I said, "let's do it."

She pulled the heavy metal latch on the cooler door, and we walked into the refrigerated room. Unlike in the movies and on television, this morgue didn't have a bunch of neat shiny drawers, each with a sterile body laying there in repose. This was just a big refrigerator, with a bunch of gurneys scattered in loose rows all over the place. On one to our right, a young man was spread out barefooted, worn jeans, blue work shirt pulled open and splattered with a surprisingly small amount of blood. And below his chin, a dark ugly hole lined with burn marks.

Toe tags, the latest fashion for today's teen.

Farther in and to our left, Conrad Fletcher was on another gurney. I hesitated for a second, drawing in a deep breath, steeling myself. Even from eight or ten feet away, I could see the ugly Y-shaped cut of the autopsy surgeon's knife, the one that started at each shoulder, met at the center of the torso, then continued down. I'd never seen an autopsy performed, but I knew how one worked. And I knew the body lying over on that table was empty of guts and of brain. Whatever made Conrad Fletcher Conrad Fletcher was long gone, and the stiff blue-gray slab on the table was just residue. I told myself that as I stood there, a feebleminded attempt to distance myself from the awfulness that I knew the corpse represented.

"You okay?" Marsha asked.

"Yeah, I just needed a second. I never could get used to this."

"C'mon, Harry, this one really isn't that bad. You've seen worse."

"I know. Just been awhile."

She walked over to the table. There was a small sheet draped roughly over his crotch, but modesty was something that was neither called for nor particularly appreciated here. No neat white sheet covering him over head to toe. Just something thrown over his privates, almost as an afterthought.

She crossed around the gurney and stood, arms folded over the file in front of her. I ambled over and stood on the other side facing her. Conrad was between us, unaware that he was the topic of the day. I studied his face. It was a little sunken, his eyelids pulled down. His color was all wrong; the embalmer hadn't had a chance to pretty him up. I was grateful that he had enough hair to cover the scalp incision, the one that's made from ear to ear across the head, the one that Marsha had cut to remove his skullcap, and then his brain.

It was a strain to imagine her in this line of work.

"This wasn't real hard to figure out," she said, unfolding her arms and opening the file. "A first-year intern could have gotten most of it."

I felt a sudden wave of dizziness pass over me as I stood there staring down at the huge stitches across Conrad's chest.

"How do you do this stuff?" I asked, woozy.

"Should've seen him before I sewed him back up," she said offhandedly.

I looked up at her. She was staring down at her notes. "So what killed him?" I asked.

"All the classic symptoms: blue mottling of the brain tissue. Paralysis of the musculature of the esophagus, larynx. Diminished ventilation of the pulmonary alveoli. Chronic and progressive congestion of the bronchial tract." She looked up at me as if she expected me to understand what she was talking about.

"Okay," I commented.

"Mucus in the lungs," she continued. "Textbook anoxia. Acute respiratory paralysis."

"So what's that mean in English, Marsh?"

"Harry, dear," she said, cocking an eye toward me, "the man drowned in his own snot."

I was trying to keep my brain working, trying to understand all this, mostly to keep from heaving.

"What, you mean somebody smothered him?" I thought of Spellman's comment about the pillow.

"Nobody smothered him," Marsha said. "He was poisoned."

"Poisoned?"

"Your acute respiratory paralysis . . ."

I stared down at Conrad, cold and dead and poisoned. For the first time, I felt sorry for the poor bastard.

"What kind of poison?"

She walked around to the foot of the gurney, then stuck her thin hand inside the right pocket of the lab coat. "Tox screen'll take a week or so. Samples went off to the T.B.I. lab this morning. My guess is, especially given that this went down in a hospital, that it was one of the anesthetics. Pavulon, maybe. More likely succinylcholine or protocurarine—"

"What in the hell is succin . . ." I stumbled. "And protocurarine?"

"Powerful anesthetic. Synthetic curares. Used for patients who are allergic to everything else. Paralyzes the respiratory system in large doses. It fits. Again, though, we'll have to wait for the lab."

"Synthetic curare. Poison-tipped arrow?"

"Try twenty-gauge needle," she said, pulling a magnifying glass out of the lab coat pocket.

"You serious?"

Marsha laid the file folder across Conrad's hairy legs. She moved her hand up his leg, above his right knee to the top of his thigh. She searched around for a second, then looked up at me.

"See? Right there."

I bent down and looked through the magnifying glass as she held it. I moved my head up and down to focus and then saw it. An unmistakable, tiny hole in the skin, with just the faintest trace of a bulge around it.

"There's a hole in his pants, too. A match."

I stood up and looked her straight in the eye, for the first time that day without any lascivious thoughts. "Why would a doctor lie there and let somebody jab a twenty-gauge needle into him—and through his pants?"

"You tell me."

"Somebody knock him out?"

"Not a mark on him. Not even a scalp abrasion. He fell back on the bed."

"Stun device?"

"I don't know. I'm no expert on that. But every one I've seen leaves either burn marks or pinpricks."

We left the cooler and its two inhabitants behind, then walked slowly back to Marsha's office. In the hall, I remembered something I hadn't thought of before.

"You know, I think he was still breathing when I first saw him."

"Probably," she said as we entered her office. "The stuff doesn't kill you immediately."

She walked behind her desk, tossed the folder onto the ever-present pile. "Want to hear a good one?"

"Sure," I said. The smile on her face was a wicked, naughty one.

"He'd just had sex," she said, almost with a note of triumph in her voice. "Ten, maybe fifteen minutes before he died."

My jaw dropped. "How can you tell?"

She raised her right index finger, her voice a bad imitation of Major Strasser telling Victor Laszlo he wasn't going *anywhere*.

"We haff ways of makink you talk."

"Marsh, that's not funny."

"Hey," she continued, "the guy went out in a blaze of glory. Besides, you know what they taught us in stiff school, don't you?"

"Okay," I said, "I'll bite."

"Rigor mortis," she said, grinning from ear to ear, "is just an all-over hard-on."

Chapter 8 _____

I knew I should head out to Green Hills and see Rachel. She sounded desperate on the answering machine. But I wasn't ready.

Besides, I was starving. The heat seemed even more intense after leaving the icy cold morgue. Between the temperature and my empty insides, a full-tilt blood sugar crash was on its way.

I crossed the river and snaked my way over to Main Street. The city changed complexion almost immediately. Downtown Nashville could be any urban city in America: skyscrapers, government buildings, plazas, bus transfer points. But cross the river, less than a mile, and you're in the middle of instant funky. That's my side of the river now, the working class, blue collar, slowly gentrifying side. No *cluster homes*, a great euphemism for ghettoes for the rich, no $80,000 condos, no upscale shopping malls. Just old homes, neighborhood bars and restaurants, and people who chug beer out of cans on their front porches. It was a daily and endless source of fascination to me.

Quite a change from my married days out in yuppie, upscale Green Hills. Personally speaking, it's no great loss. Besides, the smoking Ford would have been dreadfully out of place among the Mercedes-Benzes and the Jags.

Around the bend in front of East High School, Main Street becomes Gallatin Road. A couple of miles farther out, there's a hole-in-the-wall Chinese restaurant with the best damn Szechuan chicken that's ever cleared this boy's sinuses. I pulled into the parking lot next to a twenty-year-old rusted-out pickup truck with a pair of pit bulls chained in the back. They looked at me with either curiosity or hunger; I didn't get close enough to check which.

I'd pulled my jacket off by now, rolled up my sleeves, and decided to live with the drenching sweats soaking through my white shirt. My stomach rumbled at the aroma floating gently toward the bumper-to-bumper traffic.

"Why doan you twy somepeen else?" Mrs. Lee barked as I smiled across the counter at her. I hadn't even ordered yet, but she knew.

"And pass up the best Szechuan chicken this side of Shanghai?" I said. "No way."

"You wooden know Shanghai if it came up behind you and bit you on da butt!" She scraped a hand across her sweaty forehead, then whipped the green ticket behind to her daughter, a midteens Asian beauty that I'd been lusting after ever since I moved to this part of town. Hmmmm, maybe it's not the chicken I keep coming back for. . . .

She must have signaled to her husband to fix my order Extra Fierce. Maybe she wanted to wean me from my predictability. But as soon as I bit into the chicken, my whole face started sweating like the textbook throes of passion. I could feel the epidermis at the roof of my mouth coming loose. Every breath drawn in through my nose came from a flamethrower. It was exquisite. I took a couple of the fatter pieces of chicken, dipped them in a glass of water to get most of the pepper off, then wrapped them in a napkin and stuck them in my pocket. I wolfed down the rest of the food, drank my diet soda, then carried my plate back up to the counter.

"Almost got me that time," I said.

"What you talkeen about?" she demanded. Mrs. Lee was as genuinely fussy and ill-dispositioned as they came.

"It was delicious," I said, reaching across the counter and patting her hand. "See you later."

The sweltering air outside seemed normal now. I pulled my tie down another notch and opened the door to the Ford. The pits were gone now; the parking lot was safe for humanity. I settled in carefully on the hot vinyl car seat, and after a few deep-throated rumbles that made the Escort sound like an Alfa, I pulled back out into traffic.

I headed up Gallatin Road toward Inglewood. This part of town has more junk stores, salvage warehouses, cheap liquor stores, and pawn shops per capita than any other place I've ever seen. Off to my right, Riverside Drive ran parallel a mile or so away, changed names, then curved left and intersected Gallatin Road just ahead of me. I stopped short of the light, turned left onto some side street I never could remember the name of, and meandered back into a really seedy part of town.

Maybe it's not all *that* seedy; it's just that I've never gotten accustomed to being surrounded by junkyards, body shops, illegal dumpsites, and motorcycle gang headquarters. Down the road, on the left, next to a concrete block building that housed Billy and Sam's Expert Auto Maintenance on one side and the Death Ranger's clubhouse on the other side, sat a faded, old mobile home in the middle of a desolate, closed junkyard. An eight-foot-tall chain link fence surrounded the lot, which was littered with the rusting hulks of generations' worth of automotive dreams and overgrown with weeds and brush.

I pulled up in front of the gate and parked. I walked up, shook the gate to make a little noise, and waited for Shadow to emerge from wherever she'd been hiding out from the sun. Shadow, an aging black female German Shepherd trotted around from behind the trailer, ears at attention, a slight tilt to the left that came from age and the genetic hip displacement that seems to plague shepherds so badly.

She was slow, laid back, but I knew that was because I was on this side of the fence. If I crossed to the other side without either permission or recognition, she'd tear my throat out.

"Shadow," I said, holding a hand, palm out, against the gate. "Hey, babe, what's happening?"

She stopped about six feet away, sniffing, focusing. Then she approached slowly and ran her huge, wet, black nose up the chain link fencing to my hand. She sniffed a couple more times, then the tail started bouncing around like a clock un-winding. She whimpered a little, then backed away so I could open the gate. I lifted the chain off the hook, pressed the gate open a foot or two, and stepped inside the lot. Shadow was on my shoulders in a second, licking my face and nuzzling me. I reached inside my pocket, pulled out the napkin and unwrapped the chicken.

I took a step back; she was on the ground, jaws dripping.

"Speak. Speak to me, Shadow." She brought up a gnarl-ing growl that erupted into a bark.

"Good girl!" I squeezed the chicken into a ball, flipped it into the air. It was gone before it hit the top of the curve.

"Where's daddy, Shadow?" I said. Why do dogs and ba-bies make people talk so damn goofy? "Where's daddy, baby?"

The sun was really baking now, the bare ground cracked beneath my feet. I looked over toward the trailer, and even with the rust stains and dull, weathered paint, the reflection hurt my eyes. I walked toward the pale green hulk with Shadow flopping happily along at my side. At one end of the trailer, an overworked window unit struggled to pull the hu-midity out of the air. I knocked once and opened the door.

Lonnie stood inside, back to me, bent over slightly, staring at something on the table. He whipped his head around, shushed me, then motioned me in.

"And for God's sake, don't slam the door," he whispered.

Lonnie's office and sometimes apartment was a clutter of papers, used automobile parts, scattered books, grease, to-bacco stains, empty beer bottles. Lonnie was the smartest repo man I'd ever met, but he had strange tastes.

"What's going on?" I asked, real low.

"Shhh," he hissed. "Experiment."

Lonnie was barefoot, dressed in jeans and a T-shirt. In his outstretched hand, he held a few straws plucked from an old broom. He moved slowly toward the massive wooden table that normally served as his desk, but which had been swept clean for the drama du jour.

I strained in the low light to see what that was. Behind us, from the other room, the air-conditioner chugged away like an old steam locomotive. He padded slowly forward, reached out toward the middle of the table, then turned his head around and blindly moved a little closer. I bent down, looking around him, just as the straws touched a tiny pile of what looked like dirty table salt on the wood.

There was a terrific boom and a flash of white, followed by an acrid stink that made Mrs. Lee's Szechuan chicken smell as benign as Cream of Wheat. I jumped back, slamming against the door. I was blinded for a second, then dived on the floor with a yelp.

"Jesus H. Christ!" Lonnie yelled from the floor next to me. I looked over at his arm to see if I needed to start calling him Stumpy. "It works!"

His arm was intact, which was more than I could say for my ears. The smoke was dissipating. I stood up. A scorched circle on the wooden table outlined a gouge maybe an inch or so deep and a foot around.

"You jerk!" I yelled. "Why didn't you warn me?"

"Damn, man," he panted, standing up. "I didn't know it would be that powerful. I mean, the book—"

"Damn it, Lonnie" I moaned. "Which one this time? *The Anarchist's Cookbook?*"

He looked from the table to me, electric delight on his face. "No, man. I just got a copy of *The Poor Man's James Bond.*"

I looked around the room. On the moth-eaten couch, a paperback about the size of a telephone directory lay open. I picked it up.

"ANTI?" I asked, reading the page.

"Ammonium Nitrogen Tri-Iodide. Stuff's a pistol, man. In fact, it's more a fulminate than an explosive. Easiest junk in the world to make."

I scanned the article. "You trying to get yourself killed?" This was not the first time I'd walked into Lonnie's Playhouse just in time to almost get my head blown off. The last time, he was making ersatz napalm out of gasoline and Styrofoam cups.

"No, man, this is great! All you do is soak iodine crystals in pure ammonia, then press the goop through a coffee filter. What's left is ANTI. As long as it's wet, it's harmless. But when it dries, it's the nastiest stuff you've ever seen."

"Yeah, great," I said, dropping the book on the couch. "One of these days I'm going to have to come in here and scrape your ass off the walls with a spatula."

Lonnie grabbed a greasy rag and wiped his hands. My ears still rang from his little demonstration, and my nostrils were filled with what I now recognized as the stench of ammonia with a faint burning tinge added. Sort of like being at the landfill the day they burn the Pampers.

Lonnie reached into a dented, thirty-year old Kelvinator and pulled out a beer. "You going down to Shelbyville with me?"

"Ain't got the time this time, bro."

"I picked up the early edition of the *Banner.* Saw your name. You sure you don't want to get out of town for a while?" Lonnie popped the top and passed it over to me. I held out a hand to decline. He shrugged, lifted the can to his lips.

"Not this time. I mostly came by for information."

"Information?"

"Yeah. About the murder."

"You got any sense, you'll go to Shelbyville with me. Pick up that Trans Am. Drive back with the T-tops off. Have yourself a good time. Forget that murder shit. You look like death warmed over now. Don't make it permanent."

"Fine talk from a guy who sets off bombs in his office."

Lonnie lifted the can to his lips and downed the rest of it in one gulp. He tossed the can behind him, into the hallway leading back to the bedroom, then let loose with a long, deep belch.

"Okay, what you want?"

"That doctor who was murdered. He worked at the University Med Center, was on the medical school faculty. His wife said he was a real compulsive gambler. Owed his soul to a bookie."

"So?"

"So who'd it be? Who controls the action out 21st Avenue, Division, the West End Area?"

Lonnie tightened his lips and furrowed his brow. That meant he knew but was wrestling over whether or not to tell me.

"You not careful, you gonna get in over your head. You know that?"

"I'll watch myself."

"Okay, it's your funeral. You know where Division splits off Broadway?"

"Yeah, there at the triangle."

"Right, so you go down Division to where the restaurants are. That vegetarian hippie place on the left, you know where it is?"

"Those are the Seventh-Day Adventists, Lonnie. Not vegetarian hippies."

"Whatever. There's a little market there. You know, convenience market. Beer, bread, milk, cigarettes. Guy owns it, his name is Hayes. Bubba Hayes. He's about three-hundred pounds, tattoos, Brylcreem, used to be a preacher. Guess he got to backsliding. Anyway, he's got the action for the whole area."

"So if Fletcher was betting, that's who he'd be making book with?"

"If it wasn't Bubba, Bubba'd know who it was. He runs the whole area. Got a bodyguard, ex-pro football player. Used to play for the Falcons. Name's Mr. Kennedy."

"Okay," I said. "Mr. Kennedy. I'll keep an eye out for him. All I want to do is talk to the dude. See if what Rachel was telling me was right."

Lonnie got off the stool he'd climbed onto, came over to me, and poked me in the shoulder.

"You watch your ass," he said. "You're a good driver. I'd hate to have to replace you."

"Don't go dramatic on me, Lonnie. This is real life, not TV. I ain't Jim Rockford, and this ain't *Columbo*. I'm not going to do anything stupid."

"Yeah, well," he said, picking up *The Poor Man's James*

Bond and flipping through the pages, "you be careful all the same. I hear tell Bubba Hayes is a real Mustache Pete, a for-real freaking gangster."

Chapter 9

The Reverend Bubba Hayes, or Mustache Pete, or whoever the hell he was, was going to have to wait awhile. I needed to check the answering machine in my office, then get over to see Rachel as quickly as possible. Down Gallatin Road, a car pulling out of the Taco Bell got rammed by some old guy smoking a green cigar in a rusted blue Cadillac Coupe de Ville. That took twenty minutes to get past, and then there was a procession coming out of the funeral home. By the time I'd gone a dozen blocks from Lonnie's, I was dripping wet and the Ford was overheating.

For ten minutes, I drove around inside the three-story parking garage on Seventh Avenue, the one where my monthly rent gives me the right to look for a spot. Finally, on the top level, I found one subcompact slot left. I wedged the Escort into the tiny space and crawled out between the two cars. I made my way, sweaty and dizzy from exhaust fumes, down the concrete slab ramp to the street.

Cars were lined up bumper to bumper in all four directions at the intersection of Seventh Avenue and Church Street. Horns blared, sweat poured, engines belched steam in the summer heat. Southern Fried Gridlock.

I tiptoed between two cars out into the middle of the street, then jackrabbited onto the sidewalk just as two blue-haired little old ladies in a Chrysler New Yorker scraped a NO PARKING—TOW IN ZONE sign trying to get around the jam. I caught a glimpse of the driver's face as the car went by: thick glasses, too much rouge, false teeth bared like a dog in combat.

I walked into my dusty, rundown building, past the watch

72

repairman's office, and climbed the stairs to my office one shuffle at a time. By the time I got to the top floor, I was ready for another trip to the emergency room. Down the hall, I could hear Slim and Ray arguing over whether the second line in the chorus ought to be "Hey, baby I'm coming back home!" or "Hey, darlin', you're on your own. . . ." I decided to forego dropping in for my usual chat.

I silently opened my office door and quickly slid inside. With a little luck, no one would bother me for a while. I was feeling pretty antisocial, what with a lousy night's sleep, a bum ankle, and an aching set of butterfly closures on the crown of my head.

The red light on the answering machine was firing away like popcorn in a hot-air popper. I loosened my tie even further and opened the top two buttons on my shirt. If I pulled my necktie down any lower, I was going to trip over it. I settled back in the chair as the answering machine began reciting.

Message number one was from my old newspaper: "Hey, listen, friend. I know we're probably the last people on earth you want to talk to, but we could sure use an interview with you on the Fletcher killing." The voice was Ed Gibson's, the city editor. Ed had been sorry to let me go; had, in fact, always been decent to me. He was told to fire me. They made him do it. He's got three kids, was only doing his job. I understood.

Screw him.

The second message was from Channel 4, the third from Channel 2, the fourth from Channel 2, the fifth from Channel 2, the sixth from Channel 5, which finally got through when Channel 2 gave up.

Three more messages from the media types, then Rachel's voice: "Where have you been? I've been trying to reach you all day, and you're phone's either busy or I get this blasted machine. Please call me."

I opened my notebook and flipped through the Fs. I punched her number in, then waited through two rings.

"Hello?"

"Yes, Rachel Fletcher, please."

"I'm sorry, Mrs. Fletcher's unavailable right now."

I could hear the voice fade as the hand on the other end of the line headed toward a hangup.

"Wait!" I yelled. "Could you tell her it's Harry Denton. I'm returning her call."

Too late. A loud click, then a dial tone. Wonder who that was? Sounded like an older woman. Probably figured I was another reporter. My mail was still in a pile on the floor where the postman had stuffed it through the mail slot. I'd picked up the stack: my liability insurance bill, phone bill, and six pieces of junk mail. Whoopee . . .

Nothing to do but deal with it. For some reason or other, I was hesitant to go to Rachel's house. Maybe it's because I failed her. Maybe Walter was right; she was available now. Was I sleazy enough to go after a grieving widow? Or maybe she wasn't grieving at all. I didn't want to think about that alternative.

The prospect of climbing back to the top of the Mount Everest of parking garages was no erotic fantasy either. But it was nearing late afternoon, and the rule around here is that rush hour starts right after lunch, and the longer you wait, the worse the traffic's going to be.

I threw my coat over one shoulder and walked back out into the heat. At the intersection, the play was still the same, only the actors had changed. I slithered between the bumpers and the blaring horns and made my way over to the parking garage. The Ford had been there barely long enough to cool down. And now we were going out into the mother of all traffic jams.

It wasn't that bad, actually. Thirty minutes later, I made the turn off Hillsboro road onto Golf Club Lane. This part of town was my old hangout, back when I was married and had a job making steady money. That seemed like a hundred years ago, and I realized that one of the reasons I'd been putting off seeing Rachel was that I simply no longer felt comfortable on this side of the tracks.

The houses lining Golf Club Lane aren't mansions, but

try telling that to the Laotian families on the other side of the river who live fifteen to a two-bedroom duplex that doesn't meet codes. I slowed, watching the numbers on the houses, until I got to a huge black mailbox with the Fletcher's address in proper chrome figures.

Holy Hannah, doctors do well, don't they? A long black driveway stretched maybe two hundred feet up a well-coiffed lawn to a three-story brick house with a chimney at each end. A screened-in front porch on the left side of the house was bigger than my whole apartment. Wrought-iron yard furniture off to the left sat in the middle of a tiny, well-kept English garden. Something the Newport crowd would appreciate.

There were a half-dozen cars in the jet-black driveway, not a single one of them a six-year-old, oil-burning Ford Escort. The tackiest car in the lot—mine excepted—was about a twenty-five-thousand-dollar Buick. Probably the cleaning lady's.

I wondered if they'd call the police before I had a chance to identify myself. I pulled all the way up the driveway, figuring they'd be less upset if I parked behind the house where my car wouldn't be visible from the street. I only hope I didn't drip too much crankcase oil on the asphalt; that would be the automotive equivalent of breaking wind on a crowded elevator.

Then I saw it, a white Crown Victoria, one with unmarked car written all over it. If they wanted to call the cops on me, they wouldn't have far to go.

The Ford's door made a screeching sound as I pushed it open. I looked back over the wooded back lot, maybe twenty yards to an eight-foot-high fence that ran around the back. A combination carriage house-garage-office was just behind the house, with a stone and brick courtyard between it and the back door to the main house. All in all, some mighty nice digs.

I debated going around front, then decided it would be okay to enter through the kitchen. I jumped the two steps to the door and knocked once. The huge wooden door with stained-glass insets swung open to reveal the glowering stare of a Green Hills dowager.

"And what do *you* want?" she demanded. She had a deep aristocratic Southern accent, a faint hint of orange in her thinning hair, and makeup caked on so thick it was cracking in places. She stood tall, though, and was determined to put me in my place.

"I'm Harry Denton," I explained. "I came to see Rachel."

"Mrs. Fletcher is not speaking to the news media today. You could have saved yourself a trip by phoning first."

"I did, and you hung up on me. But I'm not with the newspaper. I'm a friend of hers. She left a message on my answering machine."

A painted-on eyebrow rose. Diamond earrings bobbed. "I'll go see if Mrs. Fletcher is willing to see you. Step in here."

I stepped into the kitchen. "Stay right there," Madame Dowager ordered.

I stood at attention. "Yes ma'am."

My maternal grandmother had that effect on people; could, in fact, drop you in your tracks with a change in tone. It gave me a shudder to think about it.

I looked around the kitchen: Garland stove taking up a good part of one wall; stainless-steel restaurant refrigerator just short of walk-in; butcher's block island the size of a twin bed; polished Mexican clay tile on the floor. This was a lifestyle that would be hard to support on the income of an established surgeon late in his career. Wonder what it was like for a guy my age? Conrad was doing all right, but how was he managing to pay for all this? Especially with a so-called gambling problem.

My questions were interrupted by Rachel's entrance. Her face was drawn, her hair pulled behind her tightly. Madame Dowager hovered behind her, like she expected me to run up and hump Rachel's leg. And she had the wadded-up newspaper ready.

"Harry," she said, her voice tense, strained. "Where have you been? The police are here. It's been awful."

She lunged and was in my arms in a second. I hugged her close, tighter than I would have expected. Her hair was freshly shampooed; everything about this woman was clean, scrubbed, still young after all these years.

"I saw their car. Sorry it took me so long to get here. The police kept me most of the night, and I've been putting out fires ever since."

She pulled back, looked me directly in the eyes. "Are you all right?" She tipped my head toward her. "I heard you got hit."

"Yeah," I said. "I'm okay. No stitches or anything. It was just a long night."

Rachel looked at the back of my head. "God, it's a nasty cut. But it looks like you'll be okay. I'm so relieved."

I stepped back, put my hands on her shoulders. "Rachel, I can't tell you how sorry I am about Conrad. If there was anything I could have done to stop it, I would have. But it was too late when I found him."

Her eyes welled, as if for a moment she'd been able to stop thinking about him, and now I'd brought it all back. "You did everything you could have, Harry. I realize that."

"Rachel, there are a few matters we need to discuss."

"Later," she whispered. "After the police leave."

She turned around to the dowager and held out a hand toward her. "Harry, this is my neighbor, Mrs. Goddard. She's a good friend and has been helping me out today, keeping the reporters off the property. Mrs. Goddard, this is Harry Denton, an old friend. We were all in college together."

"Hello, Mrs. Goddard," I said, extending a hand to her. The dowager took it gracefully and rocked it ever so gently.

"I didn't mean to be so cold to you out there, Mr. Denton. For all I knew, you might have been another of those blamed reporters."

"No, ma'am. Not me, but I imagine you've had them around all day."

"Like flies to a chamber pot, son." She gave me a sharp

grin. Maybe Mrs. Goddard the dowager had a wicked side to her, or at least naughty.

I heard voices far off in the living room, female voices melded into high-pitched insensibility.

"God," Rachel said, "the neighbors. The police. I swear, I can't take much more."

"Where's Spellman now?"

"I've got them in the den. They're questioning me about where I was, Harry. As if I had something to do with Conrad's death." There was fear in her voice, desperation, exhaustion. Her skin was pulled tight over cheekbones, her eyes tense, the purplish hollows under them deep.

"Rachel, maybe you should have a lawyer here."

Her eyes darkened even further. "You, too, Harry?"

"Rachel, I—"

"I don't need a lawyer, damn it."

She turned and charged past Mrs. Goddard into the hallway. I followed her to the den. Spellman and some other investigator I didn't recognize stood about awkwardly.

"Hello, Lieutenant," I said.

"Denton," Spellman said, nodding.

"Harry, these gentlemen presume I had something to do with my husband's death," Rachel said, straining to maintain control.

"That's not what we said, Mrs. Fletcher. It's just routine in cases like this to check the whereabouts of all the parties involved."

"As Mrs. Goddard has confirmed, I was here all night. I never left the house."

"That's right, Lieutenant," Mrs. Goddard said from behind him. I turned. The dowager didn't seem the kind of woman who'd lie to save anybody's butt. "We played bridge until eleven. When Mrs. Russell, Mrs. Winters, and the other table left, I stayed until eleven forty-five helping Mrs. Fletcher wash dishes and clean up because I only live two doors away."

Her voice was stern, solid. If this lady said she was playing bridge with Rachel until almost midnight, you could put it in the bank. I felt something inside me loosen, and it became a bit easier to breathe.

"So you see, Lieutenant," the dowager continued, "there were seven of us here with Mrs. Fletcher all night. She couldn't possibly have been in two places at once. Even you can understand that, can't you?"

"Now, Lieutenant," Rachel said, "if you've finished accusing me of murder, I'd like to get on with grieving my husband's death."

"Mrs. Fletcher," Spellman said defensively, "we—"

"I think you should go now," Mrs. Goddard said. It was not a request. Spellman flipped shut his notepad, made brief eye contact with his partner, and took two steps toward the door.

"Aren't you going to tell me not to leave town, Lieutenant?" Rachel demanded bitterly.

Spellman turned. "No, ma'am, I'm not going to tell you that." It was rare, I thought, to see a homicide investigator leave a room with his tail between his legs. Kind of fun, actually. It's not that I didn't like Spellman; I just took a certain perverse delight in seeing the mighty put in their place.

"Why don't I let you two young people talk alone? I'll go see if they need anything out there."

Rachel kept her back turned to me, following Mrs. Goddard out of the room with her eyes. When she was safely out of sight, Rachel turned to me, her blue eyes wide open, relieved.

"I've been so worried about you. What happened at the hospital last night?"

"I heard a noise," I whispered. "I went into the room. It was dark so I fumbled for the light. When I got it on, I saw Conrad stretched out on a bed. He was still breathing, though. I bent over him to see how badly hurt he was. Somebody came up behind me and knocked me silly. That's all I remember for a few seconds, which was just enough time to give the other person a chance to get away."

She held a hand up to her mouth, palm inward, almost in

horror. "Oh my heavens. The police didn't give me much in the way of details. Most of what I've been able to get has been out of the newspaper."

"That's not what we need to worry about now, Rachel. I need to know exactly what you know about Conrad's gambling. I think I may have a line on who he owed money to, but we need to—"

"No. I won't have it."

"Won't have what?"

"You're through, Harry. I want you to stop this." Her voice was tight as she strained to be forceful without being heard by her company in the other room. "I don't want whoever killed Connie to get a shot at you. I can't bear that. You have to quit."

"Rachel, I can't quit." I put my hands on her shoulders without thinking, an unconscious, spontaneous motion. I squeezed her gently; her shoulders were knotted up like cordwood. "Not now. I've got to find out what really happened."

"You've got to quit. I'm not going to have you get hurt in this, too."

"Rachel, I—"

"We'll talk about it later. We can't now, not with all these . . . old biddies . . . here. Come by tonight, late. I'll be up."

I stood back from her. "Are you sure that's a good idea?"

She put her hands on her hips, jaw clenched, eyes wide. "Of course, it's all right. We are adults, aren't we? We don't need a chaperone. I'll have the lights off. Just come up the driveway and park where you are now. The back door'll be open."

"Rachel, are you positive this is okay?"

"I just don't want to hear any gossip from this crew. They think they're helping, but the truth is they're driving me crazy. My parents are due in tomorrow night, and Connie's are going to have to fly back from Europe." She pulled some blond bangs off her forehead. "God, it's going to be a long week."

"I know you're exhausted. Are you sure you wouldn't rather be alone?"

She looked up at me, her forehead wrinkling. "Eleven tonight," she said. "Be here."

Chapter 10

I pulled out into the thick traffic on Hillsboro Road still wondering just how in blazes Connie Fletcher was paying the mortgage on that place, not to mention the requisite cars, vacations, clothes, parties, landscaping, cleaning lady, and the assorted paraphernalia that go with maintaining that kind of lifestyle.

I pulled left onto the road almost by instinct, crossed the I-440 bridge, and found myself heading back toward the university hospital. I kept thinking that there had to be some way, some contact, somebody I could put the bite on to find what was really happening with the dear departed Dr. Conrad Fletcher and his professional life. If he was in hock to his bookie, maybe he told someone. A friend, perhaps, if he had any. Judging from the reactions of people I'd met in the hospital, Conrad Fletcher wasn't a man with a wealth of friends. On the other hand, maybe I could find somebody he'd hit on for a loan, or a shoulder to cry on, or just somebody he'd shoot the breeze with. He was human, right? Even doctors need somebody to talk to, rather than at, every now and then.

Then I remembered. I'd been concentrating so hard on Conrad and Rachel that I forgot to put any connection from their life into my own. My father's closest friend, before my parents retired to Hawaii, was a doctor: Dr. Eugene Hughes. Dr. Gene, we called him. Dr. Gene was a pediatrician, and he and his wife had a surprise late baby after the rest of their children were nearly grown. And that surprise late baby, James, was now in medical school himself.

Guess where? I could have slapped myself as I drove toward Hillsboro Village. And Dr. Hughes lived about ten minutes away. I jerked into the left-hand-turn lane at Wedgewood Avenue, which becomes Blakemore, then changes names again and becomes 31st Avenue. I turned left on West End Avenue, which becomes Harding Road a mile or two down. I drove out past St. Thomas Hospital and turned right onto White Bridge Road, which is Woodmont Boulevard on the other side of the intersection before it becomes Robertson Road the other side of the interstate. What a town.

I lost track of the street names chugging around the steep curves and wandering roads of the part of town called Hillwood. Dr. Hughes's house was a big gray one; I remembered that much. But it had been years since I'd been there. The last time was my father's retirement party. My father and Dr. Hughes had flown in the war together and had been lifelong buddies after that.

There, on that corner, I thought, as I pulled into a steep downhill driveway and coasted to a stop. This looked like the right place. If not, I'd just have to hope they didn't keep many shotguns around.

Dr. Hughes raised dogs, some of the finest hunting dogs I'd ever seen. I must have smelled like squirrel that day, or maybe they got a whiff of Shadow. Anyway, the dogs went crazy as soon as I got out of the car. I headed away from them, back up the drive to the walk that led to the front door.

I had to ring twice. Dr. Hughes opened the door, stood there holding a newspaper in one hand, his glasses tipped down on his nose, trying for a moment to recognize his dearest, most lifelong friend's son.

"I'm Harry, Dr. Gene. Harry Denton."

He paused for a moment, more astonished than anything else. "Well, of course you are, son. I recognized you. I was just trying to figure out if it was really you after all this time."

He held the metal storm door open for me, and I walked in. The difference in lifestyle between a pediatrician and a hot-rod surgeon was acutely obvious here; Dr. Hughes's house was large and comfortable, but it was definitely lived in. The furniture was old, most of it from the Fifties and early Sixties, with plenty of evidence that when no one else was looking, Dr. Hughes let the dogs in.

"Good to see you, Harry. It's been too long." His voice was jovial, yet with the distinguished edge that educated Southern men start to take on when they get old. It's as if they live under some compulsion to sound like gentlemen farmers at that stage in life, as if all their great-grandfathers had been Civil War generals. If everybody who claimed to have a Civil War general in his past really had one, the whole damn war would have been fought with nothing but men wearing stars on their collars.

"Good to see you, Dr. Gene. How've you been?"

"Just fine, my boy. Just fine."

Dr. Hughes's wife had passed on about five years earlier. He'd lived alone until James finished his undergraduate work at Emory and came home to go to medical school. Now the two of them lived by themselves in this big house. And while I'm sure they had someone come by every week or so to clean house, domestic science obviously wasn't all that much of a priority to them.

"Dr. Gene," I said, after he closed the door and escorted me into the living room. "I kind of came by on business."

There was a picture of him and my father on the mantelpiece, an old black-and-white from the war; the two of them were wearing leather flying helmets and parachutes in front of a P-40.

He frowned at me and led me over to the couch, newspaper still in hand, and motioned for me to sit. He settled into his easy chair and fanned the paper out in front of him.

"I've been reading about your business, boy. I heard you lost your job at the paper, but I didn't know you'd gone into private detecting."

He made it sound like pimping. I was a long way from becoming a pimp; six or seven weeks, at least. I shrugged my shoulders. "Same old story. Seemed like a good idea at the time."

"But now you're not so sure."

"Yes, sir. I'm not so sure. But I still want to stick with this, if only to make certain my own name stays clear."

"Are you a suspect in this murder?" His eyeglasses slid a little farther down his nose as he asked.

"Not a strong one. But yes, sir, I'm sure the police are keeping an eye on me."

"But you didn't have anything to do with this, did you?"

"Of course not."

"Well, then, why don't you just back off and let the police do their jobs? You're only going to get in more trouble if you interfere."

I felt the blood pressure in my neck rising. Who was this guy? Just because he and my father fought, drank, and screwed their way across the European Theater of Operations nearly fifty years ago doesn't give him the right to—

"I'm not going to interfere." I interrupted my own train of thought. "But I am going to do some background checking. I can do some things the police can't do, mainly because I'm not the police. I want to find out what happened to Dr. Fletcher, too. It's important. It's what I'm getting paid for."

He snorted. "You think you can do a better job than the police."

"No sir, only a different job."

He paused, letting the weight of his words sink in even before he spoke them. "Harry, you came from a good family. You've got a fine education, a crackerjack mind. You had a fascinating career, and for some reason or other, you've chosen to self-destruct. And now this . . . this . . . detecting business. I don't like it."

"I appreciate that, Dr. Hughes, but for the time being, it's what I do. I'm a grown man, sir. I make my own way now."

"And what a way," he fumed. "Sneaking around some sleazy motel on Murfreesboro Road at night, taking pictures of adulterers and prostitutes."

"Doc, there's not much difference between those motels on Murfreesboro Road and the mansions in Belle Meade. Just a different class of john, that's all."

"You've become profoundly cynical, haven't you?"

"No, sir, just a realist."

"Does your father know about this mess?"

"Not yet. And I'd appreciate your not saying anything to him."

He reached up and pulled his glasses off his nose and twirled them in one hand by the earpiece. "All right. But I want you to let me know if there's anything I can do to help. Your father and mother never appointed a godfather for you, so I sort of feel like the job's mine by default."

"I appreciate that, Dr. Hughes. And the one thing you could help me with now is by letting me talk to James."

He stiffened. "What has James got to do with this?"

"Nothing, sir. I just want to find out what the medical students thought of Dr. Fletcher. I'm only looking for background."

"I don't want my son drawn into this."

"He won't be."

I sat downstairs while the doc went up to get his son. I heard water running upstairs, so I figured James was in the shower. I wandered around the living room and made my way to the kitchen. The remains of an early dinner were heaped up on the counter. I glanced at my watch and realized it was nearly seven o'clock, and that I was getting a bit peckish myself.

James came downstairs, unpressed khaki pants buttoned but still unbelted, no shirt, no shoes, rubbing a towel through his wet hair.

"Hey, Harry," he greeted me. James was a decade younger than me, with a couple of years to spare on top of it. I remembered him as a child and realized I hadn't seen him in several years. For the first time in my memory, he seemed an adult.

"Hey, James, what's happening, man?"

"Same old, same old." He took my hand and pumped it. He had his mother's reddish-brown hair and his father's deep brown eyes. He was a handsome young man, intelligent, with a bright future. I found myself envying him.

"How's medical school?"

"Tough. I'm third year, though. So apparently I'm going to make it. A lot by now is just routine. You grind it out. Next year, I start jockeying for residencies."

"Great. Hey, listen, where'd your dad go?"

James looked behind him. "He's upstairs in his office, I guess. He just came up, said you wanted to talk to me. Seemed kind of tight."

"It's my fault," I said, leaning against the counter and crossing my arms. "He doesn't approve of my present career path."

James winced. "Oh, man, I'm sorry. I hate when he does that. The old man seems to think he knows what's best for everybody."

I smiled at him. "He means well. I've just gotten myself in a mess over this Conrad Fletcher situation."

James wrapped the towel around his head and gave it a good shake. "Yeah, it's been all over the school. Not you, I mean. Just Fletcher getting murdered."

"I wanted to get an insider's point of view from you, James."

James pulled the towel off his head and wrapped it around his shoulders. "I took classes from Fletcher. We had to. No way out of it. I'd have probably gotten him next year for surgery rotation. Whoever killed him had fabulous timing. Did us all a favor."

"I got the feeling not many people were fond of him."

"He was abrasive, abusive, probably a rageaholic. Popular? No, I'd have to say not."

"Diplomat," I commented. "Any idea who might have hated him enough to kill him?"

"God, Harry," he sighed. "Who *didn't* hate him enough to kill him?"

"James," I said, pulling out my notebook and pen, "can you be a little more specific?"

"To begin with," he said, pausing a long moment, "there was me."

Chapter 11

"What?" I asked, my notebook falling to the floor. I bent to pick it up.

James laid the towel across the back of his neck and pulled both ends tightly.

"When Dr. Fletcher decided he didn't like you, you were on his list forever. And it was pretty easy to get on that list. Sometimes, you didn't even know you'd done *anything*."

"And you were on the list?"

He nodded his head. "Since first year. At the time, he taught an anatomy course. He hated it, doesn't do it anymore."

"Obviously," I interrupted.

James smiled. "Yeah, that's right. I forgot. Anyway, I was one of the herd, that's all, and content to stay that way. Somehow, I got singled out. He used to drill us, more like law school than med school. Remember *The Paper Chase*?"

"Yeah."

"He made Professor Kingsfield look like a den mother. He tore me apart one day in lecture, caught me in a weak moment. I was a target for the rest of the term. Dropped me a letter grade at the end of the semester, even though everything else I'd done was top-notch. When I went to his office to protest, he tore me apart again. Apparently, no one'd taken him on like that before. He threatened to have me thrown out of school."

"Could he have done that?"

"I've seen him do it since. I think the only reason I sur-

vived is that my dad's an alum. Still knows people. Political
bullshit. That's all it is.''

"I had no idea medical schools were such shark tanks."

James smiled. "Grow up, Harry. A lot's at stake. You
know what a doctor's lifetime earnings can be?''

By the time I left Dr. Hughes and Son's an hour later, I
had several pages filled in my notebook: petty jealousies,
betrayals, treacheries, sexual peccadillos, resentments. The
struggle for research grants, tenure, awards, and recognition
brings out the worst in people. I always had this naive notion
that somehow the hallowed halls of the university, where
learning and knowledge were prized as ends in themselves,
were free of cutthroat craziness.

*Right, Ace. And where's that oceanfront property in Ari-
zona you want me to look at?*

It was getting late, and I really needed to eat. I have this
weird blood sugar thing: I never seem to get hungry, and
then within the space of five minutes, I'm breaking out in a
cold sweat, shaking, and I'll eat anything in sight. I could
feel the onset of another blood sugar crash. Fortunately, I
was headed downtown. I made a left turn just past the park
onto Elliston Place, spotted a space just coming free in front
of Rotier's, and grabbed it before anybody else had the
chance.

Mrs. Rotier had been fixing double cheeseburgers on
French bread for the local student population for decades.
I'd been eating them since high school. She's surrogate
mother for half the under-twenty-one population of Nashville, a tiny woman with the metabolism of a runaway locomotive. Her grown kids, along with most of their spouses,
work the restaurant with her. It's one place in the ever-shifting
flood of the city that never seems to change.

I slid into a red vinyl booth near the back. A couple of the
Rotier's waitresses are notoriously ill-tempered, which only
adds to what's usually called the atmosphere of the place.
After all, what's Mama going to do, fire them?

It was my luck to get one that evening. About thirty seconds after I sat down, a plastic-jacketed menu slid across the

table in front of me, having become airborne from somewhere behind my left shoulder.

"Make it quick. I don't have all night."

I looked up to see a mass of brown hair wearing an apron, with a green order pad in one hand, a cracked Bic pen in the other. I smiled. It felt good to be home.

I flipped open the menu and scanned it. "Roast beef and gravy, potatoes, stewed tomatoes, fried okra. Unsweetened tea." I rattled off my order as quickly as possible.

While I waited for dinner, I tried to earn my money by pondering my next move. Problem was, I didn't know what the hell I was doing. I could go see Bubba—what was his last name?—Hayes. Yeah, that was it. Hayes. Or I could go track down a few of the people that James Hughes had mentioned. I opened my notebook and scanned my scribblings.

Some of them I could eliminate right off. After all, the dean of the medical school may have been hacked off about that rumor that Conrad had been sleeping with his wife, but he wouldn't have had to kill him. There would be better, more efficient, ways for the dean of a medical school to ruin one of his professor's lives.

I stared at two names I'd written down: Jane Collingswood and Albert Zitin. James told me they were two surgical residents who had been under Conrad's direct supervision. There had been a lot of friction; rumor was that he was about to bust Dr. Collingswood out of the program. There'd been a blowup the day Conrad was killed. Zitin and Collingswood had gotten into a shouting match with Conrad, right out in the hall in front of patients and staff. Everybody on Four West heard it. Most uncool. That was why, in fact, James knew about it. Tension and hostility were rampant at all levels of the institution, but open warfare in front of patients was a real breach of protocol.

Another concern had been tugging at the back of my mind ever since the police questioned me. I mentioned, in relating my linear chronicle of events, the woman I'd seen step out of the room where I found Conrad. But in my memory, I seem to remember . . . It's hard to say. It's almost as if I saw a second person. Not anybody I saw clearly, you understand. But I saw this woman, an attractive, young woman in a nurse's uniform. That is, of course, why I noticed her in the first place. But there was something else, and in my mind's eye, I was simply unable to reconstruct it.

I heard a throat clearing behind me. "You want this or not?" I looked up to see my waitress standing behind me with a steaming plate and a drink. She'd obviously been standing there a moment or two, waiting for me to come back to earth.

"Oh, sorry." I scooted out of her way and pulled my notebook off the table.

"Yeah, yeah, yeah," she said. "Here. You need anything else?"

I looked down at the plate. It was all there and looked great. "Everything's fine. Thanks."

She broke what appeared to be a human smile. "Good. Knock ya'self out," she instructed.

The food was exquisite, like dinner at home back when my mother still cooked. Meat-and-three, it's called down South, and there's nothing like it for finding a little bit of comfort in a lousy, grown-up world.

The sun had long since set even on this late summer evening when I turned left off 21st Avenue onto Division and headed toward Music Row. Way before I got there, though, I found a parking space on the street beneath an enormous umbrella of maple whose branches hung drooping and heavy out over the near lane of traffic. This part of Division was quiet at night, far from the packs of tourists that crowded the Country Music Hall of Fame, Barbara Mandrell Country, and the line of tacky souvenir shops that lined the streets all the way down to I-40. I swear, it seems that the first thing every truck driver from Tupelo who comes to Nashville and gets a recording contract does is buy himself a gift shop. Go figure. It gave new meaning and depth to the word *kitsch*, and there'd been many a time I had to slam on my brakes to keep from smashing into some hairy-legged, knobby-kneed

geek in Bermuda shorts who wandered out into traffic because the sign that read HERE ONE DAY ONLY—ELVIS'S CAD-
ILLAC had caught his eye.

And they call L.A. La-la land.

Two punkers with safety pins through their cheeks walked
past in the darkness. This town was joining the twentieth
century fast, but we were still sufficiently out of it to find
safety pins through cheeks shocking. I watched them walk
far enough up the sidewalk to where I was sure they weren't
going to turn around and mug me, then I crossed the street.
Ahead of me a block or so was the bright neon sign in the
small parking lot of Bubba's market.

BUBBA'S! YOUR 24-HOUR CONVENIENCE MART, the sign
flashed, its blue and red blazing like a visual Islamic call to
prayer for those bereft of cigarettes, beer, disposable diapers,
and munchie relief. Below that, in bright, steady white, the
guarantee: WE NEVER CLOSE!

I stepped through the heavy metal and glass doors onto
the dirty linoleum floor of Bubba's. The place was your basic
redneck all-night market. Disposable lighter displays carried
photos of half-nude women, Confederate flags, and my personal favorite: the broken down old Rebel soldier with a
drink in one hand and the Stars and Bars in the other with
the caption, "Forget, Hell!" Beer coolers lined the entire
length of the wall opposite the entrance. Wire cage displays
held every kind of goocy snack cake, processed cracker mor-
sel, and potato chip variation imaginable. The place was a
cathedral of cholesterol: potted meat product, deviled ham,
beef stick, beef jerky, pickled pig's feet, Vienna sausages,
on and on and on, ad—quite literally—nauseam.

A skinny white dude with greasy hair, wearing a dirty
T-shirt that exposed tattooed arms, stood behind the counter.
He was barely visible below an overhead rack full of cigarettes, but I got a good enough look at him to guess that he
was probably a recent graduate of the Tennessee Department
of Corrections. I moseyed up to him and tried to look casual.

"What can I do for you?" he asked.

"Bubba around?"

He looked at me, suspicious that somebody actually wearing a necktie would want to see the boss. Maybe I should have left it in the car. Maybe I should have gone home and changed into overalls.

"Who wants to know?"

"My name's Harry. Harry Denton. Bubba doesn't know me, but I think he'll want to talk to me."

The clerk's eyes wandered to the tip of my chin. Seemed this guy had trouble looking people in the face. "I don't know about that."

"Why don't you call Mr. Kennedy and ask him if it's okay." My one trump card had been played. If I knew who Mr. Kennedy was, I had to be an insider. At least, that's what I hoped he'd think.

He stared right through me for a second. Behind me, the front door opened and two teenage kids with thin, scraggly beards and bad skin walked in, a couple of Jeff Spiccoli types by way of Birmingham. I turned back to the clerk.

"How about it? Can I talk to him?"

"Well, I—"

"At least call him," I said. "He can always say no. But what if it turns out he really does want to see me and you don't call him?"

He stared at me, like screw you, smart guy. But then he turned his back to me and picked up a black receiver from the shelf behind him. He whispered something into the phone, listened for a second, then hung up.

"Mr. Kennedy'll be out in a minute," he said, turning immediately to the two guys behind me.

I took a step or two back, looked around the store. Good spot for a holdup, I thought. Wonder how many times this place has been hit? Then again, if Bubba really does have some stroke around here, maybe the local crackheads have figured out this establishment isn't a viable target.

I noticed a metal door nestled in a corner of the store, to the left of the beer cooler and facing the checkout counter. I hadn't seen it before, and then I realized the overhead cigarette display rack camouflaged it, probably deliberately. In the center of the door was a small dot framed in a ring of metal: an eyepiece.

In a moment, the door opened, and the godawful biggest black guy I've ever seen in my life stepped through. Come to think of it, this guy could have stepped through without opening the door. This hunk had to be 250, 270, all muscle, wearing a knit pullover shirt that was clean, expensive, fashionable, and a pair of stone-washed jeans that fit him like a glove. His hair was cut short, conservative, and he wore a surprisingly tasteful gold chain around his neck. What's a good-looking guy like that doing in a place like this?

He stepped toward me. I fought the urge to run like hell, figuring an ex–pro-football player could probably still outrun me in the forty-yard dash. "You looking for me?" he demanded, his voice low, serious. He was not a man to be messed with. I picked that up pretty quick; I'm a detective.

"Actually," I squeaked, my throat suddenly dry. "I'm looking for Bubba Hayes." God, I wish I'd been born with a deeper voice.

"Mr. Hayes is busy right now. Perhaps if you explained your business to me, I could set up an appointment at a later date."

"I'm a detective," I said, trying to force my voice an octave lower without sounding like a complete twit. "I'm investigating the death of Dr. Conrad Fletcher. I understand that Dr. Fletcher and Mr. Hayes may have had some business dealings."

This man had the most expressionless face I'd ever seen in my life. His face was a stone carving with a thin veneer of ebony. I could no more see what he was thinking than I could see through the metal door he'd walked out of. He stared at me a moment longer, then spoke.

"This way."

He turned, smooth and quick, and walked back toward the door. I dodged a Twinkie display and followed him. The metal door swung in hard and popped me on the shoulder. We entered a narrow hallway leading into the back of the building. It was dark, musty, with mildewed wood skids stacked against the wall and beer cases everywhere. The stale smell of beer, trash, and what was perhaps soured milk filled my nostrils. I imagined I heard rats scurrying around, although it may have been more than my imagination.

Four steps ahead of me, the imposing man moved forward silently. At the end of the hall, shrouded in shadow, was a closed door. Mr. Kennedy got to the door, stopped, then turned. I almost walked into him, but his arms were outstretched and waiting for me.

"You work homicide?" he asked. "Where's your partner?"

"No, I—"

"D.A.'s office?"

"Actually, Mr. Kennedy, I'm a private detective."

"Private detective!" He rolled his eyes in disgust, then moved so fast my eyes couldn't follow. Suddenly, I was face forward into an ice-cold, dusty, mildewed cinderblock wall.

"Hey, wait a minute—" He grabbed my arms and planted them palm into the wall, then kicked my legs apart. "What the he—"

His hands ran down each leg of my pants on the outside, then back up the inside. He bumped the inside of my crotch on his way up, then ran his hands up my sides. He pulled my wallet out, examined it, emptied my side pockets, pulled the small wire-bound notebook out of my shirt pocket. The man was a professional.

He grabbed the scruff of my neck, then pulled me back off the wall. Once I had my balance back, I glared at him. "You finished?"

He reached behind me and knocked twice on the metal door, then twisted the handle and opened it.

I stepped into a bank president's office, or at least that's what it resembled. What a shift in interior design. An enormous mahogany desk dominated the center of the room; a leather executive's chair and a cherry butler's table, surrounded by a leather couch and Queen Anne chairs, filled the rest. A color television and stereo system filled one wall, with a wet bar on the wall behind me.

Behind the huge desk sat Bubba Hayes. Remember Meat Loaf, the guy who sang "Paradise by the Dashboard Lights" back in the Seventies? Imagine Meat Loaf twenty years older and fifty pounds heavier, and you've got Bubba Hayes.

What have I gotten myself into?

The three of us stared at one another for a moment. I cleared my throat, started to say something, but was interrupted by this twisted Jabba the Hutt lookalike.

"I understand you want to talk to me, boy," he burbled.

Mrs. Rotier's roast beef and gravy did a somersault in my gut. "Mr. Hayes, I'm Harry Denton. I'm an investigator looking into the death of Conrad Fletcher, that doctor who was murdered last night in the medical center."

"I know who he is. I read the papers."

Bubba's voice was sonorous, filling the office with the same determined resonance that he must have once projected from the pulpit.

"Yeah, well. I was just wondering if you could answer a couple of questions."

Bubba leaned back in his massive leather chair. The wheels groaned under his weight, but held. "Depends on what they are. You're not a police officer. No warrant, no stroke."

Bubba smiled, revealing a row of cracked, yellowed teeth. "Right, boy?"

I was starting to resent being made to feel like an extra in a remake of *Smokey and the Bandit*. I'm nearly forty years old; it's been a long time since anyone called me boy.

"I've been asked by the family to investigate this matter. I understand from some close friends of Dr. Fletcher's that he had a . . . well, a gambling problem."

Bubba leaned forward in the chair, his bulk heading toward the desk like a flesh-colored glacier on the move. Then he stood up, moving with a dexterity and a speed that surprised me, and came around the desk. He faced me now, maybe a foot or two away. The skin of his face was pulled tight, with just a shadow of red underneath, as if he were translucent, like a monstrous gecko.

"What's that got to do with me?" he asked, his voice coming from somewhere deep inside the mound of flesh.

"I've heard that you control the action in this part of—"

Suddenly, something came out of the corner of my eye. All too late, I realized that whatever was flying upward in my direction was attached to Bubba. He caught me square in the gut, his right fist the size of a small ham.

Every bit of air shot out of my body in a second. If you've ever had the breath knocked out of you, you know the feeling. If you haven't, count yourself lucky.

My feet came off the floor, and my mind went blank. I felt myself becoming weightless, then suddenly the thick green carpet slammed me in the face.

I fought to keep down dinner, although in retrospect, I can't figure out why. I should have blown chunks all over the guy's carpet. Would've served him right.

I rolled over on my side, curled in a fetal position. One hand covered my battered gut; the other was under my head useless. As I turned, I saw Bubba's face about six inches from mine. How he could bend down that far without falling over was a mystery I'll never figure out.

"You ask a lot of questions, boy," he hissed. Then the massive hams stretched out again and grabbed my shirt, scrunching it up so hard my shirttail came completely out of my waistband.

Next thing I know, I'm back on my feet. Wish he'd make up his mind. He's holding me up, because I'm still not breathing yet, not even over the shock of getting hit yet. Which means the pain hasn't really started either. Great, I'm already hurting like hell, and it's only just begun.

Bubba pulled me up to eye level, and I got a face full of his hot breath. Something came over me, probably an attack of bad attitude, and I got just enough air to put my foot in my mouth.

"What'd you have for dinner, man?" I gasped. "Ever heard of Listerine?"

Damn if I'm not airborne again! This time, I landed in a chair against the wall near where Mr. Kennedy is watching all this deadpan. I hit the chair hard, the small of my back taking most of the impact, but my head snapping back against the wall right where the nurse put those butterfly closures last night.

It felt like a drill bit through the back of my skull. This time, I really did see red, and the shooting pain threatened to put me completely under for a second. It hurt so bad, I forgot about the first punch.

Dazed, I shook my head to bring myself to. Big mistake. That only works in the movies. After a second or an hour, I wasn't sure which, I felt behind my head and came back with blood on my hand.

Then I was really torqued; that fat bastard busted my head back open. No more Mister Nice Guy.

"What'd you do that for?" I growled, my voice lowering naturally.

"I wanted to impress upon you, in a way that you couldn't mistake, the distress that man's name causes me." Bubba spoke like a gentlemen farmer himself, when he wanted to. I was surprised, but no less mad.

"For all you know, I could be a cop," I said.

"Hah," he laughed. "I know every police officer in this town. And son, you ain't one of them. Not by a long shot."

I put a hand on each arm of the chair and pushed myself into a standing position. I'd had, simply put, enough.

"Sit down," Bubba ordered.

I kept my ground. "Listen, Bubba, I don't need this crap. You and that reject from a Lite Beer commercial over there can go to hell for all I care. You don't want to talk to me, fine. Talk to the cops."

I took a step toward the door.

"Sit down," Bubba repeated. A moment later, "I said sit."

I walked around him, settled myself on the couch. I'll sit, all right, but where I want to.

Bubba crossed back to his desk, lowered himself into the seat. "Now what is it you think I can tell the police?"

I shook my head. "No, sir. I don't think so."

"What you mean, boy?"

"After the welcome I've been given here, I don't feel like answering any of your questions. If there's any answering to be done here, I'll let you do it."

Bubba smiled, as if he couldn't believe I'd still be getting smart with him after all this. He don't know me very well, do he?

"I'll say this much for you, boy. You ain't much to look at, but you got great big brass ones."

"From what I can tell," I continued, ignoring what I guess was supposed to be a compliment, "Fletcher had two kinds of people in his life. Those who hated him enough to kill him, and those who merely fantasized about it."

Bubba looked over in Mr. Kennedy's direction and smiled. "He was not the most lovable man in God's creation."

"I keep running into people who thought the world would be better off without him. To tell you the truth, Bubba, I just wanted to find out if you were one of them."

Bubba reached down below the desk, tugged at his crotch. "The man had a problem. Loved to play. Hated to lose."

"Yeah?"

"Yeah. I've seen doctors with habits before. More of them have it than you think. I got quite a few in my territory. When he started, Fletcher was no better, no worse, than most. He played football during the season, pro basketball, some college games."

"When he started?"

"Some people just can't handle it. I told him he needed help once. Over the phone, of course. He never came here."

I thought for a second. "How much was he into you for?"

Bubba hesitated. That made me think it was quite a bit, maybe even a few thousand. He leaned against the desk, stared at me for a moment, then spoke.

"That man owed me not quite one hundred thousand dollars."

When I got my breath back, I whistled.

"Jesus," I sighed.

"Jesus hadn't got nothing to do with it, boy. At least not

on this end of the action. Right now, I'd guess Jesus and Fletcher are just about wrapping up a very long talk."

I gritted my teeth, preparing for what the next question was probably going to bring me.

"In your business," I asked, "is that the kind of scratch that would get somebody killed?"

The color shot up Bubba's fat neck. "Praise Jesus!" he yelled. "I've sinned in my time, blasphemed God in my life. But never, never, mortally sinned by taking the life of another! Besides," he added, "a doctor would be good for it over the long run. High life-style, high profile. Wouldn't want his revered name dragged through the mud."

"So you'd just blackmail a doctor. A truck driver who owed that much?"

"I'd never let a truck driver owe me that much," Bubba growled. "Now, of course, it's just a write-off. Cost of doing business."

"But you didn't kill him?"

The color came back again. "The answer to that question is *no*, boy. Don't ask it again."

Chapter 12

I was, as we say down South, dog-assed tired. Between lack of sleep, running around in circles, and being knocked silly a couple of times, the last couple of days had used up all my reserves. All I wanted to do was get home, get a cold compress on my head, clean the dried blood off, then take a nose dive between the sheets.

But then there was Rachel. I was already headed down Demonbreum Street toward the highway when I remembered. I looked down at my watch: 10:30. Just enough time to make it back out to Golf Club Lane, to the shaded, tree-lined dark street that probably had more security devices per square foot than the Pentagon.

I pulled a U-turn across the freeway bridge, in front of the nude dance club that advertises 50 BEAUTIFUL GIRLS & 3 UGLY ONES, and headed back in toward the ritzy part of town.

Twenty minutes later, I was driving up the black asphalt of Rachel's driveway. Discreetly low lights guided my way toward the darkness of the back yard. I pulled around and parked. Once the car engine was shut down, a deep quiet settled over the neighborhood. No freight trains going by a block away, no rednecks' squealing tires, no radios blaring, no gunshots penetrating the night air. Jeez, I'd hate it over here.

I padded up the steps to the kitchen door and knocked softly. A few seconds later, Rachael came to the door. The lights in the kitchen were low. Rachel wore blue jeans and a white T-shirt. Her hair was brushed loose down to her shoulders, and she wore no makeup. She'd finally, it appeared, relaxed.

"Hi," she greeted me. She smiled, a tired smile certainly, but still a smile. She was holding up reasonably well, I thought. I don't know how I'd have done under the circumstances.

"You okay?" I asked before I stepped in. "I mean, is it okay for me to be here?"

"Of course," she said, holding the door open for me. "Everyone's gone. Finally."

I stepped in. She closed the door behind me, then bent her head down slightly and came toward me with her arms open.

"God, what a day," she sighed. "Could you just hold me for a minute?"

"Yeah, c'mon," I agreed. She came to me, and I wrapped my arms around her shoulders. I felt her breath through my shirt, each movement of her chest deep, exhausted. She felt good. I had to remind myself of the circumstances; after all, her husband had just been murdered.

"This feels good," she whispered after a moment. "It's been a long time since anyone held me."

"You've been through the mill, haven't you?"

"God, you don't know. When the police started asking me where I was last night, and how Conrad and I got along, it was just too much. Then there were the phone calls, the arrangements. I had to race to the bank, close all our accounts, reopen them in my name only before the bank shut them down for probate. The insurance people, the calls from the university, the hospital. All Conrad's friends in New York and Boston."

"News travels fast, doesn't it?"

She rocked gently in my arms, leaning against me as if she needed someone to hold her up. "Yes. Fortunately, Dr. Lingo went down to the morgue to identify the body. I didn't have to do that. But they'll have him out in the funeral home tomorrow."

She raised her head. "You must be beat, too."

"It's been a rough couple of days. Yeah."

"Can I make you a drink?" she said, pulling away from me, on her own two feet again now.

"It might put me to sleep."

"Then you can crash on the couch," she said. "I could use one, myself. What can I fix you?"

She reached over, turned the dial that controlled the kitchen lights. The level rose enough to where we could get a good look at each other. She looked even better in the light. Apparently, I looked worse.

"What happened to you? What's that? Harry, you've got blood on your shirt." She gasped.

I looked down. A few splatters of red stained the front of my white shirt. Damn, that stuff's hard to get out, and I don't have that many decent dress shirts left.

"I had a little run-in with someone. Seems I did a bounce or two off a wall. Fortunately, it was just my thick skull."

"Oh, God, let me see." She spun me around, turned the lights up all the way. "Harry, this looks nasty. What am I going to do with you?"

She disappeared into the small bathroom just off the kitchen. I heard her fumbling around in the medicine cabinet.

"Rachel, it's no big deal," I said. "I probably just need to wash it off."

"No big deal, my eye. Those closure strips are hanging there like laundry on a line. You'll be lucky not to wind up needing stitches."

"Really, it's okay." Now that she'd mentioned the drink, I wanted that more than anything else.

She came back in with hydrogen peroxide, bandages, antibiotic ointment. "Here, sit down." She motioned toward the kitchen table. It was easier to take a chair than argue about it.

"You're a mess," she chided. "Can't you stay out of trouble for a minute?"

"I usually don't have a problem with a minute or two," I said. "An hour, though, and I'm pushing it."

Her hands were gentle, professional. She was the only

person who'd touched me in the last two days without causing me pain. "You're a pro," I said.

"Thanks. Actually, I am. I used to do this for a living."

"What, patch banged-up detectives?"

"No, silly. I went back to school after Conrad and I got married, when he was in his residency. Got my degree in nursing."

I turned. "You were a nurse?"

"Yeah, I worked full-time at it until we moved back down here." She brought her hands up to the side of my head and moved me back into position. "This might hurt a little. I'm going to pull these old closures off and replace them."

I got set for some serious pain, but got only a minor sting instead. "You are good. So how come you quit working?"

"I don't know. Connie was making such good money. I worked part-time, but there wasn't the driving need for it like when we were younger and he was in school. I hate to sound clichéd, but those really were the good old days. Our salad days. We were young, up to our ears in debt, living on Hamburger Helper. Sometimes without the hamburger."

I laughed. She wiped the last of the dried blood off my scalp and got everything taped down. She started pulling the wrappers from the bandage together, knotting them into a neat ball to throw away. Her voice became almost wistful.

"Connie and I loved each other then. Things were really going well for us. Something happened somewhere. I never quite figured out what."

I thought for a moment. "Why don't you fix me that drink now? Then I'd like to hear about it."

She fumbled around under the kitchen cabinet for a minute or so, and came up with a perfectly iced down, exquisite Scotch and soda.

"You remembered," I said.

"Oh, I'm sorry." She was suddenly embarrassed. "Do you not drink Scotch anymore? I can get you something—"

"This is fine," I said.

"Would you like to go into the den?"

"Sure, as long as you think the old biddies aren't spying on your house."

She laughed quietly as she stood up and pushed her chair back under the kitchen table. "It's past their bedtimes."

We walked out of the kitchen and down a long carpeted hall. Off to the right, the living room was dark and unoccupied. I could see enough to tell, however, that it was filled with expensive antiques, the kind you can only afford to keep when you're doing exceptionally well and don't have children.

"How come you and Connie never had kids?"

She stepped down into the sunken den and turned a knob on the wall. The lights came up. The room was much more relaxed without homicide detectives hanging around. A comfortable couch sat in the middle, with a projection screen TV against the opposite wall. The room was lined with books, an expensive stereo, and shelves of records and CDs.

She sat on the couch and set her drink down on an end table. "Connie didn't want them," she said. "Frankly, I never felt the urge either. So I never made an issue of it."

"What happened between you two?" I asked, settling into the couch a space or so over from her. Instinctively, I knew I wanted to sit next to her, but not *too* next to her.

"We were married twelve years," she said after a moment. "A lot can happen in that time. The stresses of professions, especially medicine. Connie worked eighty, a hundred hours a week. We got to where we went days at a time without seeing each other. That puts a strain on a marriage. It's a brutal system, but you can't do anything about it. Marriages are a casualty."

"I can imagine."

I sipped the drink. She'd made it strong, the Scotch as old as their marriage. It burned down my throat for about three seconds and then exploded into pure pleasure. Good thing I don't drink much; I'm too prone to enjoy myself at it.

"Then there were the other women."

"Other women?" I asked, shocked.

Her stare said: oh, you naive and innocent young boy.

"Infidelity is another occupational hazard in the medical profession. Think about it. Men and women, intelligent, educated, thrown together in a high-pressure, tense, dramatic environment where lives are lost and saved every day. It's pure romance. I'm no fool; I knew Conrad was handsome, charming when he wanted to be. And I know nurses, especially the young ones. The ones who go wild over being on an open heart team. Real living on the edge stuff."

"Rachel," I asked, cautious, tentative. "Were these just momentary indiscretions, or did Conrad have a steady girlfriend?"

She stared into her vodka and tonic. Her knuckles were white; condensation from the side of the glass leaked through her fingers and ran down her hands like tears.

"I don't know," she said slowly. "I know there was more than one. But I don't know how many, and I don't know how serious."

I wanted to comfort her. Her marriage to Conrad may not have been successful, but it was obvious she still cared for him in some way. And it was equally obvious that with her husband's death, there was a great deal of pain in Rachel Fletcher's life that would never be resolved.

"Rachel, I'm so sorry," I said. I scooted over next to her on the couch, set my drink down on the table in front of us, and put my arm across the back of the couch. She stared at me blankly for perhaps thirty seconds, our eyes meeting over the two feet or so separating us. Then she put her glass back down and came into my arms again.

I held her there, her head nestled in the crook of my shoulder for a long time. We were very still, very quiet, with only the ticking of the grandfather clock in the living room to remind us that time was still passing.

"I'd forgotten how good you feel," she whispered. She brought her arms around me and pulled herself even closer. My arms were around her shoulders, my hands buried in blond hair. Okay, so maybe there was something besides comforting going on here. But it was late at night; it had been a long time for both of us. Who can blame two people for grabbing what comfort they can in the world?

She pulled herself away from me for a beat, then raised her head with a look in her eyes I hadn't seen since we were in college together, involved with each other, young and inexperienced and passionate and still untouched by the worst surrounding us.

I wanted to kiss her, wanted that more than anything else in the world. But I knew if I kissed her once, I was in over my head.

"This's not a good idea," I said. Words never had to work harder to get out of my mouth.

"Why?"

I pulled myself away from her while I still could. "Not now, Rachel. Not with all this going on. Maybe after it's over, after things settle down."

"Harry, I'd forgotten what a noble old fool you were."

I grinned at her. "Noble old fool is right."

I finished my drink, and we talked a little while longer. Finally, I was exhausted. It was nearly one in the morning, and it had been a very long day.

"Yeah, I need to get up early, too," she said. "If I'm going to get in my usual three miles before all this craziness starts, I'd better do it early."

"Oh, you run?" I asked.

"Well, not professionally, you understand. But yeah, I took up running back when I was a med school widow. Oh, God, I can't believe I said that."

"Med school widow?"

"That's what med students' wives call themselves. We used to joke about it, call Code Blue when our husbands came home. The shock would nearly kill us."

"Shock would nearly kill you, huh?" I smiled, glad she was able to joke. That was, I thought, a good sign.

"Go on, my brave white knight, who's suffered the slings and arrows of outrageous fortune to protect the one he used to love." She put her arm around my waist and steered me down the hall.

"Yeah, well. I'm getting paid pretty good for it," I kidded.

"Cheap at the price. It's hard to get good help these days."

"Hey, can I see your living room?" I asked, following an impulse. She stopped, reached in, turned on a light. Rows of framed pictures on a baby grand, furniture so expensive and cultured I didn't even recognize it, art on the walls that wasn't bought at the hotel starving artists' sale. About what I expected.

There were lots of pictures—family, friends—in a cabinet in the corner as well. I stopped, stepped into the room, scanned everything out of curiosity more than anything else.

"I used to jog a lot," I said, continuing the small talk until I got to the door, "Maybe we'll go trot a few sometime."

"That sounds great," she said. "Call me."

She stood on tiptoe and pecked me on the lips. A buddy kiss, not the one I was stupid enough to turn down in the other room. But a nice one, anyway.

Rachel felt good. There was still something there between us. I'm a detective; I can tell these things.

As I pulled slowly down the driveway, headed at long last to my grungy little apartment on the other side of town, the thought occurred to me that with all the family pictures, the homey little displays of friends, nephews, nieces, parents, grandparents, pets, and old school pictures, one thing was missing.

I couldn't remember seeing a single picture of Conrad.

It was eleven the next morning before I wandered into the office. There were definite advantages, I'd discovered, to self-employment, despite never knowing where your next pay-check was coming from.

The swelling in my leg was diminishing. In fact, a decent night's sleep had left it almost painless. I could make my ankle hurt if I twisted it a certain way, so I made a mental note not to do that. What little residual swelling was left on the back of my head was gone now, and I even managed to cover most of the bandage by combing my hair back over it. I was determined to spend the day as normally as possible.

I made a pot of coffee and settled back to sift through the mail. Nothing exciting, certainly nothing even potentially lucrative. No messages on the answering machine, either. I appreciated the chance to kick back, but I knew Rachel's money wasn't going to last forever. Pretty soon, I guessed, I'd be repo'ing cars with Lonnie again.

I drank coffee and stared out the window for the better part of an hour. I was feeling as flat as a two-day-old open can of beer. Outside, through the yellow film that had coagulated on the window from years of interior cigarette smoke and exterior pollution, the traffic drifted by in a never-ending spasmodic flow of belching smoke, color, and noise. The stream was more choked than usual, thanks to some fool in a long black Lincoln stopped in a loading zone down Seventh Avenue from Church. Inconsiderate jerk.

I watched the drama of honking horns and middle fingers while, in the back of my mind, I tried to figure my next move. Every place I'd looked, I'd been stymied. If Bubba Hayes didn't smoke Connie Fletcher, then who did? And why?

I needed answers. I also needed lunch. I glanced down at my watch, realized it was 11:55, and that I was a twelve-minute walk away from my noon lunch with Walt Quinlan.

Some creative jaywalking and a little luck got me to Satsuma's on Union Street just in time to join a line of lawyers waiting to get in. Walter was third in the group, and I stepped ahead of a group of high rollers in gray suits to join him.

"Hey, guy, sorry I'm late."

"No problem, fella," Walter said, in good spirits. "Today's white bean soup and turkey supreme. Nothing can ruin that kind of day."

"You seem unusually happy."

Walt smiled deeply over the top of his silk paisley tie. "I decided that making partner's not the world's most important goal, that's all."

This from a lawyer? I thought.

"My God, don't let these other suits hear you say that," I said, looking around at the crowd. "They'll have you committed."

"Not to worry. The situation is well under control. If things work out as planned, I'm going to be set up. For good . . ."

"For good? What are you up to?"

The mischievous smile continued. The crowd moved forward four people. We were next in line for a table.

"Okay," I said after a moment, "forget it."

He folded his arms in front of him, the black sleeves of his Armani suit wrinkling loosely over his forearms.

"You're cooking up some kind of deal, aren't you?" I grinned at him.

The hostess pushed her way through the crowd and looked at us, a sweaty wisp of hair down across her forehead. "Smoking or nonsmoking?"

Walter, as he predicted, was soon slavering over the turkey

supreme. I was raking up the white beans over corn-
bread, washing it down with iced tea as sweet as pancake
syrup.

"Ahh," Walter sighed, wiping his mouth with a crumpled
napkin. "Life in the fast lane."

I leaned back, even sleepier and flatter than I had been up
in the office. I'd hoped lunch would rekindle my pilot light.
Instead, all I wanted to do was slide back into bed. I
knew, with what little measure of self-discipline I still pos-
sessed, that this was impossible.

"Visiting hours start at two today," I said. "You going?"

Walter looked at me, confused, as if for a moment he
couldn't connect. "Oh, yeah," he said, shaking his head.
"I'll be there after work. When you going over?"

"I guess Rachel'll be at the funeral home right at two. I'll
show up a little after that. I figure she'll need moral support."

Walter leaned back in his chair and ran his tongue over
his front teeth. "And you're just the guy to do that, aren't
you?"

I stared at him for a second. "Maybe. Being around Rachel again could become a habit. When the time's right."

His eyes narrowed. "Be careful, buddy. You don't have
any idea what you're getting into."

"And you do?"

Walter smiled. "Fair enough. I don't have any idea what
you're getting into either. But I'd be very careful if I were
you."

"If you were me, you wouldn't be wearing that suit. How
much'd that thing cost you, anyway?"

"If you got to ask . . ." he began.

"I know," I interrupted. "Believe me, I know."

I managed to kill a couple of hours in my office, mostly
running around in mental circles. Then I collected the Ford
out of the garage and headed out West End. It was just before
three, middle of the afternoon, which downtown means the

rush hour had already started. It took twenty minutes to make it back out to the triangle where Division splits from Broadway.

Funny, I thought, the funeral home where Conrad Fletcher lay stretched out was only a few blocks up from Bubba Hayes's stop-and-drop. I kept thinking that of all the people I'd met, or heard about, who didn't care for Conrad Fletcher, Bubba Hayes was the only one I could imagine killing him. And yet something told me—for the time being—that he wasn't a murderer. Maybe it was the timbre in his voice; maybe it was that if I didn't believe him, he'd beat the snot out of me again. Either way, I just had a feeling that while he might know more than he was telling, he hadn't killed Connie Fletcher.

I brought the Ford to a shuddering, smoking stop in the back parking lot of the funeral home. The last time I'd been here was when a distant uncle of mine died a few years back. As a child, funerals terrified me. As a man, they still do.

I walked in the back door of the funeral home, past a desk where a pasty-faced woman sat behind a telephone desk console that could have been the main switchboard at IBM. Didn't know funeral homes were such busy places.

This particular funeral home was more like an antebellum mansion than anything else, with a winding staircase in the central foyer that led upstairs to offices, and parlors off to each side of the great hall where the bereaved families gathered in front of the usually open coffins. Funerals, especially Southern funerals, are pageants, deep-fried dramas, ripping passionate catharsis. I've been to funerals where fat ladies tore their pearls off and fainted in puddles of sweat, foam spreading across their lips as they spoke in tongues. And food . . . God, the food. Some poor high school dropout clerk in a 7-Eleven gets blown away at two in the morning by a demented crackhead, and what does the family do? Scream in agony, tear hair out, yell for the death penalty, then chow down like a bunch of linebackers in spring training.

I hoped that wasn't on the agenda for this one. There was a black signboard with little white letters in front of each parlor. MR. E. GIBSON was in the room off to the right. The front room, to my left, had a sign that read DR. C. FLETCHER.

I walked into the room silently, my footsteps muffled by the thick red carpet. Long blue drapes hung down in front of floor-to-ceiling windows fourteen feet high. Victorian parlor lamps with engraved purple and gray cherubs in the glass shades lit the room dimly. The room was jammed with flowers, and the air was thick and heavy with their perfume.

And I was the only one there. Except Conrad, of course, who was lying face up in an open bronze coffin on the other side of the room. He wasn't much company, though.

I discreetly glanced at my watch. Visiting hours had started nearly an hour ago. Where was everybody? Even in death, it seemed, people didn't want to spend too much time around the good doctor.

I backed out of the room and checked out the visitor's register, opened to the first page on a white stand near the door. There were three names, one a doctor. That was all. Conrad wasn't going to break any box office records at this pace.

Back inside the parlor, I stepped across the room over to the coffin. Connie lay in the box, wearing a white shirt, striped tie, pressed blue suit. On his left lapel was an American Medical Association pin of some kind. At least I think that's what it was; the snake wound around the shaft, anyhow.

I'll say this much for him—he looked a hell of a lot better than he did the last time I saw him. He had some color back, his face had filled out some, probably from the funeral director's padding, and the ghastly sunken purple under his eyes was gone.

Yeah, he looked a lot better. Not that it mattered.

I backed away from the coffin, thinking how weird it was that nobody else was there. It was still early; most people had to finish the work day. Yeah, that was it. Had to be.

The funeral home had conveniently set up a coffee room

in the back of the building so the grieving and the bereaved
could grab a cup of hot java and a smoke between hysterics.
I went back and discovered why the front parlor was empty:
everybody was in here on break.

Rachel sat at a Formica table behind a sweaty can of diet
soda, dressed in a severe black dress with a white lace collar.
She was staring down at her hands when I came in and didn't
notice me for a second. Mrs. Goddard, Rachel's protective
neighbor, sat to the left. She nudged Rachel when she spotted me.

"Harry," Rachel sighed. She stood up and crossed in
front of the table, her arms held out to me. "I'm so glad you
came."

I took her properly in my arms and gave her the usual
shared comforting hugs one gives at a funeral home. After a
few seconds, we disengaged and stood back from each other.

"How you holding on?" I asked.

"Okay. Mostly tired. The rough part's going to be when
the family arrives. My parents get in at six tonight. Connie's
are probably at the airport now."

"That's going to be tough, isn't it?"

She smiled gamely, took my arm in hers, and led me out
of the coffee room. "I'll be okay," she said, pulling me with
her down toward the parlor. "I just need a little time."

"Yeah," I agreed. "You'll get through this okay."

We strolled casually into the room. Standard practice at
the funerals I've attended calls for the closest, most grieving,
family member to guide each visitor up to the coffin to pay
respects by remarking how natural the person looks in death.
I genuinely hated that custom, mainly because nobody looks
natural in death. They just look dead.

Two other people were already in there now, standing close
together a few feet away from the coffin. The woman was
my height, within an inch or so, with striking black hair
flowing down over squared shoulders. Even from behind, I
could tell she was a looker. The guy standing next to her
barely came to her chin: rumpled khaki suit, slightly dumpy
around the waist, thinning curly mousy brown hair. Odd

pair, these two, I thought. I sensed from their proximity that they weren't strangers.

Rachel led me around them to the open lid of the coffin. She stared down at Connie and let loose with a deep sigh, then squeezed my arm tightly.

"God, I can't believe it," she said, sniffling and pulling me close. I put an arm around her and scrunched her shoulders. She stifled a sob, largely without success.

"I'm so sorry, Rachel," I said. And I was.

She raised her head again and stiffened her neck, as if gathering strength for the next two days.

"I know, Harry. I appreciate your being here. It means worlds to me."

She stepped back, turned from the coffin toward me. "I'm sorry it took this to get you back into my life," she continued. "But I am glad you're my friend again."

"I never wasn't your friend, Rach. Things just happen the way they happen, that's all."

She gazed at me for a long time, intently, seriously, a look that was as much troubled as saddened, as much afraid as grieved.

"Maybe it's not too late to get it right this time," she said, almost a whisper.

I was close to being embarrassed, standing here in front of Conrad Fletcher's coffin, talking to his wife this way. Then, I thought, what the hell, he can't hear us.

"Yeah," I whispered. "Maybe."

A throat cleared behind us. I suddenly remembered that we weren't alone. I turned. The guy in the khaki suit was staring at us uncomfortably, the pale light mostly unflattering on his sallow complexion. The woman, though, was as elegant and as lovely as I'd guessed from a rearview shot. Her skin was smooth, flawless, her features sharp and beautifully defined. Her cheekbones would give Katharine Hepburn's a run for their money.

"Mrs. Fletcher?" he asked.

"Yes," she answered, holding out a hand, "I'm Rachel Fletcher."

"I'm Al Zitin, Dr. Al Zitin. And this is Dr. Jane Collingswood. We were taking our surgical residencies under Dr. Fletcher. We're so sorry about this."

Zitin and Collingswood, I thought. What a nice surprise.

Chapter 14

This voice inside my head said: think fast, boy. Rachel obviously hadn't met these two and couldn't know that Jane Collingswood and Albert Zitin were firmly established in the ranks of Conrad haters. I knew she was about to introduce me to them, but as who? Did I want them to know I was an investigator? Did I *not* want them to know? I wish I'd read a few more books on this business. . . .

"Thank you for coming," Rachel said, extending her hand now to Jane Collingswood. "This has been a terrible shock to all of us. All of us who loved him, respected him."

I thought I detected a slight twitch in Al's right eye. Dr. Jane, though, was beautifully sculptured ice.

"This is Harry Denton," Rachel said, pointing to me.

"Hi," I interrupted. "I'm an old family friend. I'm pleased to meet you."

We shook hands and made pleasantries for a moment. Then we all turned, as if choreographed, toward the coffin. It was a profoundly uncomfortable moment.

"We just came by to pay our respects," Al Zitin said. "We've got to get back to the hospital in a bit."

"Yes," Jane Collingswood agreed. "I'm sorry we can't stay too long."

"When is the service?" Zitin asked.

"Tomorrow at three. I didn't see any reason to delay. This has been bad enough for all of us without dragging it out."

Jane Collingswood looked at Rachel for a second, then said, "I think you're being very brave. I don't know how I'd hold up if I were in your shoes."

I did. Jane Collingswood could survive the sinking of the *Titanic*. Her eyes were deep, intelligent, determined. And, by the way, incredibly lovely.

"Don't let all this fool you," Rachel said. "I've had my bad moments. But I know that Connie would have wanted me to hold up. He had such high standards, for himself and everyone else."

There went that twitch again in Zitin's eye. "Yes, he certainly did. He was a tough taskmaster."

"But no tougher on anyone else than he was on himself," Jane added.

"We'll all miss him," Zitin concluded.

"Yes, we'll all miss him."

"Thank you," Rachel said, taking both their hands in hers. "Connie's work meant a lot to him. People meant a lot to him. He would have appreciated your coming by today."

Amidst Rachel's incredible graciousness, I noticed out of the corner of my eye that people were starting to file into the visitation room in some number now. James Hughes, wearing a crumpled green sport coat over a white shirt that he might have slept in, wandered in with four other obvious medical students. I didn't recognize any of the others.

I turned my attention back to Rachel.

"Thank you so much for coming by," she said, finishing her speech.

"We were glad to do it," Jane Collingswood said, unwrapping her hand from Rachel's and extending it toward me. "Glad to meet you, Mr. Denton."

"Pleased to meet you," I said, taking her hand. There was something solid, slightly cold, in her grip. Jane Collingswood was an unreadable woman, reserved, cards held close to her chest. Could she kill a man? I asked myself. "I'm sorry it had to be under these circumstances."

Zitin extended his hand to me as well. I shook it. His palms were wet, his grip slightly unsure. "Maybe we'll get to see you again, sometime," he said.

"I hope so." Zitin didn't impress me as the kind of guy

who'd have the nerve to kill someone in cold blood. Then again, he's a doctor. He'd know what he was doing.

Rachel looked over Zitin's shoulder at the crowd milling in, then disengaged herself politely to take care of her other guests. How do people get through these ordeals? I wondered. I watched Zitin and Collingswood as they meandered toward the door, pausing to speak to a couple of colleagues, shaking hands with a student, making more small talk. People shook their heads sadly, as if wondering how anything this horrible could disorder their safe professional world.

I watched them until they left the room, then shifted through the crowd as quickly as possible and followed them. Their pace inside the room had been slow, respectful, dignified. But once they got out into the hallway, their heels clicked away like a mechanic's ratchet. I picked up my pace to stay ten feet or so after them, then watched as they went through the double doors into the same back parking lot where I'd left my car.

This was one of those times when I really had to wing it. I wanted to talk to them, to ask the kind of questions that would provide some indication of whether they might really be involved in this mess. But what questions? How could I feel them out without putting them so on guard they'd lock down completely?

Damn, man, I'm going to have to take some lessons in this one of these days. But then I remembered something I learned a long time ago as a newspaper reporter, something that helped me get past the suspicions and distrust that people naturally seem to attribute to reporters: when all else fails, tell the truth.

I shuffled up behind them just as Zitin was fumbling with the key to his 300Z. He crossed around in back of the car to the passenger's door, then opened it and held it for Jane.

"Excuse me," I said, "you guys got a minute?"

They turned to me. Jane, I noticed, was cool, subdued. Zitin flicked his eyes over to me, then back at her, then back and forth a few times. Nervous already.

I walked up to the deep-blue sports car, wondering just

what surgical residents make to afford this kind of wheels. Maybe he came from money, I thought.

"Yes, Mr. . . ." she said, "Denton, was it?"

"Yeah, Harry Denton." I hesitated a moment, then plunged in. "What Mrs. Fletcher said in there is true. I'm an old family friend. I've known Rachel and Connie since we were undergraduates together. But I'm also a private investigator, and I've been retained by Rachel to look into Conrad's death."

Okay, so I wasn't being entirely truthful. I'd actually been retained by Rachel to get Connie out of trouble with his bookie. But all things being relative, this truth was close enough to the real truth, and would serve for now.

Zitin flushed visibly. The doctor was about as smooth as a fourteen-year-old caught locked in a bathroom with last month's *Playboy*. Jane narrowed her eyes and looked at me. I thought she was being somewhere between suspicious and sexy, then I realized the sun was coming over my shoulder and blinding her. I grinned on the inside, remembering what my father told me about his World War II flying days: always come at your enemy out of the sun.

"Private investigator," she commented. "I thought I'd heard your name before. You were the detective who found Dr. Fletcher's body."

"Yeah, that's more or less how it happened."

"I should think you'd be more worried about the police investigating you," she said coolly.

"Let's just say I've had a talk or two with them."

"I'll bet. And what do you want from us?"

Zitin, I noticed, was nervously shifting his weight from one foot to the other. I'm no expert on body language, but I know anxiety when I see it.

"I'm trying to get a portrait of Dr. Fletcher's relationships with his colleagues at the hospital, the med school. I understand that you and Dr. Fletcher didn't necessarily get along that well. I just wondered if you'd be willing to tell me about it."

Zitin pursed his lips, seemingly irritated now, as if he had somewhere he needed to be and I was keeping him from getting there. Which was probably true.

"Now's not particularly convenient," Jane said. "We both have commitments."

"Can I drop by the hospital sometime?"

"We're awfully busy there," Zitin shot back.

"I won't take up much of your time."

"I don't know—" he said.

Jane interrupted him. "I suppose if we don't talk to you, then you're going to be suspicious of us. Right?"

I smiled at her. "Probably."

"Then I'll make time to talk to you. Check in at the switchboard. They'll page me. That all right with you, Albert?"

Zitin scowled, not wanting to have anything to do with this, but not wanting to buck her either. "Yeah, I guess so."

"Thanks. I'll be in touch."

Jane Collingswood started to slide past the door Zitin held open for her. "There is one thing," she said.

I turned back. "Yes?"

"Most of us came down here primarily to make sure he was really dead."

"Jane!" Zitin said. He practically tripped over himself helping her into the car. Then he scrambled to the driver's side. He peeled out of the parking lot, jerking into traffic without stopping. I stood there in the hot sun, grinning.

I could see why he was in love with her.

Back inside the funeral home, James spotted me in the main hall.

"I see you met Dr. Collingswood and Dr. Zitin," he said, as we stood in a corner away from everyone else, kind of underneath the curving staircase.

"Yeah, but they wouldn't talk to me. We set up an appointment for later. So tell me, guy, how come you showed up here? You didn't like Fletcher very much. Why pay respects?"

James hung his head slightly, a lock of his long hair falling down on his forehead. "Most of us came here to make sure the guy's really dead."

"You're the second person to say that to me in the last five minutes. What's the story here, babe? How come everybody hated the guy? Really."

James surveyed the room, making sure no one was close enough to hear.

"Med school's rough enough without being nailed just because some smart s.o.b. doesn't like you."

"C'mon, James. Didn't like you?"

He bristled a little but kept a cool head. "I'm no dummy, Harry. And I work my butt off. What I'm not clever at is sucking up. And the only way to get anywhere with Fletcher was to suck up to him or, if you were the kind of woman he took a notion for, to hop in the sack with him."

"That's a pretty rough accusation these days," I said. "How come he hasn't been brought up on sexual misconduct charges? Women don't put up with that garbage like they used to."

"I don't have any doubt that he would have someday, one way or another. In fact, a couple of women came forward, but they mysteriously wound up leaving school before anything could happen.

"You see, Harry, he knew that for every med student, just surviving medical school's the be-all and end-all. You know what you do when you flunk out of med school, Harry? You go to work as a pharmaceutical salesman, or you wind up running a place like this. . . ." He swept a small arc with his arms, taking in the surroundings.

"Fletcher had a way of getting to you," James continued. "He knew that most of us would do anything to stay in school. He was cutthroat, and he was politically powerful. I don't know if he had pictures of the dean with a goat or what, but nobody crossed Fletcher. I hated the guy. I admit it. Rumor was that he was trying to bust Jane Collingswood out of her residency program. He had the hots for her, and he figured if she wouldn't put out for him, then he'd drill her out of the program."

I had a hard time visualizing Jane Collingswood in the same thought with the term *put out*. High school cheerleaders put out. For women like Jane Collingswood, something much more elegant is required.

"And Zitin's obviously gaga for her," I said.

"Half the hospital is," James said. "But I'm not sure Zitin's got any further with her than the rest of us."

"And when Fletcher didn't have any luck either," I reflected.

"He was going to ruin Jane's life. Professionally speaking, anyway. Getting busted out of a residency program means you're still a doctor. But you're not likely to get anywhere with that on your record."

"What was that you were saying about doctors making a lot of money?"

James smiled. "If they're any good, they do."

"Enough money to kill for?"

He shook his head. "Wake up and smell the coffee. In a heartbeat, Harry. In a heartbeat."

Chapter 15

I ducked out of the funeral parlor, cranked up the Ford, and drove out to the intersection of Division and 21st, near the law school, then out 21st until I found a parking spot in front of the Medical Arts Building. I had no idea when the shifts changed at the hospital, but there was something I wanted to chase down.

While hanging around the funeral home, I replayed the night of Fletcher's murder over and over again in my head. I was walking down a long hall, and I saw this nurse come out of a room. I can't be sure, but I seem to remember it was the same room where I found Fletcher. But the lights were down low; it was late. I was tired, and my leg was bothering me. My eyes aren't what they used to be, and when you stand in the middle of a long hall peppered on both sides with identical pastel doors, they all blend into haze.

Then it came to me, and I could have slapped myself for not figuring it out sooner. I would have, too, except that I'd already had a years' worth of slapping in the past couple of days.

I remembered the nurse, and I remembered the maybe-two-second good look I got at her as she buttoned the top buttons on her uniform and nervously smoothed out the wrinkles. But what I mostly remembered was Marsha Helms, my buddy at the coroner's office, telling me that Conrad Fletcher had managed to ride the hormonal roller coaster one last time before somebody whacked him. Not to put too indelicate an edge on it, Conrad didn't strike me as the type to be in love

125

with his right hand. So I figured somebody else had to be there. And I figured that nurse was my best bet.

All I had to do now was find her.

Time was a factor as well. I knew, from my newspaper days, that the one advantage I might have over the police was that dear Dr. Marsha had let me in on the autopsy results in advance. Ordinarily, the full report wouldn't be given to the police until the toxicology tests were completed, and that took at least seventy-two hours. Which meant that for about the next twenty-four hours, I was the only one who knew that Conrad Fletcher's last moments on this earth had been spent basking in a post-sexual glow. If I were going to make use of what I knew, I had to hustle.

It was loads of fun being back in the hospital. My playback of Fletcher's death night became even more vivid. I walked down the hall, past the information booth, to the elevators, then rode up to the fourth floor. Instinctively, my ankle began to throb, as if the mere return to Horror Hospital brought with it an aura of pain.

I smiled once again at the irony of a doctor being murdered in his workplace. It was damn funny as long as you weren't the doctor doing the dying. Hospitals are a good place to die, or so I'm told. As good a place as any, I guess.

I stopped briefly at the nurses' station, where the same woman who'd been there two nights ago still sat in front of the computer terminal, punching in numbers while the green glow of the screen danced in front of her. She didn't turn around; it was still early enough that there were visitors around. There was nobody else behind the glass with her just then, so I turned and walked down the same hall I'd been in the other night. The hair on the back of my neck crinkled.

Carts filled with plastic food warming trays lined the halls, mixed in with an occasional medication cart. Nurses buzzed around carrying sphygs, stethoscopes, clipboards. It was the busy part of the shift, before patients drifted off into oblivion and families left for the night. I was grateful for the activity and all the visitors milling around in the hallway; I'd stick out less amidst the chaos.

I casually scanned each person's face as I walked by, trying not to be recognized, looking for the nurse in the hall, or anyone else who might have been there that night. I was sure the police had questioned everyone, but they still didn't know what I knew. Not yet, anyway. Walking around these halls somewhere was a woman who shared the last moments of a dead man's life. Maybe she killed him. Maybe she didn't. Either way, I wanted to talk to her.

Only problem was, nobody I saw looked like her. I walked on. The bright red exit sign at the end of the hall still blazed like before. I struggled to recall which door I'd opened to find Fletcher. The last one, I believe. I was ten feet away from it when that door opened, and she stepped out.

We stopped dead in front of each other, our eyes meeting in a hint of recognition. She stared at me for a second, her mouth dropping open, her clipboard held tight to her chest.

"You —"

"Yeah, me," I said. Then I realized she wasn't the nurse I'd seen coming out of the room that night; she was the young one who found me in the hall after I'd been bashed in the head.

"Hey," I said, holding out a hand, "I didn't get a chance to thank you for helping me out the other night. If you hadn't come along, I might have lain there for who knows how long."

She lifted one hand off the clipboard, took mine loosely. Her nameplate read JACQUELYN BELL, R.N.

"No problem," she said, her voice cautious. "How're you feeling?"

"Lots better." I smiled at her as pleasantly as I knew how. Maybe she could help me, but I had to warm her up a bit first. "The bump on the head's almost gone. Say, Nurse Bell, I was actually looking for you. Is there someplace we could talk? Privately, I mean. This won't take long. Honest."

"Well," she hesitated. Her voice was riddled with a deep drawl, the voice of a young girl who'd grown up in the country, gone to school in Nashville, and fallen in love with the big city. The kind of girl who drove an expensive car she couldn't afford, lived in an apartment complex catering primarily to singles, and plastered her walls with hunk posters. "We're pretty busy around here."

"It's important, Ms. Bell. You were one of the few people up here who actually knew what happened that night."

"Wait a minute, I don't have any idea what happened that night. I told the police that. All I did was find you and—"

"No, that's not what I mean. Of course, you don't know what happened with Dr. Fletcher's murder. I'm talking about what happened after you found me in the hall."

I paused awkwardly, trying to figure out how to articulate this. "Listen, Jacquelyn—may I call you Jacquelyn?"

She nodded her head.

"C'mon, is this room empty? Can we step in here for just a second?"

She looked around nervously, as if I were a dirty old man in a trench coat offering her a piece of candy just outside the school playground. "It would really be better if we talked alone. What I've got to tell you, nobody else should hear."

That got her. Her curiosity primed, she opened the door next to us and led me into an empty hospital room. We stood in the dim glowing light of the fluorescent tube at the head of the bed.

"Jacquelyn, I'm Harry James Denton. I'm a private investigator." I pulled out my license and flipped it open, with my impressive gold and chrome badge that I'd bought from a mail order supply house. The badge was damned impressive. And absolutely meaningless.

"A private detective?" she whispered, intrigued.

"Yes. I was up here that night trying to find Dr. Fletcher. I'd been hired by the family because they thought, well, they thought he was in some trouble. And they wanted me to help him out. Anyway, I was trying to track him down, but I was a little slow. Somebody got to him before I could, and they killed him."

She nodded her head. "Yeah, I know that."

"What you don't know, though, is that I've got a . . . well, let's say a friend, who let me take a peek at the autopsy results before they were released to the police.''

Her eyes widened, a young woman dying to be let in on something no one else knew. ''Yeah?''

''Before he was killed, and *just* before he was killed, Dr. Fletcher had just . . . well, he'd just had sex, Jacquelyn.''

''No kidding,'' she spewed, ''you mean?'' She pointed behind her.

''Yes,'' I said. ''In that room.''

''Wow! I knew he was a sleaze ball, but boinking somebody right here on the floor. Wow!''

''Well, you knew the kind of guy he was, right?'' Talk about leading a witness.

''Oh, yeah. We all knew it. He hit on everybody. He was gutter slime.''

''Yes, Jackie, he was gutter slime. But his family loved him. Don't ask me why. And they've hired me to keep digging, to try and find out who really killed him.''

''But what about the police?''

''Well, you know how the police are,'' I said, fully confident that she had no earthly idea how the police are. ''They have their own agenda, their own methods. Sometimes the interests of the police don't jibe with the family's. I'm involved in this to represent the family's interests. To make sure they're taken care of. You can understand that, can't you? If something like this happened in your family, even if it was somebody you didn't care for, you'd want your interests protected. Wouldn't you?''

She thought for a moment. ''Actually, I've got a cousin who reminds me a lot of Fletcher. If somebody killed him, yeah, I'd want the family protected.''

''So help me out here, Jackie. I've got to find whomever it was Fletcher was having an affair with, if you want to call it that. You know what's going on up here. Who could it be?''

She backed off a couple of feet and laid the clipboard down on the bed. She was young, pretty, naive, thrilled to be the center of attention. "Well," she cooed, "I've heard a few rumors."

She was teasing me now, only I knew it, and I'm not sure she did. "Yeah," I said, taking a smooth step toward her. Maybe she expected me to hit on her. Maybe I should. What is it about hospital rooms that make people so frisky? Then I remembered Rachel's assertion about the amount of playing around that goes on when the patients' backs are turned. "So what have you heard?" We were flirting now, big time.

I had this flash of Humphrey Bogart charming the bookstore clerk in *The Big Sleep*. Lemme see, now, could I remember my Doghouse Riley imitation?

"Well," she whispered, lips pursed, "we change shifts at midnight. It's kind of late to be going out, so we all kind of stick together. Usually we go out as a group, maybe three nights a week, over to the Commodore Lounge at the Holiday Inn, you know. But lately, one of the girls on the shift hasn't been around after work. Somebody said she'd been dating one of the doctors. A married one."

I grinned at her, a motion that brought a devilish grin to her face as well. "And you think it might have been Fletcher?"

"Well, that's not to say he was the only doctor who'd cheat on his wife. But if you ask me, he'd be near the head of the line."

"Jackie, darling, I did ask you. And I'm glad I did. You've been a great help. Who is she?"

Jackie shut down for just a bit, either playing coy or honestly wondering if she'd talked too much. I tried to figure out a ploy to keep her talking.

Suddenly, she shook her head and put her hands on her hips. "Oh, why not? I'm sure LeAnn didn't have anything to do with this. She's a sweet girl. I've known her for months now. She's just the cutest thing you ever saw."

Yeah, I thought, doll freaking precious. "What's LeAnn's last name, Jackie? I just want to speak to her. That's all."

"Oh, I'm sure everything's all right. LeAnn won't mind. Her last name's Gwynn. LeAnn Gwynn."

I spelled the last name out loud, making sure I got it right. Then: "Where's LeAnn now, Jackie? She on the floor?"

"No, tonight's her night off."

"You know where she lives?"

"Well, not exactly. I've never been out to her apartment. Somewhere on Franklin Road, though."

"I'll check the book."

"Oh, she's got an unlisted number. She told me some guy'd been calling her, hassling her. The usual trash, you know. I had to have my number changed just last month."

"Gee, I'm sorry to hear that."

"Don't be," she said. "The guy was a jerk."

"So how do you get in touch with her in emergencies?"

"Oh, that's easy. We call Personnel during business hours, or at night the information operator can pull it up on the computer. Only nobody's really supposed to know that. Say, Harry, we're going to be over at the Commodore tonight. Why don't you drop by, join us for a drink?"

I was old enough to be her father, or at least her much older brother. The truth is that I'm at the age where the thought of being at a table full of twenty-two-year-old nurses is more intimidating than arousing. My God, what would I say to them?

"The Commodore at midnight, huh? Sure, I'll try to make it."

She smiled. "I've got to get back to work. I'll see you tonight."

"Okay, Jackie. Hey, listen, thanks for your help."

She smiled again, sweetly, innocently, as she walked out the door. Maybe it was that bad attitude of mine kicking up again, but I had a feeling that if Jackie Bell was an innocent young maiden, then I'm a left-handed Japanese pole vaulter.

I headed down the hall toward the nurses' station again. I stopped at the pay phone in front of the bank of elevators and flipped through the thick phone book that dangled from a chain. Sure enough, no LeAnn Gwynn, L. Gwynn, or any variation thereof.

The elevator opened in front of me and a crowd of people

stepped off. One had on a white lab coat, with DR. GORDON
EVANS, M.D. sewn across the left breast pocket in green
thread, and below that DEPT. OF NEUROSURGERY. I shut the
phone book, walked back down the hall, and found another
empty room.

I picked up the phone, dialed *O*. A moment later, the
operator's voice came on. "May I help you?"

"Yes, this is Dr. Gordon Evans, Neurosurgery, up on
Fourth Floor West."

"Yes, Dr. Evans."

"Is the personnel office still open?"

"No, sir. They closed at four forty-five."

"Oh, blast it. We've got a patient up here that went on
some medication yesterday, but the nurse who did the paperwork didn't write down what time it was started. I'm afraid
we're all screwed up unless I find out when he went on the
meds. And I can't do that because it's the nurse's day off and
nobody up here's got her unlisted number."

"I can pull that out of the computer for you, Dr. Evans.
What's her name?"

I smiled. Some letters are magic, like the ones *M* and *D*.

"Nurse Gwynn, G-W-Y-N-N. First name LeAnn."

"Okay, hold just a second."

She came back on. I scribbled down the number. Sure
enough, a Melrose area exchange. "That all you need, Dr.
Evans?"

"That's it for now. Thanks."

"My pleasure," she said.

And I'm sure it was.

Chapter 16

I could go back to my office and check the Criss-Cross Directory, but those damned things are notorious for being out of date or just plain wrong. This was something I had to be sure of.

I hung up the phone and listened carefully inside the empty hospital room, hoping that I wouldn't be interrupted for at least a couple more minutes. I pulled out my reporter's note pad, flipped through to Lonnie's number, and dialed it.

Among Lonnie's other talents—besides repo'ing cars and blowing up objects with common household items—was his computer expertise. He could do more with a computer than anyone else I'd ever met; only problem was, he usually had to keep quiet about it.

The number rang a few times, then an answering machine picked up. There was no message, just a long moment of silence followed by the distinctive *doodle-doodle-do* of the machine.

"Three two seven," I said, then looked down at the phone and called out the last four numbers. All the patient rooms were direct dial.

I hung up. If Lonnie was anywhere near, I'd get a callback in about forty-five seconds. I fidgeted almost two minutes by the side of the bed, checked my watch, and was about to give it up when the phone rang.

"Yeah?" It was Lonnie.

"Need a favor. You in the middle of anything? Nuclear warhead, perhaps?"

"Depends. What you got?"

"I got a number. Need an address."

"Speak."

I read the number, then heard the sound of the phone being laid down. I stood there perhaps another two minutes, devising excuses if hospital security walked in on me. Then the sound of fumbling came across the wires.

"5454 Franklin Road, Apartment 3-F. Think that's the Ponta Loma Apartments."

"Thanks, pal. Owe you one."

"Don't worry. I'll collect."

The phone clicked down immediately. Lonnie had several phone lines going into his junkyard. On this one, you didn't stay too long, and you never mentioned names.

I glanced out the door into an empty hallway. It didn't take long for me to cut a rug out of there.

It was close to seven, and I was starving. I figured if LeAnn Gwynn was out for the evening on her night off, she'd be already gone. If not, she was probably staying in. Either way, I had time to eat. I had a hankering for breakfast, so I walked down 21st to the IHOP, the International House of Pancakes. Restaurants come and go like crazy in this city, but the IHOP, like Mrs. Rotier's, was an establishment that would be around forever. I'd eaten many a meal there, and I had the blood cholesterol level to show for it.

I finished my third cup of coffee and stared down at a plate scrubbed clean of egg yolk and pancake syrup, reasoning that if LeAnn Gwynn had any involvement with Conrad's murder, she wasn't likely to chitchat with me about it. Unless, of course, she thought I was visiting her in an official capacity. I'd never done anything like this before, but I figured that if I walked a thin enough line, I could get away with it. I took my license case out of my pocket again and looked at it: picture I.D., fancy badge.

What the hell, why not?

After all, I couldn't claim to be a police officer. But was it my fault if someone else chose to infer otherwise?

* * *

I drove out Eighth Avenue until it became Franklin Road, past the old Melrose Theatre, the shopping centers, pawn shops, liquor stores, convenience markets, and on under the freeway cloverleaf. Dark had settled in over what was a fairly redneck part of town, with a nearby housing project adding just enough of an air of danger to keep respectable people off the streets. To cap things off, the most popular gay bar in the city is right in the neighborhood as well. Most nights, parking lots for blocks around are packed with people headed for the Mine Shaft Cabaret.

I pulled into the Ponta Loma Apartments and slowed the car. The Ponta Loma was just another apartment complex: built sometime around the early Seventies, hip at the time but aging not very gracefully. In the real estate crash of the late Reagan/early Bush years, places like the Ponta Loma really suffered. The new apartment complexes had fire-places, ceiling fans, saunas, Jacuzzis. The Ponta Loma was considered far out twenty years ago because it had two pools.

I'm lousy at snap judgments, but I couldn't figure out why LeAnn Gwynn lived here. I always thought nurses made decent money. She ought to be able to do better than this.

I drove around through the parking lots slowly, looking for F Building. Not surprisingly, it was past the E Building and just before the G Building. And you thought I couldn't handle this detective shit. . . .

The two-story building was long, narrow, with apartments off either side facing inward on a long hallway. If LeAnn's apartment was 3-F, it was a safe bet she was on the first floor. If she was in the back, her apartment had a great view of the parking lot and the Dempster Dumpsters. If it faced the other way, she looked out on another building. Nice life, LeAnn. No wonder you were—how did Jackie Bell put it?—*boinking* a married man on the job.

I parked the car and doused the lights, then sat there for a few minutes, trying to get a feel for the place. It was quiet; no kids running through the parking lot, no splashing coming from the pool, no parties in progress spilling out into the common area. Not at all what I expected.

Each building had a bank of painted gold mailboxes, the kind you usually see in apartment houses. I looked at 3-F. There was a small white label showing, but neither LeAnn nor the apartment manager had bothered to write her name on it.

There was nothing else to learn by hanging around outside LeAnn's apartment. This reminded me of my days on the paper, when I'd be checking out a story and preparing to question somebody who probably didn't want to be interviewed. I'd get nervous and my gut would knot up, and I'd hang around outside thinking up excuses not to go in. Felt worse than a job interview sometimes, although that may be stretching it. Finally, it's like diving into cold water; the best recourse is to hold your nose and jump in.

I knocked on the door to 3-F.

Inside the apartment, I could hear soft music playing, the kind of music that's euphemistically called Lite Rock: elevator music for baby boomers.

I knocked again. I couldn't hear footsteps or any change in the music. I was about to give it up, when the peephole went dark. I stared into it, to let her know I'd seen her.

"Ms. Gwynn," I said, "may I talk to you for a moment?"

The peephole went bright again; then there was a fumbling with the doorknob. The door cracked a fraction, held by one of those flimsy security chains that could be popped by a loud belch. I pulled out my license and badge.

"Ms. Gwynn, I'm Detective Harry Denton. I'd like to ask you a few questions, please, if I may."

Jesus, Mary, and Joseph, I thought. Spellman's going to chew my butt ragged if he hears about this.

The half-hidden face behind the door studied the license, the badge, my picture. "You got a search warrant?" she asked.

Search warrant? What the hell has she got in there?

"No, ma'am," I said, giving her the most insipid smile I could muster. "There's no need for a search warrant. I just want to ask a few questions, and it won't take very long."

Her hair was coal-black, straight, cut short and sprayed.

She was a little shorter than I remembered, but then I'd only seen her from a distance. In fact, I wasn't even certain she was the woman in the hallway. She stared at me through the crack, then pushed the door closed. I heard the clicking of the chain being unlatched, then the doorknob turning. She opened the door, stood there for a moment, and I knew it was her.

LeAnn looked at me strangely, as if she were trying to place me as well, which was something I didn't want her to do. Whatever misconceptions she was operating under, I wanted her to continue under them for a while longer. Time to distract her.

"Ms. Gwynn, I know it's a little late to be making a visit, but when you're investigating a murder, especially a murder of someone so prominent, you can't delay on anything. May I come in?"

"Sure," she said, tense and brittle. She turned and held the door open for me. I walked in and looked around, then stepped aside as she closed the door and led me toward the couch.

The place was a mismatched hodgepodge of rental furniture, bargains that she'd moved from one place to another over the years, odds and ends she'd picked up from friends, family, whoever had bought new and needed to hand me down the old.

LeAnn Gwynn was a surprise as well. Like I said, I'd never seen her up close. But if Conrad Fletcher was having a sleazy, disgusting, lurid affair with a hot, passionate, lusty nymphomaniac nurse—which was the scenario I'd always assumed—then LeAnn Gwynn would have been the last person I'd have cast in the role. In fact, she wouldn't have even made the callbacks.

To begin with, she was attractive, but in a plainspoken, solid way. No randiness, no overwhelming sexual energy radiated from this woman. No surgically enhanced body parts. And she certainly didn't have the kind of monied, sophisticated tastes that one assumed would appeal to Conrad Fletcher. In fact, unless this apartment was some kind of front she was using to mislead everybody, LeAnn Gwynn didn't have much in the way of taste at all.

She wore jeans and an untucked man's white shirt that hung down to midthigh, sort of early Patty Duke show. I wondered if the shirt belonged to Conrad, but decided to hold off on that one. She walked over to the radio—one of those late Fifties or early Sixties hi-fi floor models—and turned down the puke rock, thank God. Then she sat in the easy chair across from me, the one with lace doilies barely covering worn fabric.

"So, what can I do for you, Lieutenant, Sergeant—?"

"No, please, I'm just a detective. Detective Denton."

She smiled uncomfortably through eyeglasses that were probably ten years old, the kind with the heavy plastic frames that today were unfashionable, if not downright geeky.

"Okay, Detective Denton, what can I do for you?"

I pulled out the pad and clicked my ballpoint, then held the two in position in front of me. "I'm investigating the death of Dr. Conrad Fletcher. I understand you knew the doctor." A two-beat pause. "How well *did* you know Dr. Fletcher?"

She crossed her legs in front of me, a worn sandal tipping forward and dangling off the end of her foot. I could feel her fear, could tell that her calm was all surface and barely that. Finally, she sighed, as if she was relieved to get on with it.

"C'mon, Mr. Denton, if you didn't know the answer to that already, you wouldn't be here."

Some color returned to her face. I saw now that her complexion was almost olive, her eyes nearly as black as her hair. When her face relaxed, she was lovely in a sort of different way, but there were the beginnings of crow's feet around her eyes and even the faintest trace of wrinkle around her mouth. She was older than she looked.

I laid down the pen and notepad. "Now that we've got that out of the way," I said, "you want to tell me about it?"

"I don't know what you've heard, but most of it isn't true."

"Why don't you tell me what is true," I suggested, my

voice lowering to its warm and comforting why-don't-we-be-friends? level.

She leaned back, almost as if to relax. "Yes, of course, I'd been seeing Conrad. And I'm sure all those obnoxious gigglers at the hospital were just delighted to dish the dirt. But it really was different with us."

"Different? How?"

"I met Conrad Fletcher about a year ago. I did a rotation in I.C.U. We met there. He was, as I'm sure everyone's told you, demanding, insensitive, tactless, not an easy man to like. Unfortunately, I always seem to wind up with those men. My first husband, for instance."

"And?"

She sighed again, a noise that emerged somewhere between this side of sadness and the other side of despair. Funny, I'd shown up here convinced I was going to be dealing with a sleazoid vamp; what I had, instead, was someone who came off as a real nice person who'd been just another victim.

"I've got a boy and girl, Mr. Denton, and an ex-husband who hasn't made a child support payment since the first month after the divorce came through. I don't even know where he is. The kids live with my mother in Alabama. My son's got muscular dystrophy. I went back into nursing because I had to, but I couldn't work the hours I do and still raise my kids right. Every spare nickel goes for their schooling and his medical expenses. Which explains why I live . . ." She motioned with her hands. "Here."

I was starting to feel like a damned fine imitation of a slimeball myself.

"I get up to see the kids about every other weekend. I don't smoke, drink rarely, don't do drugs, and don't indiscriminately date married men."

I leaned forward, put my elbows on my knees, trying to relax her as much as possible with my slim mastery of body language. "So how did you meet Conrad?"

"We met in I.C.U. He was doing his usual—the ranting and raving, ordering everyone about, making a jerk of himself. He also managed to offend every woman on staff. There was a doctor's lounge on the same floor as I.C.U. One evening, we had a question about one of Conrad's post-surgical patients, and somebody mentioned he was still on the floor. None of the other nurses were willing to go with him alone into the doctor's lounge. It was not so much that they were afraid; it was more like they didn't want to get dirty.''

"Yeah, I understand," I said. And I did.

"I volunteered. I figured I was the last person he'd try to hit on. Anyway, I went into the doctor's lounge. It was late at night, close to midnight, near shift rotation. We were all wondering why he was still on the floor, why he didn't go home."

She stood up nervously and walked around the back of the chair. I followed her with my eyes, seeing something in her and in my mental portrait of Conrad that I'd never seen before.

"He had his back to the door, sitting in a conference room chair, his elbows propped on the armrests. I walked in, cleared my throat, trying to get his attention. He never moved. He just sat there, staring out the window over the campus. It was very dark. The campus is dimly lit at night. He was just staring."

She gazed off herself for a moment, remembering what she'd seen that night. "I walked around in front of him," she continued, "and stood there looking down at him. His eyes were locked in front of him, as if he were in a trance. And he was crying, tears just running down his face."

Conrad Fletcher, I thought, *crying*?

"But he was real quiet," she went on. "No sobbing, no sniffling. Not a sound. Just tears. Anyway, I knelt down in front of him and asked him if he was okay. I thought maybe he was having a stroke. He looked at me for a long time without answering. Then he reached out and took my hand. I flinched. I mean, I thought for a second that he was just up to his old tricks or something. But he was just looking for some kind of human contact, I think. He was very gentle, very sweet. He never said a word at first, just held my hand.

Then he said 'I'm sorry.' And he shook his head and kind of brought himself to. I asked him about his patient, and he gave me some instructions and that was the end of it. For then . . .''

"What happened after that?"

"I rotated off nights. I didn't see him for several days. Then I went back on late, and one night I saw him in the hall. We were alone. He walked up to me, started talking. I thought again maybe he was hitting on me, but to tell you the truth, I'm just not the kind of woman who gets hit on very often."

Only because most men have no taste, I thought.

"He started talking to me, telling me about his marriage. Asking me about myself. Once he dropped his act, let go of all the yelling and screaming and power stuff, he could be quite vulnerable and very charming. He wasn't a happy man. I actually felt sorry for him. That's funny, isn't it? Me feeling sorry for somebody. He asked me out for coffee when the shift ended. Coffee, mind you, not drinks. We went in separate cars, met at an all-night restaurant. He was very proper. Never got out of line. We talked a couple of hours. I asked him back here for a nightcap. He spent the night."

She turned away from me, clearly embarrassed. This part, I could see, was tough for her. She paced back and forth for a few steps, then turned back to me.

"I don't know why I did it. I'd never done anything like that before. And heaven knows, my judgment in men has never been brilliant. But no man had ever talked with me like that before. Lots of men have talked *to* me. He's the only one I can ever recall talking *with* me. People didn't see that in him, because he would never let them see it, but he could be very sweet. What made it easier for him with me is that I caught him alone that first night, in the doctor's lounge, in a weak moment. It's no secret that doctors are egomaniacs and very much into power issues. Conrad was no exception. But for some reason, he let go of that around me."

To say that I'd never expected this was like saying Saddam Hussein never thought anybody'd kick his butt out of Kuwait.

Either LeAnn Gwynn was one hell of a liar, or I'd finally found somebody who had some fondness for the late, great Doc Fletcher. Could it be that he was human?

"So were you getting serious?" I asked.

She raised her head and focused on some invisible point beyond me. "I honestly can't say I know. Toward the end, we saw each other frequently. But I never asked him about his wife. Never mentioned anything permanent. I don't even know if I was in love with him, or he with me. We talked, spent time together. And yes, Mr. Denton, we had one dynamite time together in bed."

I couldn't help but grin a bit. I'd asked for honesty from her; by God, I'd gotten it.

"Why do you think he kept coming around?"

"That's easy. I don't know what I gave him. Whatever it was, though, he wasn't getting it at home."

"Where were you the night he was killed?"

LeAnn Gwynn's eyes widened as she looked at me. I saw fear in her.

"Who are you?"

"Ms. Gwynn, I told you, I'm—"

"No," she said. "I remember you now. Damn it, I remember you now! You were in the hall that night. I thought I'd seen you before!"

"LeAnn, I—"

"Who are you?" she yelled. "You said you were the police!"

"No, I said I was a detective."

My chest went into overdrive. Control of the situation was slipping away fast.

"You're not with the police?"

"I've been hired by the family to—"

"She hired you! I don't believe that lying bitch. She hired you to come after me, to pin Conrad's murder on me." Tears welled up in her eyes. Whatever tenderness she felt for Conrad was buried by her anger at me. Her fear was gone as well; now she was just plain mad. "You get out of here," she ordered, stalking to the door. "And you tell her that if she thinks she can dump this on me, she's in for a hell of a fight!''

LeAnn twisted the knob and yanked the door open before I had a chance to stop her. Not that I would have; I'd pressed my luck enough for one evening.

''Ms. Gwynn, I'm just trying to sort out what happened to Fletcher.''

She grabbed my arm, spun me around, and planted a hand in my back. Then she shoved.

I turned around out in the hallway. There was a look on LeAnn's face I hadn't seen before, a determined set to her jaw.

''You tell Rachel Fletcher I didn't kill her husband,'' she said. ''I had to spank him a few times when he got naughty, but I didn't kill him.''

Then she slammed the door in my face.

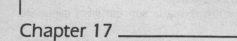

Chapter 17

Interstate 65 heading back into town was as crowded as Friday afternoon rush hour. Where in hell does all this traffic come from? I remember when this whole city shut down at ten. Then again, I remember when nobody had color television.

So somebody loved Conrad Fletcher. LeAnn Gwynn claimed she didn't know whether she was in love with him or not, but I knew love when I saw it. Something told me I'd just met the only person on earth who was going to miss Connie.

It was late; I ought to go home and grab some sack time. But my conversation with LeAnn Gwynn had been a profoundly disturbing one. I'd learned as a newspaper reporter that the worst way to chase down a story is begin with a preconceived notion of how the story ought to be. But I also knew that everybody, no matter how hot a reporter or investigator, *does*. It's as natural as looking outside, seeing dark clouds, and grabbing your umbrella. You see clouds; you figure it's going to rain.

Only sometimes it doesn't rain. Sometimes the sun breaks through and illuminates the landscape in ways you've never seen before. That's how I felt now. The lay of the land was different.

Not that I knew what to do about it. But all my assumptions were called into question.

First, there was a side to Connie I hadn't seen. No matter how he appeared to other people, at least one person saw

144

him as gentle and vulnerable and—how did she put it?—
charming.

Second, and this was the most subtle yet disturbing reve-
lation: I'd assumed Conrad Fletcher was running around at
night, sleeping with any nurse who'd have him, laying bets
with Bubba Hayes, partying down like a real lech. Now it
turned out that what he may have been doing was sitting
alone in dark hospital rooms with silent tears pouring down
his face.

Why?

There was only one person who could answer that question. I hoped that she was still awake. I cut right, a little too
closely to the long black limo behind me and to my right,
and swerved to hit the entrance ramp to the Four-Forty Parkway. I heard the blast of a horn as I cut the guy off and
realized he was veering to follow me.

Great, I thought, as much as I've got on my mind, and I
get into a traffic hassle with somebody. This is a bad town
for that. In New York City, drivers honk at each other as a
way of communicating. Down here, it's an invitation to a
gunfight. And I wasn't in the mood.

I laid down on the Ford, valves clattering away like Fla-
menco dancers under the hood, and pulled away. Around
seventy, I checked the rearview mirror and saw that he'd
dropped back. Guess the guy figured it wasn't worth it. He
was right.

I greased onto the exit chute for Hillsboro Road, squealed
tires through the horseshoe turn, and melted into the traffic.
Up ahead of me, the exclusive Green Hills homes sat darkened, quiet, well-tended, well-guarded.

I turned right onto Golf Club Lane and slowed. A couple
of blocks up, I slowed even further to make the turn onto
Rachel's driveway. The house was mostly dark, except for a
few lights in the upper right corner of the house that were
still burning.

I turned into the driveway and geared down to pull the
slight hill. I was halfway up the driveway when I spotted it,
slammed on the brakes quickly, and doused the headlights.

There was another car in the driveway. One I hadn't seen before: silver, looked foreign. Maybe a BMW, perhaps a Mercedes. Too dark to tell. I could just see the tail end of it poking out of the shadow cast across the backyard by the house. I couldn't see much of it, or read the license plate, but I knew I hadn't seen it there before.

Rachel had company. I looked at my watch: 10:15. I sat there for a second, wondering if I should go on up and knock on the door. Probably just a neighbor. But what if it wasn't?

No matter what, I hadn't called first. And it would be unspeakably intrusive, I thought, to drop in uninvited this time of night. That just isn't done in polite society. Besides, it was probably either her parents or Conrad's. They might not appreciate an unknown man dropping in on the widow unexpectedly. Might give them the wrong idea.

After all, Conrad's funeral was tomorrow. Out of respect, I ought to wait at least another twenty-four hours before moving in.

What followed was a restless night, full of dreams that shot at me like movie clips, disjointed faces: Conrad lying under me again, the police, the bash on my head, lying on a hospital floor with the young blond nurse kneeling over me, only this time the nurse was Rachel, then she was LeAnn Gwynn, and then finally, Marsha Helms. I woke from the dream when I was lying on an autopsy table with Marsha standing over me.

I came to in a cold sweat, the sheet twisted around me in knots, the chattering window unit straining to blow cold air on me in my attic apartment. I focused on the clock and discovered it was a little past seven. They were burying Conrad today, in less than seven hours, and I didn't even have a handle on who he was. I untangled myself from the sheets and stumbled over to the air conditioner. On especially humid, close nights, the damn thing tends to freeze up. I turned it off and pulled off the plastic cover; it was frosted over in white.

No matter. My cold sweat had evaporated into goose bumps, and I found myself shivering in the morning air. I wandered into what passed for my kitchen, plugged in the coffee, then went for the bathroom.

I don't usually shower first thing in the morning. I like to wake up slower than that, ease into the day with a cup of coffee and the newspaper. But this morning, I needed a bigger jolt than caffeine could handle. The hot water ran over me and felt marvelous, warming me up, bringing color back. Then for the last fifteen seconds, I twisted off the hot water faucet and let the cold sling down on me like a shower of needles.

The outside door to my apartment led onto a rickety metal landing, with a flight of rusting stairs down to my landlady's backyard. I walked down and grabbed my paper off the front lawn, then trudged back to get my coffee.

There was a short article on the front page of the Metro section headlined SLAIN DOCTOR BURIED TODAY. There was nothing in the story about the cause of death, so I hoped that meant the autopsy results weren't in yet.

The more I thought about it, the more I thought all hell was going to break loose when the autopsy results came in. If Marsha's suspicions were on target—and I knew from years past that they usually were—then this investigation would blossom from almost no official suspects to a truckload of them. The drugs Marsha suspected, one would assume, could only be obtained in a medical setting. That meant virtually anyone at the hospital could be guilty: James Hughes or any other medical student; the exceedingly lovely Dr. Collingswood or the infatuated Dr. Zitin or any other resident; or any nurse Conrad ever hit on, including LeAnn Gwynn, the one who loved him.

LeAnn Gwynn's story, which had seemed so convincing last night, didn't hold up so well in the hot light of the day. I believed every statement she made except the last. Maybe she didn't kill him. But if she did, she wouldn't be the first person to kill a lover. Maybe he'd decided to end their affair. Murder's been committed for less.

And what was that business about spanking? Was she kidding, or did Conrad, besides everything else, have a kinky side?

I picked up the phone and dialed the morgue. It was probably too early for Marsha Helms, but I knew my old buddy Kay Delacorte would be there. The shifts changed at seven, but she always came in at least a half hour early to make sure everything was under control.

"Forensic Science Center," she said.

I deepened my voice. "Hello, darling."

"Well, if it ain't Conway Twitty."

"In the flesh, my love," I said, back to normal.

"Yeah, but whose flesh?" She laughed out loud. "Bad joke to make at the morgue. Too early."

"You got that right. Listen, Kay, I'm looking for Marsha. She in yet?"

There was a long, tense pause over the phone. Kay was messing with me again.

"Business or pleasure this time?"

I thought for a second. "Maybe both."

"Yeah? In which order?"

"Definitely pleasure. Pleasure's always first whenever I see you guys."

"You slick bastard, you. Hold on, I'll ring her."

A second later, Marsha picked up the phone. Her voice was too bright and cheery to be fully real; either she was glad to hear from me or she wasn't awake yet.

"Morning, Harry. How are you?"

"Great, babe. How you doing?"

"That's Dr. Babe to you. And I'm fine."

"You going to Conrad Fletcher's funeral today?"

"I hate funerals," she said, voice fluttering with horror at the thought. "They're so morbid."

"And doing autopsies for a living isn't?"

"Hey, that's just business. Besides, you get used to it after awhile. It's like playing with jigsaw puzzles."

"I've never seen a jigsaw puzzle where the pieces would squish through your hand when you tried to pick them up."

"To answer your question, Mr. Smart Guy, no. I'm not going to Conrad Fletcher's funeral. If I went to the funeral of every stiff that came through this door, I'd be a professional funeral goer-toer."

"Good point. Well, I've got to. I not only knew the guy; it's business for me."

"So have fun. Sing a hymn for me."

"Listen, Marsh, I got to be at the funeral home at two. Thought maybe you'd like to get lunch before. What do you think?"

There was more silence from her end. "So what are you looking for this time?"

"Nothing," I said, which was at least partly true. "I just remembered what you said the other day. About calling you. What do you say? C'mon, you gotta eat."

"Where you want to go?"

"Make it easy on you. Someplace close to the hospital. Maybe that sushi bar on Second Avenue."

"You want to take a forensic pathologist to a sushi bar? You're a sick puppy, Harry."

I laughed. "Okay, that restaurant across the street from you. What is it this week, Thai or Korean?"

"Korean, I think."

"Great. How about noon?"

She exhaled deeply into the phone. "I'll probably regret this, but okay. Noon it is."

I'd never seen Marsha Helms outside work before, but I knew her well enough not to be surprised when she pulled into the parking lot in a black Porsche 911 Turbo Carrera convertible with a vanity plate that read DED FLKS. All I could do was put my head down on the table for a moment and think: great, I'm having lunch with a woman who thinks autopsies are cute.

I looked up just in time to see her bend over to lock the car door. Bizarre sense of humor aside, Marsha was attractive and growing more so by the day. Unlike some very tall women I'd seen in my life, she didn't try to hide her height.

She wore clothes that looked as if a tailoring genius had designed them just for her. She tended toward dark colors, but they were bold and vivid, not muted. The Addams Family came back to me again. I couldn't help it; I wanted to be Gomez to her Morticia: Marsh, you spoke French. . . .

She walked into the restaurant carrying herself high, a zest to her footsteps that belied her grim work. Maybe dealing with death makes you appreciate life all that much more. Come to think of it, since this business with Conrad started, I'd found my senses sharper, keener. Images were more distinct, voices were clearer, more piercing, flavors more intense. As grim as this whole business was, for the first time since I entered this line of work, I was enjoying myself. I've always tended to go from one obsession to another, which helped make me a pretty decent reporter. Maybe the skills were beginning to transfer. Maybe someday, I'd be able to make a living at it.

And maybe I was flattering myself. After all, I was no closer to figuring out who killed Conrad than I was the night he was murdered. I just had a sense of how many people might have wanted to. No matter how hard I tried, though, I couldn't stop racking my brains. So many questions remained, not the least of which was the big one: why would Conrad lie there without a struggle and let somebody jam a syringe into his leg?

My seemingly endless mental monologue was interrupted by the elderly restaurant owner accompanying Marsha to the table. I stood, smiled at her appreciatively, and found myself strangely tongue-tied as she took her seat.

We exchanged pleasantries as she unfolded a cloth napkin and spread it across her lap. We were seated at a large window overlooking Hermitage Avenue, the noontime traffic passing in an endless stream. The morning cloud cover had burned off; the sky was a bright blue. It was turning into a gorgeous day.

"Funny," I said. "I'm a little nervous."

"Me, too. I've never seen you outside—"

"Yeah. Say, love your car."

She grinned sheepishly. "I'll let you drive it sometime."

The waiter came. We ordered a couple of glasses of an Australian chardonnay, an unusual indulgence for both of us, and a couple of Korean dishes I'd never heard of. Lunch is seldom an adventure for me, but I was delighted to have it turn into one. We made small talk and swapped stories, just as people do when they're on what amounts to a first date. I swear; I'm nearly forty years old, married and divorced, and a decorated veteran of the relationship wars, but I still get nervous when something starts feeling like it's about to happen.

On the other hand, I'm also old enough to enjoy the nervousness, to celebrate that someone can still give me butterflies, even if just for lunch. And maybe I was seeing something that wasn't there. But, hey, she seemed to be having a good time.

"By the way," I asked, as we were finishing our coffee, "whatever happened to the tox report on Fletcher?"

She looked over the top of her cup, her eyes darkening. "Well, I was wondering when you would get around to it."

"Now wait a minute, Marsh. That's not why I invited you to lunch."

"Oh, it isn't?" She put the cup down hard. This little voice in my head muttered an obscenity, and I figured she really was steamed at me.

"No. Listen, I'm interested, and yes, I need to know. But you got to believe me. I've been wanting to do this for a while."

She softened a bit. The wine, along with a sinfully good meal, had taken the rough edges off both of us.

"Well, I'll tell you what," she said. "I'll believe you if I give you the poop and then we wind up doing this again."

"If that's the deal, I'll take it."

"That's the deal." She smiled and leaned across the table, her voice dropping to a conspiratorial whisper. "The report came in last night. I was right. Protocurarine. I forget the blood concentration, but he was packed to the gills. Whoever did it wasn't taking any chances. Bombed him good."

"Where would it come from?"

"Well, Sam Spade, since he got whacked in a hospital, I'd say that's an excellent place to start."

"Would the stuff be locked up?"

She thought for a second. "I don't know. Probably. It's certainly a narcotic. But it'd be held with the other anesthetics. Outside of putting somebody way under, I don't know of any other medical use. It certainly wouldn't be routinely kept in a drug locker."

"Has the report been released to the cops?"

"Oh, yeah. First thing this morning. Homicide's holding a press conference late this afternoon. They figured they'd wait until after the funeral as a sign of respect to the family."

"Damned decent of them," I said. "They'd probably like to keep it under their hats altogether."

"It'd never work. Too big a story. The media'd bust their chops."

I looked down at my watch. Conrad's funeral was in less than an hour. I pulled out my credit card, the one least likely to be maxxed out, and laid it on top of the check. Then, on impulse, I leaned across the table and kissed her. Nothing heavy, no slobbering passion at lunchtime, but a kiss. A for-real, unmistakable, not-just-a-friendly-peck-on-the-cheek kiss.

"Thanks," I said.

She smiled at me. "Anytime."

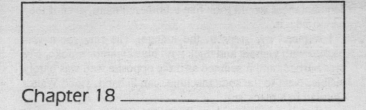

Chapter 18 _____

Conrad Fletcher picked a beautiful day to be buried.

The silver hearse and two black limousines were already parked on the side of the funeral home, with rent-a-cop security cars on either side of the parking lot. The television stations were there as well. Conrad's murder was considered particularly intriguing and juicy by the media vultures, and they didn't even know the whole story yet.

The back lot was filling up fast. I parked the Ford between two larger cars and sat there, discreetly watching the proceedings. I recognized several doctors, some other people who looked vaguely familiar from the hospital, and groups of younger people who were probably Conrad's students. I wondered what the proportion of mourners to rejoicers might be, then decided that kind of speculation was not called for.

Inside the funeral home, the crowd resembled spectators at a dull trade show or convention rather than a group of souls lost in sadness. People milled about, gossiped, made the idiotic small talk that's been the grease of human interaction since humans gave up grunting and shaking sticks at one another. Occasionally, a too loud voice would break forth in laughter, then just as quickly hush. I wandered around the outside fringes of the throng, then slowly began working my way toward the front of the funeral home. Conrad's coffin had been moved into the chapel to accommodate the larger crowd. Despite the solemnity of the occasion, even inside the chapel itself there was little in the way of melancholy. I found myself hoping that when I crossed over, at least a few acquaintances would look like it bothered them, even if they had to fake it.

I retraced my steps to the lounge. The tiny room was packed with visitors and thick with blue cigarette smoke. My eyes burned, and it seemed as if the opposite wall was barely visible. Next to the soda machine, can in hand, stood Walter Quinlan in a black suit.

"Hey, buddy," I said, walking up to him and sticking out my hand. He looked stressed, not at all the happy exuberance I'd seen the other day.

"Hi, Harry. How are you?"

"I'm hanging in there, man." He shook my hand tightly. "I'm glad to see you. I was wondering if I'd run into anybody I know."

"Don't worry. They're all here."

"You seem strung out, my man. What's the matter?"

"All this, I guess. I hate funerals." There was a redness in his eyes. Had he been crying? Didn't seem likely. Walter wasn't the type. More likely, he'd had a few drinks and a lousy night's sleep.

"You been here long?"

He hesitated for a moment. "I don't know. Maybe an hour."

"Seen Rachel yet?"

"Oh, yeah. I came by the other night, too. Sorry I missed you."

"Me, too. I had to leave earlier. Had to check something out."

He grabbed my arm and pulled me closer to him. In the crowded room, with a buzzing conversational din all around us, nobody was going to hear anything we said. But Walter wanted to make sure.

"Are you still working on this, Harry?" he whispered.

"Yeah. Of course."

"Harry, I want you to stop. This is killing Rachel. It's not what she wants."

"What do you mean?" I demanded. "She wants the person who murdered Conrad, doesn't she?"

"Yes, she wants him. Bad. But she doesn't want anything to happen to you. And you have a lousy habit of getting yourself into places where you shouldn't be."

Tension radiated through my shoulders, and I found myself wanting to tell him to mind his own business. This was, after all, between my client and me. Walter, though, was my lawyer and he was a buddy. So I guess he had the right to butt in if he wanted to.

"Walter, we've been on this ride before. I can take care of myself. This is important to me, damn it. And I'm not quitting."

"Suit yourself, you jerk," he snapped, letting my arm go with a push. "But when you get hurt, don't come yelling to me for help."

I walked away without saying anything else. He'll cool off, I thought. Everybody's walking the edge today.

Inside the chapel, Rachel stood in a simple black dress, her hair pulled back in a bun, with just enough makeup to cover the dark circles under her eyes. She was at the head of the aisle, a few steps away from the coffin and the still-expanding circle of wreaths and flowers. No tears had been expended by the mourners, but I'll bet some checkbooks had been strained. It was a great day to be a florist.

I stood halfway down the aisle for a moment, in the long line of people waiting to extend condolences, when I spotted Howard Spellman at the back of the chapel. He sat off in a corner by himself, at the far end of the last pew. I broke from the line and walked back down the green carpet, then cut in toward him. He watched me without getting up, and I slid into the seat next to him.

"Lieutenant Spellman," I said. "How nice to see you again."

"Hello, Denton."

I followed his eyes toward the front of the sanctuary. He was watching Rachel, along with several other people I didn't recognize, as they shook hands in the receiving line.

"Her family?" I asked.

"The two on the left are her parents. The silver-haired one

on the right is his father. I understand Fletcher's mother had to leave. Too much for her.''

"How about the tall guy at the end?"

"Mrs. Fletcher's brother, I think. The man and the woman on the other end are Fletcher's brother and sister.''

"Fletcher had siblings?" I asked.

Spellman turned to me. "He *was* human, you know.''

"So I've heard.''

"People do have brothers, sisters, cousins.''

"Funny," I commented, "I'd have guessed that Fletcher was an only child. Maybe it was the combination of being an overachiever and difficult to deal with.''

"He was the oldest.''

I looked down at my watch. The funeral was going to start in about fifteen minutes.

"If I'm going to make it through the receiving line before the kickoff, I'd better get on up there. You staying for the whole ball game?''

Spellman looked up at me as I stood up. "Not if it means you're going to come back and sit with me.''

"Lieutenant, I hope you don't think my presence here is a case of the killer coming by to check out his own handiwork.''

He went stone-faced on me. I took my cue and walked off. I couldn't help jibing him; he was such a tough guy. Cop works homicide for twenty years, he's going to get a little jaded. Just thought I'd put a little humor back into his colorless, dreary life.

The line sped up a little as the clock wound down to show time. Funerals make me so uncomfortable that my mind runs around in unconnected, disjointed, extremely inappropriate patterns to avoid feeling what's happening. Sort of a mental Tourette's Syndrome. Thank God, we can't see inside each other's heads. The world would be even crazier than it already is.

Finally, I got to Rachel. I hugged her, her form warm and vibrant in my arms. This, I thought, is the roughest of duties. Amazingly enough, she had not yet reached that point where she was on automatic pilot. She was still actually hearing the words of sympathy from each person, still feeling the loss, the conflict of despair, sadness, along with the good dose of anger we all feel at the dead. *How dare you die on me, you rat bastard?*

She sobbed in my arms, her face tightening, although her eyes remained dry. The tear ducts can only work so hard before even they give out. But the heart continues.

I felt like hell for her. I wanted to wrap my arms around her, take her away from this grim room. I even found myself with that old familiar burning down below that she'd always fired in me. I had to fight to suppress that one, let me tell you. Nothing like getting frisky at a funeral to get yourself dropped off the A-list at party time.

"Thanks for coming," she said, pulling away from me.

"What can I do to help you?"

"You can take care of yourself. Be my friend. Come see me after all this is over."

"You got it," I said. "No problem."

I wove through the rest of the line, meeting the relatives and the in-laws, shaking my head in sadness and agreeing that this was indeed a terrible tragedy. Then I took a seat in the chapel about midway down the aisle. I looked around and saw Dr. Collingswood and Dr. Zitin sitting next to each other. James Hughes sat farther back with a group of other medical students. I looked around for LeAnn Gwynn, then realized she was in the back of the chapel with Jackie Bell and a covey of much younger nurses. All we needed was Bubba Hayes to complete the cast, but I doubted if bookies were in the habit of showing up for their customers' funerals. After all, how could they collect?

Yes, I'd agreed with someone from Conrad's family in the receiving line: this was a terrible tragedy. But for at least one person, and probably one person who was somewhere in this room, this was not a terrible tragedy.

It was simply and completely a job well done.

Chapter 19

I can't decide whether I was born a good liar, or it was simply a skill I acquired over time out of the necessity of need and the tedium of practice. I guess it's lucky I was born with a sense of moral value as well, because I have no doubt that had I been so inclined, I'd have made a pretty fair grifter.

"This is Dr. Evans, Neurosurgery," I said to the hospital night operator.

"Oh, yes, Dr. Evans," she said. "I recognize your voice."

"I'm trying to locate two residents who should be in the hospital tonight. Do you have any way of checking the scheduling?"

"Why, you know better than that, Dr. Evans. Of course, I do."

I thought quickly, then laughed. "No, of course, I know you can do it. I meant, have I caught you at a bad time?"

"Oh, no, Doctor. Things are quiet around here tonight. Who are you trying to locate?"

"Doctors Albert Zitin and Jane Collingswood."

"Please hold."

I leaned back in my office chair and put my feet up on the desk. Outside, the traffic was finally thinning, and the temperature was taking a slide out of the nineties. Conrad's funeral had been a long one, what with the drive out to Mount Olivet and all. I'd stayed for the duration. For Rachel's sake, I'd told myself. Most of the people, though, had chosen to do otherwise. And outside of the family, a couple of TV cameras, and the university hotshots, there probably weren't twenty people at graveside.

"Dr. Evans?" the pleasant voice came back.

"Yes."

"Dr. Zitin is not on call tonight. Dr. Collingswood is doing a rotation in E.R."

"Thank you," I said, equally pleasant. "I really appreciate your help."

"That's what I'm here for," she said, clicking off.

It occurred to me that if the real Gordon Evans ever called this woman, he was going to have an awful time avoiding arrest for impersonating a doctor.

So Dr. Jane's in E.R. I'll be damned if I'll go out and bung up my leg again just to see her. The swelling had gone down almost completely, and I'd now been almost twenty-four hours without a twinge. All that was left were some nasty blue and yellow streaks that would probably be around for at least a month.

I lowered my pair of good legs to the floor and stood up. Down the hall, I could hear a guitar strumming and the sound of voices. Slim and Ray were holding their nightly songwriter's cocktail hour. I thought I might drop in on them. I hadn't said much of anything to either of them since the day Rachel Fletcher walked into my office. They were good people; I'd best reconnect with them.

I spread my jacket across the back of the chair and rolled up my shirtsleeves. Casual was the order of the day at Slim and Ray's office. In fact, I'd be the only one down there out of denim, not to mention the necktie. I was about to leave the office when I heard the squeal of tires and a blaring horn outside.

The corner of the building blocked part of the view, but apparently somebody had taken the curve at Church and Seventh a little too tightly and almost collided with a car illegally parked in the loading zone for the drugstore on the corner. Idiots, I thought, turning away.

Then I looked back.

It was a Lincoln, a long black bear of a car. You didn't

park a car like that; you docked it. Was it the same one that had been in the loading zone the other day? Maybe the one that followed me on the parkway last night? I wasn't sure, but something set off bells and whistles.

I stood there scanning the car, trying to recognize the driver. But the windows were smoked just enough, and the setting sun was striking the glass at just the right angle. It was impossible to see inside.

If I went down there and knocked on the glass, one of two things would happen. If the person inside was tailing me, then I'd blow his cover, and there was no telling what might happen next. If the guy wasn't tailing me, he'd just think I was another urban crazy.

I turned away from the window. I knew I'd seen a long black car a couple of times in the past few days. But was it *that* car? Where had I seen it before? If I could only remember . . .

The boys down the hall struck up another tune. Slim and Ray's office looked directly out the front of the building. I could keep an eye on the Lincoln from their window even better.

I walked down the hall. Their door was cracked, but I rapped a couple of times with my knuckles.

"Yo!" a voice inside yelled, halting the strumming of guitars.

"Yo, yourself," I said, stepping in.

"Hey, Harry, you dirty rascal. Where have you been, boy?" Ray jumped up from a desk with his guitar in his left hand. He stuck his right hand out and jerked mine like a pump handle.

"Must be a special night," I said. "You've got the Martin out."

Ray's prized possession was a thirty-year-old Martin D-28. It was a work of art, as preserved and cared for as the day it was brand-new. Even a musically ignorant, tone-deaf brick like me knew it was a classic.

"Yeah, we been working on this new song. Think it's going to be our next hit, don't you, Slim?"

Slim looked up from the strings of his Ovation, smiled at me, and shook his head. Slim was decidedly not the lyricist in this team. I doubt I'd heard him say twenty-five words in the months that I'd known him.

There were four other people as well crammed into the tiny, two-room office: a bleached blonde in worn jeans and a T-shirt, two other cowboys, and a girl who looked maybe sixteen. I tried to figure out who was with whom, without any luck. The woman had an old, beat-to-hell guitar with nylon strings. Cowboy No. 1 had a shirt pocket full of harmonicas, and Cowboy No. 2 had a fiddle.

A bucket full of longnecks in ice cubes sat on the floor.

"Mind if I listen?" I asked.

"You know better than that, boy," Ray said. "And grab that one on the left. It's got your name on it."

I reached down and pulled an amber Pabst Blue Ribbon bottle out of the bucket and popped the top with the opener on Slim's desk. Slim was an interesting kind of guy; year or two younger than me, frame like a body builder, thick, wavy light-brown hair, blue eyes that cut right through you. He was more than handsome, almost the kind of man that could be called pretty, although you better not call him that to his face.

Ray, on the other hand, was thin, somewhere way over forty, and had the skid marks on his face and thinning gray hair to show for it. Ray had come to Nashville in the Fifties, played Tootsie's Orchid Lounge down on Lower Broad and the Stockyard Restaurant for twenty-five years before giving that up to save his liver. Now he just wrote songs, except for an occasional appearance at the Opry or on the Nashville Network. He'd been through a lot, yet seemed to me the least scarred veteran of the music business I'd ever met. I kept thinking I ought to get him and Lonnie together sometime, but Ray was too busy writing songs and Lonnie was too busy repossessing cars and making homemade explosives.

The beer was as cold as a mountain stream in January, in contrast to the thick, hot air of our old office building. All

the tenants kept saying we were going to have to complain
to the management company, but nobody ever did. Besides,
autumn was just around the corner. Another month or two,
the worst of the heat would break, anyway. If I could stand
it without air conditioning in the car, I could stand it in the
office.

An old, thirteen-inch black and white flickered away in
the background as Slim and Ray, accompanied by the other
four on either instrument or voice, began their new song. I
don't know much about country music, but I have to admit
I was impressed. It sounded good to me, a fusion between
traditional country and modern pop, without all the over-
produced studio effects and the other crap that goes into music these days. Slim and Ray were on the last verse of the
song when I glanced over at the television. "The Scene at
Six," the local newscast, was just starting, and the lead story
was Conrad.

"Excuse me, guys. Gotta hear this." I crossed to the
corner of the room and turned up the sound just enough
to hear.

"Friends, family, and colleagues of surgeon and professor
Dr. Conrad Fletcher mourned his passing today, as police
reported startling new evidence in the murder." The an-
chorwoman's face was earnest, serious, begging us to trust
her and be her friend.

I turned the volume up another notch. Behind me, the
music stopped.

"The results of Dr. Fletcher's autopsy were released today
by the Metro Nashville Medical Examiner's office, and the
findings lend only more credence to police suspicions that
the murder was an inside hospital job. We turn now to Daphne
Fox with more."

The station switched to a videotape of a reporter standing
just outside the hospital, with a university building in the
background.

"Police now say that, as a result of the autopsy done on
murdered surgeon Dr. Conrad Fletcher, Nashville private
investigator Harry Denton is no longer a suspect."

Ray let out a cheer behind me, then slapped me on the back. "Way to go, dude! Ya'll didn't know we had a celebrity in our midst, did you?"

"Hush, Ray," I said, "I'm trying to listen."

"The coroner's office announced today that Dr. Fletcher was murdered by an injection of a lethal synthetic anesthetic, protocurarine, which hospital security officials indicate would have only been available to hospital personnel. Police are now turning their attention to reports that Dr. Fletcher may have been murdered by one of his colleagues at the hospital."

The videotape jumped again, this time to Lieutenant Spellman behind a podium in the police press conference room.

"Yes, that's correct, Mr. Denton is no longer a suspect in this homicide."

Man, I thought, I'll bet he had to pry those words out with a crowbar. It hadn't occurred to me, though, that I really had been a suspect. It just seemed too ridiculous. If I'd have known I was held in such high regard by the homicide squad, I'd have been a little less chatty over the past couple of days. Especially with Spellman . . .

"We have a number of clues, however, and several leads that will be very helpful in light of the autopsy findings and the T.B.I. toxicology lab results."

Videotape switch again, this time to Dean Malone at the med school looking shocked and concerned: "It's beyond me that anything like that could happen at this university. However, I want it known publicly that we intend to cooperate with the police in every way possible to bring the perpetrator of this horrible crime to justice."

I laughed. Wonder how this was going to affect admissions next year. *You're going where? I hear they don't flunk you down there. They kill you!*

Back to the reporter now: "All evidence then points, police say, to an inside job. With over five thousand employees and medical students at the medical center, however, finding the one who killed Dr. Conrad Fletcher may be more like looking for a needle in a haystack than anything else. For "The Scene At Six," this is Daphne Fox."

"Yeah," I whispered, "especially when the haystack is full of needles to begin with."

I turned down the volume knob. Raising the beer bottle to my lips, I noticed that everybody in the room was staring at me. The bottle froze in midair as I looked out over the top of it.

"Did you really find him?" the young girl asked.

I nodded my head yes.

"Was it awful?" she asked, her drawl becoming even more syrupy as she drew the words out.

"It was no tiptoe through the tulips," I said, wanting more than anything else not to discuss it. "Hey, Ray, why don't you let me hear that song again?"

Ray hit a lick on the Martin, filling the room with notes as clear and loud and sweet as heaven's doorbell. I backed away toward the window, to listen to the song as they all let go again. Over my shoulder, I could see the black Lincoln still parked in the loading zone. The driver's side window was rolled about halfway down now, but I couldn't see anything because of the angle.

Ray and Slim really had written a winner. The chorus was catchy, the bridge was bridgey. The more I listened to Ray and Slim, and the new, younger voices of country music, the more I grew to love it. The work of songwriters like Bob McDill, Jim Glaser, Randy VanWarmer, sounded more like poetry than pop to me. And I'll take Garth Brooks, Randy Travis, Kathy Mattea, any day over Metallica and Poison and the obscene urban MTV warfare raps.

The two sang on, their voices blending in a harmony as sweet as clear sunshine. The verses were not sophisticated, but they were genuine and earthy and touching. I felt like I was sitting in on something pretty impressive. Ray and Slim played guitar licks off each other at the end of the song, then note by note, traded off the resolution, hit the final chord, and let the sound echo away into silence inside the office.

Then there was a scream.

Chapter 20

We sat there a moment, stunned. That definitely was not part of the song. "What the hell?" Ray said, stretching out the word hell into about four syllables.

I couldn't even tell where the scream had come from. I shrugged my shoulders.

"I don't know," Slim said. It was one of the more profound statements he'd ever made.

"Where'd it come from?" the bleached blonde asked.

"Beats the shit out of me," Cowboy No. 1 offered.

Then we heard it again, muffled, from a distance: a solid, human scream bellowing from a healthy set of lungs.

I looked over my shoulder at the Lincoln. Someone stood next to the driver's side window, with a shopping cart full of cardboard boxes, rags, and garbage, held with one hand to keep it from rolling down Seventh Avenue. A bag lady, I realized, and just then she released the shopping cart, raised both hands to the side of her face, and let loose with another long, bloodcurdling howl. The shopping cart rolled down Seventh Avenue, picking up speed as it went, then hit a pothole and toppled, sending the bag lady's prized possessions arcing off into the street and blocking both lanes.

"Ray," I said, "I think we got trouble downstairs."

Ray laid the Martin down carefully on the desk, then was behind me only a couple of steps as we bolted for the stairs. No time to wait for the elevator, I realized, as we pounded down to the landing, pivoted, and took the next flight down three or four at a time.

On the landing just above the main floor, I hit the wrong

way. My bum ankle twisted and pain shot like a bolt of lightning up the side of my leg. I slammed against the side of the wall, pulled my knee up to my belt, and let out an old-fashioned obscenity.

The young girl stopped beside me; everybody else flew past in the, by now, mass hysteria.

"I'm all right," I grumbled, rubbing the ankle through my socks. "C'mon, let's go."

I hobbled down the hall as fast as I could, then pushed through the front door and down the steps to the sidewalk. Across the street, a crowd was already gathering around the car and the bag lady as she continued howling like a demented wolf, both hands to her face, staring through her dirty fingers at the heavens.

Traffic had stopped now in both lanes. I skipped across the street to the crowd and pushed my way through the first layer. Ray reached inside the window to unlock the car door.

"Wait a minute, Ray," I yelled as I got next to him. "Hold up."

"I just want to help him," Ray said, turning to me. "We got to get the door open and get him out of there."

I elbowed him out of the way and bent to look inside the car. On the edge of my consciousness, I could hear the faint high pitch of the police sirens growing louder by the second. Inside the car, the crumpled body of a huge black man lay slumped over, held up only by the armrest folded down on the front seat.

There was a small hole about the size of a dime in the left side of his head, just above and ahead of his ear. Barely visible gray powder and burn marks starbursted out from the wound on his dark skin. Chemical tests, I knew, would bring out plenty more.

There wasn't much blood, just a small trickle down the side of his face. He wasn't breathing. That much was obvious. There wasn't anything anybody could do for him now.

I leaned inside as far as I could go, which wasn't far, trying to get a better look at him. It worked. I recognized the man, and everything in my gut went liquid. It was Mr. Kennedy, Bubba Hayes's right-hand man.

Make that ex-right-hand man. Mr. Kennedy wasn't anybody's anything anymore, except a fading memory.

They carted the bag lady off to the Middle Tennessee Mental Health Institute, formerly known as the Central State Asylum. Apparently the sight of a corpse in a thirty-thousand-dollar car on her turf was more than she could handle. Come to think of it, I could say the same for myself.

For the second time in less than a week, I found myself sitting in an interrogation room at the Metropolitan Nashville Justice Center.

"You know," Spellman said, "just when I think I've gotten you out of my hair, boom, you wind up next to another stiff. What is it with you? You got a thing for dead bodies, son?"

What is it with you, I wondered, and the legions of other Southern men that makes them think they can call anybody they want to *son*, no matter how old they are, or how little the chance of any blood relation? The way I was feeling about Spellman right then, I'd trace my roots all the way back to the slime pool to deny any connection to him.

"Lieutenant, I was sitting in a room full of witnesses who've told you I was with them until we heard the street lady screaming. I couldn't possibly have had anything to do with this death."

He loosened his tie. It was late, the end of a long day. We were both tired and stressed out. I'd had one beer up in Ray's office; I was ready for another.

"Do you know who he was?" Spellman asked.

"I didn't check his wallet." A true statement.

"We did. His name was Kennedy, Roosevelt Kennedy. Ex-TSU star, All-American, drafted by the Falcons in the early Seventies."

"Explains the wheels," I said.

"No it doesn't, and you know it. For the past six or seven

years, he's been working for the Reverend Bubba Hayes. Ever heard of him?''

I screwed my mouth into a tight turn. "Name's familiar.''

"It should be,'' Spellman said. He bent down in front of me, put a hand on each armrest of my chair, got real low, right in my face. "He controls most of the action for the university area. We keep a close eye on him. And we know he was Conrad Fletcher's bookie. And we know you knew that.''

"So when did knowledge become illegal?''

"Knowledge isn't illegal,'' he said. "Interfering with a police investigation is. I know you've been all over the hospital, questioning nurses, questioning doctors, and I know you've been to see a cutie by the name of LeAnn Gwynn. That one, I could probably make a case for impersonating an officer. But frankly, I don't have time for pissant private investigators who've been watching too many episodes of "Magnum, P.I." The paperwork is more trouble than you're worth.''

He backed away, paced the room, then turned toward me again. "You're a smartass, Denton, and I don't like you very much. You've been defecating in my nest, and I don't like that either. To make matters worse, you're an incompetent. You couldn't find your ass with both hands and a set of instructions. If I catch you so much as spitting on the sidewalk around this investigation again, I'm going to have your license yanked, and I'm going to have you up on charges. You savvy, boy?''

I stared at him, a long bout in an ice-cold staring contest. "You finished?'' I asked him finally.

"Maybe, maybe not.''

"In that case, I want my lawyer. Now.''

He glared at me, disgusted. "Get out of here,'' he spat.

I felt sorry for Mr. Kennedy. Even if he was muscle for a scumbag ex-preacher-turned-bookie, there was something about him that radiated more class in an afternoon than most lowlifes could muster in a lifetime. I don't know what he was doing following me around, but I regretted that doing so got him killed. The only people winning this contest, it seemed, were the grave diggers.

My frustration was doubled by what Mr. Kennedy's death meant in my search for Conrad Fletcher's murderer. The best candidate all along, especially given that I was sure he was innocent, was Bubba Hayes. My newspaper days taught me that the guy who looks the cleanest has probably got the most to hide. So while I didn't have any way to prove Bubba's guilt, I was certainly remaining open to the possibilities.

Only problem now was, it didn't make sense, at least not based on what I knew and what I'd observed. There was a bond between Bubba Hayes and Mr. Kennedy. I figured there was no way they could work together, given their differences, without it. They were like two components of a machine that operated so smoothly, so tightly, that it seemed effortless. It didn't make sense that Bubba Hayes would kill off somebody like Mr. Kennedy. Good help's too hard to find these days.

It had to be somebody else.

I sat back on my old couch and wrapped my palm around a lukewarm bottle of beer. I was still smarting from the verbal working over Spellman had given me, still sore from where I'd taken the landing wrong, and still torqued that the day had gotten so screwed up.

On top of it all, I couldn't sleep. And I was beginning to have some heavy-duty doubts about finding Conrad's killer. I figured that with all the people who hated the guy, it ought to have been easy. It would have been my first big case, the kind of case that could give me some serious stroke in a very competitive marketplace. The private investigators in this town take up a complete spread in the yellow pages, and then some. But there was more to it besides business, although going months without a case had been bad enough. There was more to it than that.

Lanie, my ex-wife, was an assistant vice president at the city's largest advertising agency when we were married. Since we divorced, she's become a group V.P. in charge of acquisitions for a fifteen-state region. Don't have to look too hard to find out how she's handling the breakup. Lanie's tough, ambitious, attractive. She's also ten years younger than me. We met when she was new in the business and hustling reporters to get press releases published. She brought in a couple one day, and I offered to take her on a tour of the paper. What the hell, she was a looker, and I was currently unattached. I wound up taking her to lunch in the company cafeteria. It really knocked her panty hose off when, in mid-bite, the publisher himself came up and patted me on the back over a story I'd just done about the lack of sprinklers and fire-code violations in one of the downtown office buildings. We called each other by first names, laughed around a bit. I introduced her to him, and he kissed her hand, European-style. Lanie thought she was in high cotton, and she thought I was freaking Walter Cronkite or something.

Six months later we were married. The paper did a feature on the wedding. One of the television stations even did a spot. Her parents were awed by it all. Mine were pretty blown away, too.

It was only after we'd been married a year or so, and had the chance to share a joint checking account and file our taxes together as married people, that Lanie figured out that she was fresh out of college, two years into a career in business, and was already making more than me. I explained to her that most newspaper people rarely make more than about thirty-five grand a year under the best of circumstances, no matter how hot they are, and my circumstances were no-where near the best. And while I might move on to a larger paper in a bigger city someday, for now I was pretty happy and didn't plan on going anywhere.

When she was made assistant V.P., the trouble started. It wasn't merely that she was doing better. We both could have lived with that. It was more that I didn't *want* to do any better. She couldn't imagine that I could work the hours I worked, get as many front-page bylines as I did, and still be willing to settle for a three percent annual raise every year.

She encouraged me to go into television, where the truly big bucks are. For a while, I considered it. But even more than print journalism, broadcast journalism is as much entertainment as anything else. There was no way I could endure the happy horseshit that permeates the local news every night and still keep my lunch down. Sooner or later, I'd wind up pushing somebody's button and get fired, which I figured would never happen on the paper.

Reality, of course, had a way of figuring differently.

Anyway, my lack of ambition doomed the marriage, and pretty soon, when we couldn't qualify for the loan she wanted to buy the house out in Belle Meade, and we couldn't take the European vacation because the paper didn't give me that much vacation time, and not only could I not pay for a Jaguar, I didn't even want one. . . . Well, things went down the dumper fast. I got called out one night to cover a major apartment-complex fire. It wasn't my usual beat, but the late night cityside guy was doing twenty-eight in an inpatient dryout unit. When I got back in at five in the morning, Lanie'd packed a bag and moved out. I got served a week later. And that was, as they say, all she wrote.

It wouldn't be so rough if I hadn't gotten myself ashcanned on the paper. There was a certain satisfaction in knowing that when Lanie drove her Alfa into the parking lot of her West End condo, took the elevator up to her well-furnished living room, poured herself a glass of twenty-dollar-a-bottle wine, and settled back to look at her daily paper, she was more likely than not to run into my smiling name, still there in her life and in her face. Now even that satisfaction was gone.

I don't usually allow myself to drift into self-pity. Ironically, I didn't realize how much being a hotshot newspaper reporter meant to me, how much seeing my name on page one above-the-fold made up for so much, not the least of which was the relatively puny paycheck. In one of our last conversations, Lanie insisted she was leaving me because I lacked ambition. She said that the contacts I'd made and the influence I had on the paper and in the community were wasted—because I refused to take advantage of them.

Maybe she's right. I could always get a job as a P.R. flack

for somebody and make double the dough I was making at the paper. Buy a nicer car, get a nicer place. Go back to pinstripes and drinks after dinner at Maude's Courtyard and Mario's. This business of being a private investigator's just not worth it. I didn't have any idea what I was getting into, don't have any idea what I'm doing, and am probably going to do more damage than good if I don't cut and run while I still can.

I finished off the last inch of flat, warm beer. Somehow, it felt appropriate to be sitting in the middle of the country music capital of the world crying in my beer. Any minute now, I was going to break into a chorus of some George Jones song. Only I don't know the words, and it's hard to sing George Jones when the crying in your beer only extends to two over the whole evening. I just don't like beer well enough to drink enough of it to cry in.

Hell, I can't sing, I can't drink, and I can't detect. Maybe I can sleep.

I got up, limped into the kitchen to turn off the lights— though my leg wasn't really hurting anymore—and to see if there wasn't some orange juice in the fridge. Maybe there was an old movie on television.

The kitchen clock said 12:20. The neighborhood is finally quiet about that hour. Downstairs, Mrs. Hawkins, my land-lady, would have removed her hearing aids, put her four cats out, and be snuggled under her handmade comforter. I felt alone, maybe a little lonely, but I was all right with that. Maybe I'd blow this whole business off and find something else to do with my life.

I leaned across to douse the kitchen light and lock up. Just as the light disappeared, the kitchen door imploded, the heavy brass doorknob bouncing off the wall behind it. A black form came at me out of the darkness, blocking out all light behind it. Something caught me in the chest, threw me backward. I felt myself airborne for a split second. Then I slammed down on the kitchen floor and lay there helpless, random sparkles going off behind my eyelids, and the back of my head pound-ing like a drumbeat.

Then there was weight on me, and I couldn't move my arms, an oppressive, awful heaviness that was crushing my chest, pinning me to the floor, with the world going blacker around me by the second.

In what I was afraid was going to be my last coherent thought, I realized I couldn't breathe anymore.

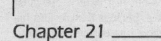

Chapter 21

It felt like the whole damned house had caved in on me. But then, in the darkness of the kitchen broken only by dusty shafts of silver cast by distant streetlights shining through the windows, I felt hot breath on my face.

"You and I are going to talk," a gruff, low voice said. I struggled to recognize the voice and couldn't. But I recognized the peculiar smell that came with the hot breath.

Bubba Hayes.

I'd been in trouble before, had seen times in my life where I wondered if I were going to see another day. Like when I did the undercover story on suburban kids going into the projects to buy crack and nearly got my head blown off in the crossfire of a street corner shootout. But never have I felt as close to the grim reaper as I did that very second, with the three-hundred-pound-plus Reverend Bubba Hayes sitting on my chest.

There was one thing Bubba had to realize: until he got off my chest, it was going to be a somewhat one-sided conversation. "Can't . . ." I managed to whisper, "breathe . . ."

He bent over, the dark vague shape looming over me now, blocking out even the streetlights' glow.

"Neither can Mr. Kennedy. Unless you want to join him, you'd better do exactly what I tell you."

I could feel drowning man's panic washing over me. For a second, I hoped that terror and its ensuing adrenaline rush would give me the strength to toss him off, like the little old lady who lifts the Volkswagen off the mechanic when the jack gives way and traps him underneath. Only I could tell

175

after a few quick muscle twitches that there was no way. He had me pinned. My thoughts were coming slower now, the sparkles again in the edges of my vision. I'd have been better off if the house had fallen on me.

I managed to nod my head yes but just barely. He must have felt me move; a moment later, his legs flexed, and his huge backside came up off my chest just enough for me to suck in one desperate, loud gulp of air. The rush of oxygen into my lungs left me light-headed, and the stretching of my rib cage hurt so acutely I almost cried out.

But it felt wonderful to be breathing again.

"I didn't have anything to do with it," I said. "I didn't kill him."

"Do you know how long he worked for me?" Hayes demanded. There was a whooshing sound in the air, like the sound of a golf club, and then his palm slammed into the side of my face. The slap caught my left cheek and the very tip of my nose. Strange, I thought, it burns more than anything else. I imagined, in one of those ridiculously irrelevant thoughts that invade human brains in times of crisis, that I now knew what it was like to have my head shoved against a hot waffle iron.

"Do you know how good a friend he was to me?" Another whoosh, and this time the slap came on the right side of my face, like somebody closing the waffle iron. Something wet ran down the side of my face; I hoped it was blood and not snot. I'd hate for this s.o.b. to think I was crying.

I lay there, sucking in breath, figuring that his questions were purely rhetorical. I hoped he'd yell the next question a little louder and that Mrs. Hawkins downstairs might hear him even without her hearing aids and call the police.

Both of his hands, which looked in the dark like cast iron skillets coming at me, encased the side of my head and locked it down.

"All right," he hissed, "who did it? Who did Mr. Kennedy?"

"I don't know." I felt his hands clamp even harder onto

my head. He lifted it an inch or two off the wooden floor-boards, then slammed it back down with a loud crack.

An explosion went off, like Lonnie's little homemade goodie blowing a crater in his office table. I wished I had a cupful of the stuff right now; I'd blow us both to hell just to get this guy off me. Blinding pain turned everything red, and I thought, damn, man, there go the closure strips again. I'm gonna need those stitches yet.

"If you didn't kill him, you know who did."

My arms were pinned at my sides, running beneath his huge thighs down the side of my leg. I shifted a shoulder on the floor. If I could get one hand up just a few inches, I might be able to get one hand into his crotch. Then he'd see what it was like to have the room turn red on him.

Only it wouldn't work. The Reverend Bubba Hayes was obviously experienced at using his bulk as a weapon. He had me, and more than anything else, more than the pain and the fear, it made me mad. Who the hell did this guy think he was? If I could only get close enough to bite him.

"You talk to me, boy." He was back in my face again, his breath less rotten now that my nose was swollen shut. "I had to see his wife, his children, tonight. You know what that was like?"

I panted there quietly for a moment. He'd decided to give me room to breathe, but it was still no picnic. I opened my mouth, tried to form words.

"I can't talk like this. You got to let me up."

His bulk came down on me heavy again and my rib cage crunched into my lungs. I tried to hold my breath, to keep him from forcing all the air out of my lungs, but I knew I couldn't hold on long. I felt the panic again, only I was too battered, too weak, to get much strength out of it. Maybe he was going to kill me after all. And it came to me that it was really stupid of him to do that. It didn't make sense. To die senselessly filled me with sadness and regret, and I felt tears coming into my eyes. Had he broken me finally? Is this the way people died? I wondered. Crying and wishing that it didn't have to be this way?

"If I let you up, boy, you're going to spill your guts. And if you try anything stupid, I'm going to break you in half. You understand?"

The breath I was holding spewed out of me in a wet spray. I shook my head as enthusiastically as I could.

Then he was off me.

As soon as I felt my body relieved of his mass, I went completely limp, as weak as a newborn. I hadn't realized I'd been pushing so hard against him, but every muscle must have been locked tight. I was exhausted to the point of nausea.

I heard a scraping across the linoleum, then the creaking of the floor as the man who weighed over a sixth of a ton settled into a ten-dollar kitchen chair. I raised my head, and in the dusty silver shafts breaking through the kitchen window I saw Bubba Hayes at my table, his elbows propped up, his head in his hand.

He sobbed. I stared at him slack jawed for a moment, a three-hundred-pound criminal sitting at my kitchen table crying. Who'd have thought? I rolled over on my side, pushed against the floor, and painfully rotated up onto my haunches. I pulled my knees up into my chest, stretching, trying to figure out how many ribs were broken, feeling alertly for the sharp pain in my chest that might indicate a punctured lung.

Get a grip, I told myself, and brought my arms behind me and pushed myself up into a kneeling position.

The room spun around me. I was apparently overreaching myself once again. I leaned across the floor, grabbed one of the other kitchen chairs, and pulled it toward me. Then I climbed into it, feeling the soft vinyl pad beneath my butt, glad to be up off the hard cold floor.

"So what's next?" I asked, still panting. I felt a sharp cramp in my right side and massaged my ribs with my left hand, trying to work it out. With the other hand, I grabbed a dish towel off the kitchen table and ran it across my face as gently as I could. It came away with an ugly dark smear, but it was a mostly dry smear. I sniffed, feeling for the sensation of wet on my face. Nothing; my nose had clotted.

Bubba raised his head. Even in the darkness, I could see the filmy reflection off his eyeballs like sharp points of light. I was glad the lights were off; if I saw the look on his face, I probably would have been frightened into paralysis.

"I want the man who did this," he said, his voice like a bulldozer in low gear pulling a hill. There was no evangelical flair in his voice, no theatrics, just cold, murderous rage. I was glad I didn't kill Mr. Kennedy for more reasons than just the law.

"Well, you ain't got him yet," I said. "Why did you have Mr. Kennedy following me?"

"Mr. Kennedy was following several people. You were just one of them."

"What were you doing? Playing private eye yourself?"

Bubba dropped his hands to the kitchen table. It shook like I'd dropped a thawed frozen turkey on it.

"I wanted to know what's going on. It's bad for business when people think they can get whacked for owing Bubba money. I'm a moral man. I don't kill people. I give them what they want."

Yeah, right, I thought: the same old tired argument they all use. Call it sin if you want, call it vice. But don't call it victimless. But I wasn't about to say that to Bubba. "So who else was he following?"

Bubba turned away from me. He was heaving and panting now himself, overcome with either emotion or exertion. I neither knew nor cared which.

"I trusted Mr. Kennedy. He was on his own."

"So you don't know who else he'd been trailing?"

"I intend to find out. And when I do . . ."

A silence as threatening and cold as any I'd ever endured lay between us. I felt sorry for whoever killed Mr. Kennedy. If the killer were lucky, the law would get him before Bubba could, and all he'd have to face was the electric chair.

Now he had me thinking. Why would somebody kill Mr. Kennedy?

"There're only two reasons somebody would have killed him," I said.

"And?"

"One, Mr. Kennedy was getting close to figuring out who killed Conrad Fletcher. Two, Mr. Kennedy was getting close to someone who was getting close to finding out who killed Fletcher. And they killed Mr. Kennedy to keep control of the situation."

"You ain't making sense, boy."

"No, think about it." I stood up, energized by the notion that maybe I was closer to figuring this out than I had imagined. One thing was certain: if reason number one was not the motive for killing Mr. Kennedy, then reason number two almost had to revolve around me. There was nobody else out there.

"Except for the police," I said, "I'm the only one who's actively looking for Conrad's murderer. If I'm getting close, then the killer's going to have to play his hand. But he has to play his hand when it suits him. And with Mr. Kennedy in the picture, there was one more thing he'd have to control. With Mr. Kennedy out of the way, it's just me and the killer.

"To paraphrase a disgustingly racist, politically incorrect saying," I ventured after a moment, "Mr. Kennedy was the Ubangi in the fuel supply."

The Reverend Bubba Hayes swiveled in the tiny chrome and vinyl kitchen chair, a squeal cutting the air from where the legs screwed into the base. If the chair didn't give way with him on it, it might last the night. But it'd never be the same again.

"I don't completely understand what you're saying, boy." Then there was silence for a moment, until he spoke again. "But what I *do* understand makes sense."

I closed my eyes, trying to concentrate through the pain and the fatigue.

"Something's wrong here," I said. "And I'm not seeing it. I'm closer than I realize. Don't you see, Bubba? I'm close. The answer's out there, and I'm just not seeing it."

He said something, but by then I wasn't paying attention

anymore. I stood up and rubbed my temples. Damn, it's here somewhere. I know it is.

It's got to be.

Chapter 22

Bubba Hayes's last remark before he left at three A.M. was that if he found out I had anything to do with Mr. Kennedy's death, he was going to make damn sure I was looking out at the world from inside a dog food can.

Talk about raising the stakes. I knew I didn't have anything to do with Mr. Kennedy's death, but now I had to convince Bubba. And while I'm at it, I should work on convincing the Metro Homicide Squad I didn't kill Fletcher. Spellman had announced to the media I was no longer a suspect. But the police, I knew from hard experience, could be less than forthright.

Everybody thinks I killed somebody. Wonder if I can get my old job back.

Not to sound like a Pollyanna, but one bonus did come from Bubba's nocturnal visit: the realization that I wasn't as far off the mark as I thought. That was good. On the other hand, I'd personally seen two dead bodies that were the result of the killer's handiwork, and if he killed once, he'd kill again. Maybe me. That was bad.

Suddenly, I had this sensation that I was dealing with some really serious stuff. I don't know why, but up to now it felt on some level like a game to me. I go up, I go down, I go all around, chasing after something as if it's some kind of 3-D, real-time version of Clue. Colonel Mustard did it with the pipe wrench in the drawing room.

Only this time, if you lose the game, Colonel Mustard does you. And it's for real.

That dose of reality kept me up all night. When Bubba

finally plodded down the metal staircase to Mrs. Hawkins's backyard, thankfully not pulling the side of the house down as he went, I pushed the door to and leaned a chair against it, figuring I'd repair the splintered doorjamb tomorrow. Then I checked all the windows. I settled into bed, but as close as I could get to sleep, it may as well've been in the next county.

Finally, around six, I rolled out of the sack and made a pot of coffee. I looked in the mirror and saw that my nose was still swollen, with a few disgusting flakes of dried blood on my cheek, a little more mixed in with my hair. There'd been a little blood seepage as well from the closure strips on the back of my head. Damn, that thing was never going to heal if people didn't stop slamming me around like a fifty-pound sack of dried dog food.

Dog food, again. Bad joke.

I cranked the shower up full blast and stood under the spray until the hot water ran out. Every muscle in my body, it seemed, ached. I was hurting in places I hadn't hurt since I'd gone out for football my freshman year at prep school. All it took was two workouts; I never came back for the third. My father called me a quitter, until the coach told him I was, at 125 pounds, the smallest kid he'd ever seen go out for varsity football, and he was surprised I made it through two days.

I'd felt like a quitter last night as well, at least until Bubba Hayes showed up and had the unfathomable kindness to beat some sense into me. He'd never know what a favor he'd done, and while somewhere inside there was part of me that wanted to tie him down and jump on his head for an hour or two, I was strangely grateful to him.

Put back together as well as I could be, I finished the coffee and headed to the hospital. I had no idea if Jane Collingswood was still on duty or not. I knew residents pulled some god-awful shifts, so I figured she might be there. I was going to hunt her down, and Zitin, too. It was time to get some answers.

There was the usual midday construction on the freeway; I could see as I crossed the Shelby Street Bridge that traffic was backed up in both directions all the way to the horizon. I decided to skip that experience and threaded my way through the downtown traffic, up past the Union Rescue Mission, just over from the downtown bus terminal, and maneuvered my way onto Broadway. There was construction there as well, with traffic slowed to walking speed. The Ford began overheating, the indicator moving up fast toward the "oh, hell" range. I loosened my tie, having already thrown my jacket into the seat next to me. I rolled my shirtsleeves up past my elbow. Life went on like that for nearly forty minutes before I found a parking space six blocks from the hospital.

Lack of sleep, physical abuse, urban stress—by the time I walked into the air-conditioned lobby of the medical center, I was a dripping mess. By now, I pretty well knew my way around, so I walked past the lobby, down a hall, turned left onto a corridor that looked as long as a football stadium, and walked about twenty minutes. At the end of the hall, two closed beige metal doors supported a sign that said EMERGENCY ROOM—AUTHORIZED PERSONNEL ONLY and below that ALL OTHERS USE OUTSIDE ENTRANCE.

I walked out a glass door and into the heat. A curved drive wide enough for ambulances three abreast ran from the street, under a concrete canopy, and back out onto the street. The drive was empty save for one quiet orange and white van that had emblazoned on the side in blue paint: PARAMEDIC EXTRICATION UNIT.

I didn't even want to speculate on that one. I walked past the van onto the breezeway that led up to a series of glass doors, the same ones I'd gone through what seemed so many nights before, back when life was simpler and nobody was threatening to kill me, jail me, fill-in-the-blank me.

The emergency room was its usual buzz. The E.R. people seemed frenetic, even when there was only a couple of patients waiting around with skateboard injuries. Stress junkies, they've got to be. Otherwise, they'd never last.

The calm, suited woman in the middle of this maelstrom sat behind a high circular desk with a row of clipboards set out in front of her. I walked up to the counter and leaned over to look at her.

"You'll have to fill out these forms, sir," she said before I had a chance to open my mouth.

"Wait," I said.

"We can't do anything for you, sir, until you fill out these forms."

"I—"

"Sir, you must fill out these forms before we can help you." She reached over, grabbed a clipboard with a Bic pen and a stack of papers already loaded, and thrust it at me. "Please cooperate."

I must have looked desperately in need of medical care. I was sure having trouble getting through to this woman on any other level.

"Ma'am," I said, pulling out my license, flipping my badge at her, then shutting the case before she had a chance to examine it. "Harry Denton. I'm a detective, and I'm looking for Dr. Jane Collingswood. She went on E.R. rotation last night. If she's still here, I'd like to see her."

She appraised me for a moment, but she didn't ask to see the license again. "Have a seat over there, Detective, and I'll see if I can locate her."

I took a seat in the waiting area, my gut doing a bump and grind at the thought that I'd once again borderline impersonated a police officer. If these people assumed I was a cop, that was their problem. Spellman, however, probably wouldn't see it that way.

For about ten minutes, I thumbed through a two-year-old copy of *Reader's Digest*. Then the woman behind the counter stood up.

"Things have gotten a little quiet down here today, Detective," she said. "Dr. Collingswood's on a break, in the third floor doctor's lounge."

I stood up and flipped the magazine onto the table. "Thanks," I said, turning my back on her before she got a better look at me than she already had.

Back inside the main building, I trekked to the lobby and

up to the information desk. The fat lady behind the desk had wires coming out of her everywhere: headphones, telephone mike, Walkman.

"Third floor doctor's lounge," I said. "This way?" I pointed down the hall.

"Sorry, sir. Doctor's lounge is restricted."

"I know that," I said irritably, "I'm Dr. Evans, Neurosurgery. I just got confused out here. Now which way is it?"

"Oh, yes, Dr. Evans. Follow the red line around to the second bank of elevators. Go up to three, take a right."

I turned around and walked away from her. Doctor's aren't known for passing out polite thank-yous to just anybody. Upstairs, I stepped out of the elevators and took a right, down past the nurse's station, a row of offices, what may have been a classroom, and stopped in front of a door with a plate on it that read DOCTOR'S LOUNGE—AUTHORIZED PERSONNEL ONLY.

I'd had enough of that authorized personnel crap. I took out my license and looked at it. Yep, I'm authorized.

I pushed open the door and stepped in. The room was dark, cool, with a color television, floor model, flickering silently away in the corner. It was a comfortable room: subdued, pastel-blue carpet, heavily padded and equally heavily used sofas lining the walls, with the center of the large room occupied by wooden tables and cafeteria chairs. There were two sleeping bodies on the sofas, backs to the rest of the room, the wrinkled white of lab coats rising slowly up and down in breathing rhythm.

Jane Collingswood sat at a table, back to me, sipping something out of a Styrofoam cup and flipping through a magazine. She hadn't moved when I walked in. I padded slowly up behind her and stopped.

"What, you couldn't sleep?" I asked, my voice low.

She twisted around in the chair. It was comforting to see that even someone as attractive as Jane Collingswood could occasionally look as if she'd been on a bender. Her skin was pale in the unflattering light, her face drawn, her eyes sunken and bloodshot. I'd heard they put doctors through hell just to see if they can take it. I guess it's true. No wonder so many of them are jerks; like being a freaking Marine or something.

"What are you doing here?" she asked. It would have been a demand if she'd had the energy.

"Looking for you," I said, walking around the table and taking a seat across from her. She frowned, the motion of her jaw pulling lines on her skin. Her eyes darkened, and she shook her head slightly.

"Mr. . . . . what was your name again?"

"Harry."

"Well, Mr. Harry, I'm thirty-three hours into a seventy-two hour pull. I'm trying to get a little time alone because tonight's Friday night, and sometime around ten thirty this evening we expect to see some casualties."

"I don't know how you docs do this stuff," I said. "I didn't sleep last night, and I feel like somebody stuffed me in a microwave and punched all the buttons at once."

She almost smiled, but the weight of her lips was too heavy a burden to manage. "Right now, Mr. Harry, I don't know how we manage either. But I certainly don't have time to fool with you. Now, if you'll excuse me."

I thought for a second. Even if she killed Fletcher, and I was beginning to think she had just enough inner strength to do it, I sympathized with her. But I needed to push.

"Tell me about you and Conrad Fletcher."

The magazine fell from her hands, slid down her lap, and onto the floor. "What makes you think there's anything to tell?"

"C'mon, Jane. I like you. You're bright, determined, dedicated. And not to sound too much like a sexist, you're damnably attractive. Trust me, I know these things."

This time, she did smile. "You can flatter me all you like. There's nothing to tell."

"I know he was harassing you. I know he wanted to sleep with you. And I know he was threatening your position here at the hospital."

She blanched. "How did you—"

"And I know that Albert Zitin's in love with you. And I

know he wanted to protect you from Fletcher. What I don't know is how much he protected you. Or, for that matter, did you need protecting at all? Frankly, you look like you can pretty well take care of yourself."

"I can't believe you'd think—"

"Okay, so I don't know how medical school works, and I don't know how doctors become doctors, at least not every little step of the way. But I do know that supervisors in residencies have a lot of stroke, and a recommendation from a doctor, who's a respected member of the staff as well as chief of something or other, that you get kicked out of a program will—"

"Get you kicked out of the program." She finished the sentence for me, then sighed exhaustedly. She folded her arms on the table in front of her and nestled her head in the crooks of her arms. Her black hair splayed out over the table, long and straight. I resisted the urge to pat her on the head.

"And sooner or later, if they haven't already, the Metro detectives will learn what's been going on. And when they do, they'll ask questions you won't have any option about answering."

She leaned back in the chair. She seemed, more than anything else, weary, beyond feeling, beyond pain, even, perhaps, beyond anguish.

"And they will find out, won't they?" she whispered, so low I could barely hear her.

"Yes."

"This is one of the largest university hospital medical center complexes in this part of the country, and the way gossip travels, you'd think it was a neighborhood bridge group."

"Funny how that works, isn't it?"

"Not so funny. Not when you think about it," she sighed. She looked off toward the other two sleeping doctors. "I used to love being a doctor until I came down here and met him. Now, I think he may have ruined it all for me."

"Let me get you some more coffee," I offered.

She smiled at me, pushed her cup forward on the table. "Thanks. Black, one sugar."

I fixed myself a cup as well and brought them back to the table. We both needed help staying awake.

"I went to medical school down in Memphis, at UT. I wanted to be a chest cutter—thoracic surgeon, you know. The residency here was my perfect chance.

"Then I met Fletcher. Good old Dr. Fletcher, who decided that his incredibly gifted hands could best be used pawing anything that would stand still for him. When I met him he was very nice to me. Supportive, attentive, friendly. Not at all like he usually was with students. Surgery's like anything else, you know. It's not perfect. Mistakes happen, but you correct the mistakes and learn from them."

She paused and sipped the coffee. "I'm rambling, I know. I'm too tired to think straight."

"It's okay. Do the best you can," I said.

"Conrad Fletcher asked me out on a date about six weeks after we met. At the time, I didn't even know he was married. I went to dinner with him, but that's all. I've spent my whole adult life preparing to be a doctor. I'm human; I have the same needs as everyone else. What I don't have is time for relationships. Someday maybe, but not now."

"Yeah, I can imagine."

"So when it became clear that Fletch the Lech wanted more, I put a stop to it quickly. There was no choice; it had to be that way."

"What happened after that?"

"As you can guess, the situation changed. Suddenly, the minor mistakes were huge screwups. He got cold, angry, resentful that I'd rejected him. Every day, it seemed, he'd find some new reason to criticize me."

Jane Collingswood, even in her fatigue and discomfort at relating what could not have been a pleasant story, sat with an air of propriety and dignity. It made me like her even more, which made me even more suspicious. Just the cynic in me, I guess.

"Eventually, we had a big blowup right in front of a group of fourth-year students. He called me incompetent, threatened to bust me out of the program. Wanted to know if I'd taken my medical training at Auschwitz.''

"He said that to you?''

"In front of patients, nurses, and students. And yelled it, not said it. That's when Albert got into it. Albert's very sweet, very protective of me. He said no one had to take that kind of abuse and he wasn't going to watch Fletcher hand it out. He said he'd file a complaint with the dean of the medical school, go all the way to the university president if he had to.''

"What did Fletcher say?''

"He said that if Albert didn't watch himself, he'd wind up a salesman for a pharmaceutical firm just like me.''

I rubbed the sides of my forehead with my hands. Jeez, Conrad had a real style with people. "When was this?''

She paused, her lips tightening almost unconsciously. When I sensed her hesitation, I looked up. Her tired eyes were strained, even darker than before. "The day before he was killed.''

"So the day before Conrad was killed, you and Albert Zitin had a public blowup with him. And in this blowup, everybody wound up threatening everybody. I'm surprised the police haven't already questioned you.''

She picked up her coffee cup and drained the last inch. "They have, Mr. Harry,'' she said, placing the cup in front of her. "They have. Only no one really knows why it all happened. You're the first one I've told.''

I looked at her closely. "Are you in love with Albert Zitin?''

She smiled, looked down almost shyly. "Albert's very sweet, and he cares deeply for me. In my own way, I care very much for him. But am I in love with him?'' She stood up, pushing the chair behind her. "I don't know.''

The problem with this whole mess was that every time I felt I was getting closer to Conrad Fletcher's murderer, I ran into somebody else who got taken off the list. Pretty soon, I was going to get right next to a murderer who didn't exist. And like dividing by zero, that's impossible.

I drove out 21st to Hillsboro Village, then parked in front of the shop that sells relics from the Sixties, with tie-dyed clothing draped throughout the window. I crossed over to the Pancake Pantry.

The PP was another restaurant that had been around forever, while fancier places came and went weekly. I got a booth down near the kitchen, ordered a woodchopper's breakfast, more coffee, and settled back with the newspaper.

The news of Mr. Kennedy's death was page one on the local section, with a picture of the death car on Seventh Avenue and a reproduction of his Atlanta Falcons team picture off to the side. He had a wife and two boys. Seemed like a perfectly normal middle-class husband and father. Except that he worked for a guy who was the illegal gambling kingpin of the whole west side of town.

On the jump page, thankfully near the bottom, was a notation that I'd been questioned, but the young reporter fortunately didn't do his homework well enough to catch the connection between Bubba, me, and Conrad Fletcher's death. This younger generation! I don't know what to think about them.

I ate like a condemned man, if that's not too grim a simile under the circumstances. I deliberately tried not to think about the murder, hoping that like an artist looking for inspiration, something would burble up out of my subconscious.

Only it didn't work that way. I sat there through a pot of coffee and a stack of pancakes that would have intimidated a St. Bernard and came up with nothing. I paid my check and walked out of the restaurant in a fog. It was close to mid-afternoon now, hot as blazes, post-lunch traffic nearing gridlock. I decided to get back to work and, as long as I was in this part of town, drive out and check on Rachel. I hadn't seen her since the funeral.

The Ford was hard to start in the heat, probably some kind of vapor lock or something, and I had to sit there grinding the motor for about a minute before it finally caught. I heard a small pop in the back and looked in my rearview mirror just in time to see a puff of blue-black smoke spurting out behind me. That's all I need, to have this piece of junk die on me. I wished I still had my good car, only by now Lonnie would have repossessed it.

The stick shift made a grinding noise and shook under my hand as the gears meshed and I pulled out into traffic. It was stop and go, start and stall, all the way out past I-440 where the traffic thinned out enough to be manageable. I turned onto Golf Club Lane and followed the shaded tree-lined street up to Rachel's house. The long driveway was empty. I drove up anyway and pulled in behind the house. Conrad's Jaguar was in the garage, but there was no sign of Rachel's car.

I walked around to the back door. There was no sign of movement inside. I figured if I tried the door, I'd set off an alarm. I started to get back in the car and roll off, but I suddenly noticed how quiet the place was, how well-ordered.

What I wondered more than anything else was how so much misery could exist in a place this beautiful. I leaned against the hood of the car and craned my neck upward. The house and the grounds were like a sanctuary. But they were also filled with tension and even violence.

I stood there for a couple of minutes, half thinking/half fretting over everything. Then I heard the sound of an approaching car. I walked around the corner of the house just in time to see Rachel turn into the driveway.

She pulled in just to the left of the Ford, behind the garaged Jag, and stepped out. Her blond hair was pulled back, a wet sweatband holding it off her forehead. Her skin was still flushed.

"Must have been some run," I said as she got out.

She came around the back of the car, still panting. "There's a track a couple of miles away. Some days I jog. Others I go down there and run the clock. How are you, Harry?" she said, throwing her arms around my neck and pecking me on the cheek.

"Fine, Rachel, how are you?"

"Hot. I haven't had much chance to talk to you lately."

"You were a little preoccupied at the funeral home," I said, as she dropped her arms from my neck and led me over to the back door. She pulled a ring of keys from her fanny pack. A Chicago Ace lock in a brass plate controlled the burglar alarm; she pulled out the tubular key, worked it into the cylinder, and twisted it to the right. A tiny red light set in the plate went dark. Then she unlocked the deadbolt, stuck another key in the doorknob cylinder, and opened the door.

A blast of cold air greeted us as we walked into her kitchen. "Oh, that feels good," she said, pulling the pack off and tossing it onto the kitchen table. "I could use something cold to drink. How about you?"

"Great," I said, standing uncomfortably in the center of the kitchen. It was strange being alone with her.

"What can I get you? Gatorade?"

Truth was, I had a weakness for the stuff. "You got enough?"

"Of course. I go through several gallons a week."

She poured the green liquid into two tall glasses filled with ice. My throat went numb as I poured it down like a shipwreck survivor.

"Rachel, how're you doing?" I asked. There was a pair of tall stools next to the kitchen island. I pulled one up and sat on it.

She finished off her glass and poured another.

"Harry," she said firmly, "I'm doing great. The last few days have been rough. And I'll have some more rough ones. But I'm determined to get on with my life."

"Good," I said, meaning it. "Listen, I don't mean to be too personal, but how did Connie leave . . . well, leave things? How're you fixed up?"

"You mean can I make the house payment?"

"Yeah."

"For the time being, I'm okay. Eventually, I'll have to go back to work. But for now, I'm just going to take some time off. Recover, regroup." She took another long swallow. "Get back into shape," she added.

"You look like you're in great shape," I said, wishing I hadn't said it as the words tumbled out of my mouth.

"Aren't you sweet, Harry. I appreciate that, I really do."

We looked into each other's face for a moment, one of those awkward moments where both people are thinking to themselves: okay, what do we do next?

"I think I'd like to stay in touch with you when all this is over," I said.

"I'd like that," she said slowly. "What do you mean, when all this is over?"

I settled back in the chair. "That's one of the things I wanted to talk to you about. I wanted to see how you were and all, but I also wanted you to know that I'm certain I'm getting close to finding out who killed Connie. Just a gut feeling."

Her eyes went kind of dark for a second. "Harry, I don't want you to do this. I don't want to see you get hurt. You . . . well, you mean too much to me right now."

"We've been through this, Rach. I'm going to watch myself."

"Yeah," she said, "you've done a splendid job so far. I'm not even going to ask who punched you in the schnoz."

I instinctively reached up and cupped my hand over my nose. "You can still tell, huh?"

"I'm a nurse," she said. "I can identify a swollen nose.

Harry, I don't know what you're doing, and I'm not sure I want to know. But I want you to stop."

"I can't."

"I won't pay you any more after the money runs out. I can't. I haven't got it, and if I did, I wouldn't spend it on that."

"I don't care about the money." *Jesus, who's putting these words in my mouth?* "This is more important than that."

"Is it more important than your health? More important than us?"

"Us?" I asked. "There's an us?"

She walked around the counter, right up to me as I sat there on the stool, and put a hand on my knees. "Of course, there's an us. You know that, don't you?"

She ran her hands up my legs to my waist, then put her arms around me. She leaned over, sweat still glistening on her forehead, and moved her face in close.

She went out of focus as her lips melted onto mine. She was hot, soft, wet all over. It had been a long time since I'd been kissed like that. It wasn't what I came here for; at least I didn't think it was what I came here for. But now that it was happening, I sure as hell wasn't going to fight it.

What little semblance of a thought pattern I could muster was fading fast. I wrapped my arms around her and opened my legs on the stool, pulling her as close to me as possible, the inside of my thighs rubbing the outside of her legs. She opened her mouth, pulling mine along with hers, and we were inside each other now, hotter, wetter. I stifled a moan. I don't know why.

"It's burning up in here today," she sighed, pulling away from me a few inches.

"Yeah, summer's not over yet."

She unwrapped her arms and took two steps away from me. "I need a shower," she quipped. "Want to join me?"

The room was dark when I woke up, the last pale shafts of sunlight straining to hold on against the oncoming night.

At first, I couldn't remember where I was. But when I felt Rachel next to me, it all came back.

I rolled over in the huge bed. She was on her side, facing away from me. I settled back into the pillow, drifting, languorous, sleepy. The sheets were tangled around us, her back bare, her blond hair splayed out on the pillow. Her torso rose and fell slightly with each deep sleep breath.

Okay, okay, so I woke up feeling guilty. I'm not going to lie about this; we went at it for hours, like two passionate young college kids having their first real adult affair. Which is what we once were. I haven't had an afternoon like that in years, and I savored every moment of it.

Only problem was it was wrong, and I knew it. It was too soon for her, too soon for me. And there was something about doing it right in Conrad's bed when his corpse hadn't yet settled into the grave that made the hair on the back of my head stand up.

Having gone running, Rachel was a workout ahead of me for the day. I could tell from the stillness of her body and the deepness of her breath that she was nowhere near waking up. I eased out of bed and stood looking down at her. I'd loved this woman once. Could I love her again? A lot of time had gone by, a lot of living. I'd loved her as a young man. Did I have it in me to love her as a man standing on the precipice of middle age?

She was still beautiful, full of life and energy and passion. When we were first lovers, in college, she'd taught me things I never knew. I'd never been with anyone like her. All she had to do was walk into a room and it would light up. Funny, I think about those days and all I can come up with to describe them are clichés. But that's the way it was then: a wonderful, innocent time that lives in my memory now like my mother's oatmeal and brown sugar on snowy days, or my father's standing over the turkey with carving knife in hand on Thanksgiving Day.

What I needed was another glass of Gatorade. All this passion had left me with a raging thirst.

I slipped into my underwear and trousers as quietly as

possible. I'd spent the afternoon relearning Rachel's body, but for some reason I wasn't comfortable strolling around naked in her house. I silently left the bedroom, leaving the door cracked open, and padded barefoot down the hardwood floors of the hall and down the steps to the first floor.

In the kitchen, I rinsed out the glass I had used earlier and refilled it. I stood at the kitchen door, staring out over the deepening shadows that filled the backyard. It was so quiet, so idyllic. I wondered for a second if I'd wind up living here someday.

I took my glass and walked into the living room. The huge window that overlooked the wide expanse of front lawn down to Golf Club Lane could have been a Frederick Church painting, with the glowing blues and reds of a luminist sunset. I stood there watching for a long time in the silence, feeling more peaceful than I'd felt in a long time.

Then it came back to me: my first impressions of this room. For that matter, of this house. This was a house owned by a surgeon, a professor, an accomplished, privileged, educated man.

And yet, there was no sign of him anywhere.

Out of curiosity more than anything else, I began walking from room to room, being careful not to make any noise. I didn't want to awaken Rachel.

There were no pictures of Connie in the living room, nor any in the den. No framed diplomas, certificates, testimonials, the trinkets that men and women proud of their achievements show off for everybody else. Hell, three years ago I got a nomination for an award from the Middle Tennessee Press Association, a less than prestigious group if ever there was one. But that nomination letter—and I didn't even win the award—sat framed above my desk until the day they canned me and threw me out the door.

But nothing here. I went from room to room, thinking that somewhere in this house, Conrad must have had a study or an office. Maybe it was upstairs. Maybe I should ask Rachel, although I didn't want to come off as nosy.

I walked back into the kitchen, poured myself another

glass, and sat down at the kitchen table. Rachel's fanny pack was still on the table where she'd tossed it earlier. The zipper was halfway open, some of the contents hanging out. There was a bandanna, a ring of keys, a radio with wires leading to headphones, and, of all things, a beeper.

A beeper, I thought, *what in heaven's name would Rachel be doing with a beeper?*

I looked closer. The overheads were off in the kitchen. The outside light was fading fast. It was difficult to see. I didn't want to go messing around with her stuff, but there it was, the base of it visible just outside the bag: a small black plastic box a little smaller than a cigarette pack, with a belt clip on the flat side.

"Mmm, how about that?" I said out loud.

"How about what?" a voice said behind me.

I jumped about a foot off the chair and spun around. "Don't do that!" I yelped.

Rachel smiled as she walked into the kitchen. She wore only a man's white dress shirt, presumably one belonging to her dead husband. She walked past me, over to the sink, and grabbed a fresh glass out of the overhead cabinet. The tail of the shirt pulled up as she reached above her; she wasn't wearing anything underneath. Despite the exhausting afternoon we'd spent, I found myself wanting her all over again.

"Been up long?" She opened the refrigerator door, light spilling over her.

"Maybe twenty minutes," I said. "I tried not to wake you."

She pulled a pitcher of orange juice out. "That's sweet. I woke up a few minutes ago, and you weren't next to me. I was afraid you'd left without saying goodbye."

"I wouldn't do that." I stood up and walked around the kitchen island. She poured a glass of juice, and while she drank it, I ran my arms around her waist and nuzzled into the back of her neck.

"You feel great," I purred.

"So do you," she said, but her voice was distracted. "What were you doing down here?"

I pulled my face out of her hair. "Nothing. Just hanging around. That okay?"

She set the glass down and turned to face me, my arms still around her, her bare legs rubbing against me.

"Harry," she said, "it's going to take me awhile to get used to this. I've been through a lot. I need to know you're not going to hurt me. To tell you the honest truth, I've had enough of that."

"I know. And I agree with you, things are moving a little too fast. But we've got time, Rachel."

She came back into my arms, pressed her face into my bare chest. I could feel her breath on me, hot, short gulps of air as if she were in a panic. I brought my right hand up and ran it through her hair, rubbing her softly, feeling her next to me.

"All the time in the world," I whispered.

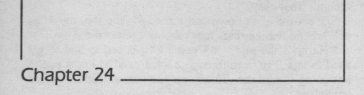
I pulled out of Rachel's driveway at 9:20 the next morning, wondering how I was going to get through the next sixty hours without seeing her. That was part of the deal: to give each other time and space, we weren't going to meet again until dinner Sunday night. She wanted it that way, not me. She was the one who needed time to recover. I understood and went along without question.

Neither of us mentioned again my searching for Conrad's killer. I was in a fog as I pulled out of her neighborhood onto Hillsboro Road, drove toward town a couple of blocks, then got on the entrance ramp for I-440.

I wasn't even sure where I was going. Back to my apartment first, I supposed, for a shower and a change of clothes. Then I had to figure out what was next. Albert Zitin, maybe. If I could track him down, check out his story against Jane Collingswood's, then maybe I'd have some idea if my suspicions were on target.

Mrs. Hawkins was in her front yard weeding a flower bed when I coasted into the driveway. She was a sweet old lady, a tad on the dumpy side, with those rhinestone teardrop glasses that were popular thirty-five or forty years ago. She reminded me in a way of my grandmother, except that my grandmother had exceptional hearing until she died. Mrs. Hawkins, even with her hearing aids, was nearly as deaf as a box of rocks.

After parking the car, I walked to the front yard just to be polite. "Hello, Mrs. Hawkins," I yelled about five feet away from her.

She looked up from her weeding. She was wearing a faded pair of stretch denims, a checked workshirt, and an old pair of work gloves.

"Good morning, Harry," she said, her voice high and loud. "I didn't hear you leave this morning."

"You wouldn't hear me leave if I'd shot my way out of the house," I said in a normal voice.

"What was that?"

"I said I left *really* early this morning," I yelled.

"Hot case, I suppose. It's so exciting having a private detective as a tenant."

"I'm flattered, Mrs. Hawkins. Listen, I've got to get back to my office. I just came by to grab a quick shower."

"Fine, Harry. By the way, do you think you could see to the lawn this weekend?"

"Just freaking great," I muttered under my breath, then raising my voice back to noise pollution levels: "Sure, Mrs. Hawkins. I'll take care of it this weekend."

"Thank you. You're such a *nice* boy."

I laughed to myself. If Mrs. Hawkins knew how I spent last evening, she'd probably evict me.

It took one last call posing as Dr. Evans of Neurosurgery for me to learn that Albert Zitin lived a block or two off West End. He rented one side of a duplex near St. Thomas Hospital. He was off rotation until ten o'clock tonight. I figured he'd be at home mustering his reserves.

The brick house sat on a corner of a four-way stop intersection. The neighborhood was quiet, middle-class, a mix of rental property and owner occupied. A pair of fir trees maybe twenty feet high and badly in need of a trim grew on either side of the concrete front porch, nearly blocking the front door from view. I parked the Ford in front and killed the ignition. The engine chugged for a few seconds, then backfired and let loose a puff of smoke before finally sighing itself into silence.

I shook my head, both embarrassed and disgusted. I walked up the long stretch of concrete to the front door.

There was a picture window behind the overgrown shrubbery with no curtains. I peeked through a branch and saw Albert Zitin lying on the couch in a pair of jeans, no shirt, no shoes. A book was propped on his chest, but it was lying facedown where it had settled when he dropped off to sleep.

I folded a branch of the fir out of the way and rapped on the glass storm door. There was no sound for perhaps thirty seconds, so I made a fist, knuckles out, and pounded on the glass a little harder. The echo reverberated in the space between the storm door and the front door.

This time, I heard a shuffling and the thud of a book falling on the floor. A sleepy voice yelled, "Hold on a minute." There was a fumbling with the lock, then a sleep-logged face surrounded by a mop of thinning, curly hair appeared at the door.

"Sorry to wake you up," I said.

"Oh, hell. It's you."

I smiled at him, trying friendly first to see how it worked.

"Jane said you'd probably find me."

"Then you've been expecting me. Mind if I come in?"

"Yes, I mind. I mind very much. But I'm afraid if I don't let you, I'm never going to be rid of you."

"Yeah," I said, drawing it out a little, "that's probably right."

He fumbled with the latch on the door, then pushed it open.

Albert Zitin's house was more my style; under-socialized bachelors who live alone for extended periods share certain similarities. Plainness of surroundings, for example. Albert had nothing on his walls, no rugs on the scuffed hardwood floors. His couch was an expensive one, but it clearly had been bought to sit by itself in a living room as the sole piece of furniture.

"At least let me make a cup of coffee first. You want one?"

"Sure, if you got it."

He led the way to the kitchen, whose cabinets doubtless held an unmatched set of dishes missing odd and random pieces. His refrigerator, I guessed, would have a scattered collection of condiment jars and a carton of milk a week past the expiration date.

"I think this is still drinkable," he speculated, opening the refrigerator door and sniffing cautiously at the lid of a milk carton. "At least for coffee."

Can I call 'em or what?

Albert boiled water and pulled two mismatched mugs from a cabinet above the stove. He spooned instant coffee into each, then poured in boiling water and handed me a cup. The instant coffee clumped up like chunks of brown mud floating in the water. I took the carton when he handed it to me and poured in a dollop of milk, which immediately clotted into rancid-looking lumps.

I stirred hard, hoping to make something drinkable out of it. Finally, the liquid inside resembled coffee, except for the truly sour lumps of milk that refused to dissolve no matter what. Think of it as yogurt, I told myself.

"Sugar?"

I took the lid off the sugar bowl; inside, clumps of brown mixed in with the white, the result of spooning sugar out with a wet coffee spoon. Yeah, Albert and I could have been roommates.

He sipped the coffee as if it were actually something fit for human consumption. I lifted the cup to my lips and took a quick swallow, surprised that it wasn't any worse than I feared.

"So what do you want?" he asked, heading back into the living room. "Here, have a seat."

I sat on the far end of the couch and set my coffee cup on an upturned fruit crate that served as an end table. "Just wanted to talk to you."

"Jane says you think I killed Fletcher, and that she was in on it."

"I don't know if that's what I think or not. It could be that way. On the other hand, there were a lot of people who wanted to see Conrad Fletcher dead."

"You got that right, He was one slimy son of a bitch."

"And I thought doctors never spoke ill of each other."

"That's one rule I'll break in his case," Zitin said, pulling his legs up on the couch under him. He sat cross-legged, the beginnings of a paunch settling over his belt. He was pale, pasty, not terribly attractive to women, I would think. But he was obviously intelligent and dedicated, as well as determined.

"Tell me how you came to meet him. How'd you wind up here?"

"Same as everybody else, I guess. I'm from up north, took my medical training at Albert Einstein. Came here to do a surgical residency under Fletcher. He's one of the best, you know. Was one of the best, I mean. I'd heard he was a tough guy, real hard to get along with."

Zitin leaned over behind him, picked up the coffee cup. "That's not news to you, though, is it? I just figured if you can survive med school, you can survive anything."

"I always heard that was true."

"Usually it is. But not in surgery. Surgeons are weird. They're gearheads, really. Highly specialized, technically oriented, with a surprisingly limited knowledge of general medicine and no insight into what it means to be human. They're not very pleasant to be around."

"And you want to be one."

He thought for a moment. "Yeah, I do. With all the drawbacks, there's nothing like it. You cut into a human body, use your skill and your knowledge, and sometimes your balls, to make a human body determined to malfunction work properly again. My father was a surgeon. He was a lousy father, probably a lousy person. But he was a great surgeon, a real miracle worker. I've wanted it ever since I was a child."

"Means a lot to you, doesn't it?"

"Everything, almost."

"What was it like for you when Conrad Fletcher threatened to take it all away?"

Albert Zitin reddened just a bit, the color rising quickly and then fading just as fast. "What are you asking me, Mr. Denton? Did I kill him, or did I want to kill him?"

"Maybe both."

He looked down at his coffee cup, stirred the sludge with a bent spoon. "I'm in business to put people back together, not take them apart. I didn't kill Fletcher. Then again, I might have one of these days, if someone hadn't beaten me to it."

"Where were you the night he was killed?"

"Right where you found me this afternoon. I'd come in off a seventy-two hour shift at six P.M. that evening. I ate dinner, went through some correspondence, and started watching a movie on television. Which I promptly fell asleep right in the middle of."

"Were you alone?"

"Absolutely. And unfortunately."

"No phone calls? Visitors?"

"Nothing. There wasn't even anything on the answering machine. I woke up in bed about four A.M. with the television still going and turned it off. It was midmorning before I woke up again."

I stared at him, figuring that he must know how weak an alibi that was. "What did the police say when you told them this?"

"They gave me the same look you just did. Then they went next door and talked to the couple who rent the other side of the duplex. They confirmed that my car was parked in the driveway exactly when I said I was home."

"But they didn't see you."

"I don't make much noise. Neither do they. We've met, pass pleasantries coming and going. That's all."

"What about Jane?"

"What about her?" he said, just a trace of defensiveness in his voice.

"Tell me how you feel about her."

He laughed. "What are you, a therapist?"

"Hey, confession's good for the soul."

"It may be good for the soul, but it's hell on your options."

"If what you say is true, that you and Jane didn't have

anything to do with Fletcher's murder, then what have you got to lose?''

He leaned back wearily in the chair. So far, what I'd learned most about doctors in training is that they're always exhausted. Zitin seemed to be thinking, perhaps choosing his words, maybe trying to figure out how he really felt.

''Jane Collingswood is an unusual woman,'' he said. ''I know that no other woman's ever had the effect on me that she has. Don't get me wrong, Mr. Denton. I'm no virgin. On the other hand, my priorities have always been elsewhere. I always figured that sooner or later, I'd find somebody, but after the internship and residency were over.''

''Then you met her.''

''Yeah, then I met her. I can't keep my mind on anything anymore. All I think about is her. I think this is what teenage boys feel when they get a first big crush on somebody. Only back when I was supposed to be taking care of all that, I was buried in a biology book.''

''Hormones have a way of catching up with us all,'' I said.

''This is more than hormones. One of the few benefits of age is that you gain perspective on life, even if your experience in life's a little limited. I'm very much in love with Jane Collingswood, and I haven't the slightest idea why I'm telling you that. Maybe it's because I know that nothing will ever come of it.''

''Don't be too sure. Fortunately, women gain perspective as well. Part of that perspective is realizing that the true value of something often exceeds surface appearances.''

''Thanks a bunch, pal. What you mean is that I'm still worthwhile even if I'm no Mel Gibson.''

''So what's wrong with that? I ain't exactly going to win *People* magazine's Sexiest Man of the Year award myself.''

''Well, all I know is she hasn't given me a hell of a lot of encouragement.''

I stood up. My guts were starting to tell me that I was wasting my time with him. ''Don't give up, fella. People sometimes wait a long time to get what they want. Only makes it better when they do get it.''

"That's what they told us in pre-med," he said. "Yeah, I'll wait for Jane. But I won't kill for her. And I didn't."

I started toward the front door. "Yeah, Albert, I know you didn't."

Damn.

Chapter 25

I'd be less than honest if I didn't say that I truly wanted Albert to be the murderer. That would have made matters so much easier. I just couldn't accept that Jane Collingswood was a killer; pretty girls don't go around committing such nasty acts.

Right, and Tricky Dick was basically a good guy who got some bad advice.

I didn't want to think LeAnn Gwynn had done it; I was too sorry for her. James Hughes couldn't have done it, either; his father and my father were best friends.

As if that meant anything.

And Bubba Hayes was out, unless he killed Mr. Kennedy to throw me and everybody else off the track. Hey, now there's a novel theory. Come to think of it, Bubba struck me as a guy who could do something sleazy like that.

Only he hadn't, and I knew it. Five suspects: five people who couldn't possibly have killed Conrad Fletcher. Only thing was, he was still dead. If everybody was innocent, then how'd he get dead? Maybe I did it in my sleep. Yeah, that's it. They sneaked some drug into me in the emergency room that made me go flappers, drove me to kill on sight anyone who'd just had sex with a nurse.

Talk about desperate. I was so deep in reverie that I didn't even swear or lay on my horn when the snooty blue-haired Belle Meade society matron in a maroon Cadillac Fleetwood pulled out in front of me onto West End and nearly drove me up on the sidewalk. I slammed on the brakes, scraped my tires against the curb for half a block, then went on without even giving the old bitch the Universal Sign Language Gesture of Disdain.

Maybe there was somebody I hadn't found yet—some person in the hospital who had some yet undiscovered grudge, some private hatred, some unknown motivation for icing Conrad. Or maybe I was letting my instincts cloud my judgment. Most of what I was relying on was *feeling*, but feeling that in each case was backed up by just enough hard fact to be solid.

Back at the office, the answering machine was as empty of messages as I was of answers. I was certainly going to rejoice when the new Yellow Pages appeared; at least my small display ad might result in an occasional call. I wasn't sure which would ruin me first, the poverty or the loneliness.

I leaned back in the chair, loosened my tie, and kicked my feet up on the desk. There wasn't much to do besides think. Down the hall, Ray, Slim, and company were already tuning up guitars for the Friday afternoon songfest. I could hear the metallic spewing of beer can pop tops as they were pulled. Outside, rush hour had already begun. Office workers were bailing out everywhere possible to start the weekend early.

Everybody, it seemed, was either having a good time or looking forward to one. Everybody except me. I wasn't even going to see Rachel until Sunday night. The weekend stretched out before me like fourth down and hopeless. I felt like breaking into a chorus of "Oh, Lonesome Me."

I left the office quietly, not wanting to be noticed by the developing party down the hall. It was hot as blazes outside, but I decided to walk to the bank anyway. Too much trouble to get the car out of the lot. I cashed a check for fifty dollars, which left me with less than five hundred in my account and no prospects. Rachel was going to get her way after all. You can't play detective when you're standing behind a stainless steel counter wearing a paper hat and going: "Hey, was that eat-in or take-out?"

I spent the rest of the afternoon back in the office waiting for the traffic to thin out. I drew diagrams on paper, outlining everybody I thought could be involved in the murder. There had to be something I wasn't seeing, some other pattern, some other possibility. I hadn't gone to detective school, but I'd read my share of crime novels. That had to be worth something.

Okay, what was it Sherlock Holmes said? "Eliminate the impossible, and whatever is left, no matter how improbable, must be the truth." Or something like that. Maybe it was Miss Marple. Hell, I don't know. I sat there, staring at the wall, going over every possibility. He owed Bubba money, and a lot of it. But if he killed Conrad, that money was gone forever. Like it is now. No, it made more sense to squeeze him, not kill him. Maybe there was some other person at the hospital who hated him for some other reason, but with five thousand people wandering that hospital in any given twenty-four-hour period, how was I going to find the one who hated Conrad Fletcher enough to do him in?

Damn it, I thought, I'm going around in circles. It was time to clear the brain. I needed something to take my mind off. What I wanted to do was call Rachel. But being pushy wasn't going to get me anywhere with her. Besides, dating the murdered victim's widow is no way to forget the murder.

Marsha Helms—that's it. She wanted to see me again. I wanted to see her, but given how things stood with Rachel, that almost felt like cheating. Besides, truth be told, I really wasn't in the mood to see anyone. At least not anyone I had to share any involvement with. What I needed was an old-fashioned dose of emotionally detached male bonding.

Walter—yeah. Split a pizza, coupla beers, maybe take in a movie. My leg was still too bunged up to play racquetball, but I wouldn't mind shooting some stick if we could find a pool hall that didn't have a bunch of bikers hanging around looking to crush some skulls.

I thumbed through the Rolodex and stopped at Walter Quinlan's card. I punched the number up and listened through five rings before the secretary answered.

"Potter and Bell. May I help you?"

"Walter Quinlan, please. Harry James Denton calling."

"I'm sorry, Mr. Quinlan's in a meeting. I expect him out within the hour. Can he call you?"

I gave her my number.

"May I say what this is in reference to?"

"I'm his racquetball partner."

"Oh," she said, pausing for a second. "Sorry to hear about your leg."

I winced. "He told you, huh?"

"Yeah, from what I hear, Walt's a real killer on the racquetball court."

Great, I thought, now even women I've never met think I'm a wimp. "He's not so tough," I said. "I've taken him once or twice."

Another hour passed before he called. By then I'd forgotten I'd left him a message. I was so surprised to hear the phone ring, in fact, I nearly fell out of my chair going for it.

"Denton Agency," I said, "Private Investigations."

"Hey, dude. What's happening?"

"Nothing much, man. Just waiting for you to call so I can close down the office."

"Rough week, huh?"

"I've had better. Listen, I thought we'd go split a pitcher, get a pizza, maybe catch a movie or shoot some pool. What do you say?"

There was this protracted silence, as if he didn't want to accept my invitation, but didn't want to come out and say he didn't want to spend Friday night hanging around with another bachelor. I knew it was a lost cause by the third second.

"Hey, man," I said, "you got plans, it's okay."

"In fact, I'm going to be tied up most of the weekend."

"Hey, great, who is she? Anybody I know?"

"Just somebody I've been seeing."

"Anything serious? She the one you were talking about before?"

"Yeah on both counts. I think it's serious. I don't know. Maybe."

"For a guy who's just found true love, you don't sound too happy."

"Oh, no, man, I don't mean to sound that way. It's just that, well . . . Damn, man, I don't know. Life's just complicated sometimes."

"Ride with it. Enjoy it while it lasts. Life's too short."

"I know that, Harry. Believe me. After this week, I know. Listen, man, I got to go."

"Yeah, I understand. Have a good weekend."

"You, too. Got any plans?"

"I'm hoping my landlady will invite me down for Cream of Wheat, maybe show off her new dentures."

"Funny, Harry. *Trezz-amuzzante . . .*"

I hung up, disappointed. I was getting more sour and grumpy by the minute, and the four walls of my office were closing in fast. I set the answering machine up, on the long shot that somebody might actually want to communicate with me. Then I flipped off my light and eased out into the hall.

Sounds of laughter and music came full tilt from Ray and Slim's office. I knew from past Fridays that the party would go on for another couple of hours, then they'd head over to Second Avenue to a restaurant. Later, they'd wind up at a songwriter's bar swilling beers and picking tunes until they got too drunk to hold their guitars steady. I'd hung with them a night or two, but not tonight.

I left the building quietly, crossed the street, and walked four floors up the parking garage to retrieve the Ford.

I drove out Main Street until it swerved and became Gallatin Road. I didn't even feel like Mrs. Lee's Szechuan chicken tonight, so I pulled into a grocery store parking lot, picked up a six-pack of beer, a couple of frozen nukeable dinners, and headed for my apartment. Catch a movie on the tube, drink a few beers, get to bed early.

After all, Mrs. Hawkins wanted her grass mowed tomorrow.

Nashville sits nestled deep within a natural bowl, surrounded by high ground on all sides. This has the effect of making the entire city a natural garbage dump for stale air, automobile exhaust, heat inversions, and organic pollution of every kind imaginable. We've got more pollen, mold, dust, and varieties of airborne fungi than any place ever chronicled in *National Geographic*. If you don't have bad sinuses when you come to Nashville, you'll soon get them. You'll wake up one morning hungover beyond belief when you haven't had a drink in weeks. Your eyes will puff up like adders. Every part of your body will itch like crazy, including some parts too intimate to scratch. And your cheeks will be so swollen your teeth will hurt. The river running down the back of your throat will make you feel like you ought to rent a canoe and shoot the rapids.

And you'll go to the doctor convinced that a terminal virus has got you in its grip, and if it's not Lyme disease or Chronic Fatigue Syndrome or Epstein-Barr, it's probably something even worse. You'll find yourself reviewing your sexual history over the past two decades wondering which one it was who gave it to you, asking God to give you enough time to track the person down and give them one last terminal bit of your enfeebled, senile mind.

Then to add mortal insult to grievous injury, you'll stagger into the examining room, every orifice from the neck up seeping stuff you neither want to think about nor endure a second longer, and you will relate your laundry list of symptoms to your trusted, faithful family physician.

And he will laugh.

Yes, he will laugh, for he has heard it all before. And he will assure you that despite desperate hopes to the contrary, you are not going to die. You do not have some awful disease. Your body has not been taken over by some alien being.

You simply live in Nashville. And like all other long-time residents of this city, you will learn to clear your throat politely, to keep a box of tissues always nearby, and to study the qualities and characteristics, if indeed not the actual chemical composition, of every over-the-counter remedy from Benadryl to Sudafed. And like all other Nashvillians, when you find one that works, you will buy it five hundred at a time and write letters to the pharmaceutical companies asking when they're going to start selling it in the large size.

And you will dread days like the one I'm having today, the days when you have to cut grass.

It was ninety degrees outside when I woke up at 9:15. The air conditioner was frozen shut again, as useless as an ice-covered airplane wing. The motor, now too hot to touch and in great danger of setting the whole house ablaze, chattered away as it strained futilely to move air through the clogged filter.

I unplugged the machine, determined to watch it for the next hour with the fire department number nearby. I made coffee, then went out on the landing with a steaming cup and sat on the hot metal in a pair of cutoffs. My night had been full of bad dreams. In them I had committed some unspecified crime and was locked away in prison. My cell was tiny. I could stand in the middle of the cell, turn to face the door, and touch both walls without fully extending either arm. I lived alone, and each day was planned, each moment accounted for. We ate at the same time every day, showered three times a week, and ate food at the same times every day seated silently at long tables.

I sat on the landing a long time, until the sun shifted in the sky and began to beat down too hard on me. I retreated inside and made a plate of scrambled eggs and polished off the rest of the coffee, read the paper, stared at the air conditioner. Finally, there was no way to delay the inevitable.

Mrs. Hawkins had a shed out back, a largely decayed wooden frame structure, that had been built by her late husband. It mostly served as a honeymoon hotel for the neighborhood stray cats and as a refuge for brown recluse spiders. As a matter of personal policy, I kept as far away from it as possible. But since she stored the lawn mower in there, at least once a week during this summer and for all my future summers there, since it looked like I'd never have the money to move, I'd risk life and limb to get what I needed to make her happy. I kept hoping one of the neighborhood urchins would crawl in to sneak a smoke one day after school and burn down the damn hovel. So far, though, my customary luck held out.

I suited up in my cutoffs, an old T-shirt, a dust mask I'd picked up at the local hardware store, and my old workboots. Just as a matter of habit, I kicked the door and rattled it on its hinges just to make sure whatever critters were inside knew I was coming.

The lawn mower roared to life after only the twenty-ninth pull. By then I was sweating torrents, covered in dust, and swearing like a drunken sailor on leave in a Hong Kong whorehouse. The cloth filter in the plastic face mask was about as effective as holding a minnow net over my mouth, and soon I was choking, spitting, and generally miserable. I pushed that unholy wheeled contraption around the yard for two hours, in the process nicking the corner of one of Mrs. Hawkins's flower beds and playing hell with some lilies.

The one good thing that came out of the day's work in the sun was that—while clogging my sinuses—it cleared my mind. For the first time since Rachel first stepped into my office and back into my life, I spent a few waking hours with my mind on something else besides murder and desire.

Only that didn't last very long. Late in the afternoon, after I finally finished trimming borders and edging the driveway, I went upstairs, cranked up the now thawed air conditioner, and sat down on the floor with a cold beer in front of the television. I was too dirty to sit on even my worn furniture, so I simply rolled on my haunches across the hard wooden floor to get the remote control.

Thirty-six channels and not a damn thing worth watching. I grazed around for a few more minutes, the choice finally coming down between Looney Tunes and that idiot preacher from Dallas with the demented look who tells people they can buy their way into heaven with a thousand-dollar faith gift. I had sense enough to take the Looney Tunes, and was soon cooling off under the air conditioner with a second beer.

Saturday night was an endless stretch of empty road. How many times had I sweated and longed for and waited impatiently for Saturday night to roll around? I used to enjoy Saturday nights, my favorite time of the week. But then I became self-employed, divorced, and now Saturday nights are a calamity of unfulfilled expectations.

This one, I promised myself, would be different. I was going to prove that a single person can spend a Saturday night alone, enjoy a good dinner, catch a movie, and not be lonely. Around seven, I showered, put on my best dress shirt with a paisley tie and a pair of jeans—nice combination, I thought— and headed out to my old neighborhood with its movie theatres, chic restaurants, and late-night music places.

I grabbed the morning paper on the way out, and over grilled Alaskan salmon and a dynamite California chardonnay at the Sundowner Grille off Hillsboro Road, saw that Janis Ian would play that night at the Blue Bird Café. The Blue Bird was always crowded Saturday nights, and especially so on nights when somebody famous was playing. I finished dinner about nine, drove over and, on impulse, picked up two tickets.

That's right, two tickets. I'd been fooling myself that I was having a good time on a Saturday night by myself. What I wanted to do was see Rachel, and the more I thought of it, not to mention the cumulative effect of a hot day in the sun, two beers, and the better part of a bottle of wine with dinner, the more I became convinced that it was silly for us to let life trickle away when we could be enjoying ourselves and making up for lost time. We had nearly an hour to go before the show started. I'd call her, run by her house, and pick her up, and—

No, don't call. If I call, she'll have the option of saying no. She'll still have that option, but at least she'll have to say no to my face, and I'll get the chance to see her. There was time to feel like a fool tomorrow. For now, I needed to hustle.

I fired up the Ford and pulled back out into the traffic on Hillsboro Road. I even hit the lights right, not missing a one all the way down to Rachel's street. I cut in front of somebody in a classic, horn-blowing, Nashville maneuver, and hammered down on it the two blocks to her house.

I turned into Rachel's driveway and noticed the lights were

still on upstairs in her bedroom, although the rest of the house was dark. I slowed the car and doused the lights, not wanting her to see me pulling in. Let it be a surprise.

I coasted up the driveway and stopped. I set the parking brake, held my breath, and prayed the car door would open quietly for once. I cut around the edge of the house into the back. I was almost giggling to myself with excitement, imagining the expression on her face when I held the tickets up in front of her.

I turned the corner and walked right into the back bumper of a car I hadn't seen.

I didn't hit it hard enough to hurt myself, but I was stunned for a second. It was pitch-black. The outside lights were turned off. Nothing but shapes were visible all around me, heightened by the soft glow from the bedroom window on the second story.

I fumbled around, straining to see in the darkness. Over past the car I'd stumbled into, I could see the outline of Rachel's car. Past that, barely visible in the garage, was the silhouette of Conrad's Jaguar.

Three cars in a driveway that normally held only two: Rachel had company. I turned back to the strange car, running my hand along the edge, trying to feel it. I got down low and followed it all the way around to the back. I was down behind the car now, trying to focus. Then, in the shimmer of a distant streetlight that reflected dimly off the bumper's chrome, I recognized the car. It was a Beemer, a silver BMW sedan. A shudder ran up the back of my neck.

The BMW was Walt Quinlan's car.

Chapter 26 _____

I sure as hell didn't feel like listening to any damn heart-break tunes. The Janis Ian tickets went out the window as soon as I coasted down the driveway and into the street.

No wonder Walt didn't want to tell me who he'd been seeing.

Once safely out of the driveway, I started the Ford and turned on the headlights, then got out of there as quickly as the clattering valves could carry me. Two blocks away, I rolled through the stop sign onto Hillsboro Road, then through two lights to the freeway entrance ramp. I ran the car up to seventy-five, the steering wheel shaking like it had the ague.

I felt like such a fool. It's not so much that Rachel slept with me; hell, people sleep with each other every day without even the benefit of a proper introduction. Happens all the time.

No, it was more that I bought into the whole charade. All my life, I'd been a sucker for this sort of thing. I get interested, misread signs, take too much for granted, get my hopes up for nothing. Jeez, at my age, you'd think I'd have learned by now.

One thing was for sure; I could hold off on packing my bags and giving Mrs. Hawkins my notice. I hadn't realized until I pulled into that driveway and saw Walt's car how much I'd been subconsciously fantasizing about a future with Rachel. I still had feelings for her. It just seemed natural that we'd slide back into life together, and that eventually we'd find what we once had with each other, before Conrad came along and ruined it all.

I passed over the Cumberland River on the I-265 bridge, the water below a ribbon of darkness cutting through the city's nightlights. A single tugboat, a pinpoint of light as sharp as a needle, plodded slowly upriver against the current. The amber freeway lights cast harsh shadows over the darkened concrete. The night air was filled with the smell of the rendering plant.

I took the exit ramp off the freeway and drove up to the entrance ramp of the Ellington Parkway, a lightly traveled bypass that ran from downtown Nashville north toward Madison. The E.P. started next to one of the city's most grim housing projects, the chain link fence separating the highway from the grounds of the project peeled away in some places, torn completely down in others.

I slapped the steering wheel, disgusted with myself and life in general. I got off the parkway at Douglas Avenue, steered my way through the roller-coaster hills to my own neighborhood, and back to the safety of my apartment. I went upstairs, locked the door behind me, and threw my clothes in a pile in the corner. I opened the refrigerator and realized I was out of beer. Damn, I thought, I ought to throw on a good drunk.

Only thing was, I'd outgrown throwing on good drunks years ago, and I never had much luck with it then. I never liked that out-of-control, reeling feeling that hits you right before you head for the porcelain.

But I wanted to be drunk, wanted to drown in the stuff until my head spun like a Ferris wheel gone wild. I wanted to forget it all—Conrad's murder, Mr. Kennedy's murder, the smell of sweat on the racquetball court, the sheen of perspiration on Rachel's face as she twisted beneath me in the sheets.

I turned out the lights and went to bed, the neighborhood strangely and eerily silent. Saturday night in East Nashville usually brought with it the sound of parties gone wild, tires screeching as teenage boys fought to impress girlfriends and one another, the occasional sounds of ominous gunfire. But tonight there was nothing, only silence.

I lay there half the night, struggling vainly to find sleep, that wonderful, empty, dark hole that I could step into and fall forever void of thought and feeling. I needed more than anything else to quit thinking, and that seemed the one thing I could not do. Over and over again, the screens inside my head played the same movies.

Conrad lying beneath me, his lights fading to black.

Rachel lying beneath me, her breath coming in short bursts.

Bubba Hayes on top of me, his thighs like tree stumps, pinning me to the floor.

Walt standing over me, dripping sweat on me, helping me up off the racquetball floor.

Rachel's face outlined against the ceiling as she sat astride me, the two of us pumping away at each other madly.

The glowing red digital numbers of the alarm clock read 4:30 the last time I looked at it. I drifted off finally, into an uneasy and troubled sleep that was anything but rejuvenating. I woke up around seven. I was exhausted.

I spread the Sunday paper out on the kitchen table, but didn't have the concentration to get very far. My eyes burned from lack of sleep. I felt brittle, old.

Even then, I couldn't stop thinking. I kept seeing Rachel's house, with its great lawn and expensive furniture, the cars, the clothes. The more I pondered, the odder it seemed that Conrad Fletcher could afford all that, yet couldn't afford to pay off his bookie. A hundred thousand dollars, Bubba said he owed. Not exactly pocket change, but probably only a few months' salary to Conrad. A fortune to me. If I owed that kind of money to a bookie, it could just as well be a hundred million. But Conrad *could* have paid it off. How come he didn't?

Maybe the truth lay somewhere else. Maybe, I thought, it was the house and the cars and the lifestyle that *kept* Conrad from paying off Bubba.

If that were true, then the mirror was cracked. All the

perfect reflections I'd seen were false, tricks put before my eyes like a magician's scarf covering sleight of hand. I sat at the kitchen table staring at the wall for over an hour, my thoughts reduced to pure, nonverbal essence.

Something's stinko.

"You rook awfuh."

"Thanks, Mrs. Lee. Good to see you again, too."

"Weah you been? It been days now."

I looked across the counter as Mrs. Lee scribbled my order down on her green lined pad. She was as crotchety as ever, the result, I guess, of risking your keister to escape to the land of freedom and opportunity and discovering that freedom and opportunity meant opening up at 7:30 in the morning and closing at 9:30 at night seven days a week for the rest of your life.

"Don't tell me you missed me."

"I nevah miss anybody," she spat. "We just made too much chicken tree days in row 'cause you didn't show up. Cost me money."

"I'll leave you a big tip."

"Oh, yeah, weah I heahd dat befoah?"

She disappeared behind the stainless steel counter between the cash register and the kitchen. I could see her husband back in there, slaving over a hot wok.

Maybe things weren't so bad for me. Then again, maybe Mrs. Lee would give me a job. I used to make a pretty mean Mooshu Pork back when Lanie and I were married.

Mrs. Lee came back around with the steaming plate a moment later. She shoved it across the front counter.

"I put exta chicken on theah foah Shadow. Doan you eat it all."

I smiled at her. "Mrs. Lee," I said, "you're one of the few truly wonderful people I've ever met in my life. I mean that."

"Yeah, and you fuh of it." She waddled off behind the counter with a load of dirty plates.

This was the longest I'd gone without a visit to Mrs. Lee's

since I moved to East Nashville. I guess I didn't realize how
much this part of town had become home for me. It's weird
to think that I used to eat at joints with names like Mario's
and Chef Sigi's and Arthur's, all restaurants where you were
as likely to run into the mayor as anyone else, or maybe the
chief of police, or maybe the head of the Nissan plant in
Smyrna. With two people, you'd walk out with a VISA that
was three figures closer to being maxxed out than it was
before you walked in.

I used to think I enjoyed that life, even regretted losing it,
but realizing that Mrs. Lee had honestly missed me the past
few days made me feel better than all the three-figure dinners
ever had.

This was home. How odd. . . .

I guess it was okay that I wasn't going to be moving back
across the tracks to live with Rachel. I ate the Szechuan
chicken with a delight that bordered on the sociopathic. I
realized that the dinner I'd paid twenty-five dollars for in
Green Hills hadn't filled me, and that the $3.95 I'd just spent
at Mrs. Lee's would do me for the rest of the day.

I pulled the last few pieces of chicken out of the gloppy
sauce and dipped them one at a time into my water glass,
washing off most of the hot pepper and chile oil. One of
these days, I was going to get in a hurry, feed Shadow some
unwashed chicken, and she was going to tear my head off.

I wrapped the chicken in a couple of paper napkins and
stuffed them in my jeans pocket. I pulled out onto Gallatin
Road at 11:30, which meant the church traffic would be just
about peaking. No matter, I wasn't in any hurry, wasn't even
sure if I could find out what I needed to know on a Sunday.

It was a gray day; the clouds overhead looked like rain. I
felt better after eating, though, and I'd set out that morning
with something that resembled a plan of action. It took twenty
minutes to make it up the street to Lonnie's. The side road
that led to the junkyard was completely deserted, the garages
and body shops closed, the bikers having locked their building down and gone off somewhere to sleep off Saturday
night's binge. I pulled up in front of the gate and stopped.

Overhead, the thick clouds grew more menacing by the minute. These late summer thunderstorms come up out of nowhere in this part of the country, and you can go from dazzling sunshine to inside a tornado in moments. I stepped up to the gate and rattled it, hoping to get inside the trailer before the gullywasher started.

Shadow padded out from her nest behind the trailer, her tail and head held low in alert.

"Hi, Shadow," I said brightly, hoping my voice would relax her. She hadn't seen me in days, and would be suspicious for a bit until her doggy synapses located the right memory bit and cleared me through security.

She approached slowly, cautiously. Then her tail began to wag and her head came up, her eyes widening from the narrow slits they'd been.

"Shadow, girl, how's it going? How you been?" I unlatched the gate catch, swung the door open, and stepped in. She was on me in one leap, her great paws on my shoulders, her stale hot breath right in my face. I wrapped my arms around her back and hugged her, delighted to see her again.

Over her shoulder, the trailer door opened. Lonnie stood there in a pair of worn jeans and a white T-shirt. He could do James Dean with the best of them, I thought.

"Hey, stranger," he said.

"Lonnie," I said, nodding. Then I stepped back, pulling Shadow's paws off my shoulder, and backed up a step. I reached into my pocket, pulled out the fist-sized wad of chicken, and held it out in front of me. I pulled the paper off.

"Speak. Speak, Shadow."

She dropped to her haunches, her head pointed up eagerly.
"Speak!"

She let out a bark that was more of a bellow than anything else, and at that moment I sent the chicken flying in a slow arc toward her. She sprang up, her jaws snapping shut like a bear trap.

"You're going to spoil her, goddamn it. I got to live with her."

"That's okay," I said, scratching her ears, then walking past her to the porch. "She deserves it."

"Yeah, right," Lonnie said. I stuck out my hand to him, which was promptly refused. "Wash that crap off your hands first."

He led the way into the trailer, the door swinging to on its own behind us. I walked over to the filthy sink, with auto grease and used, dried crankcase oil caked around the edges, and turned the water on.

"You won't shake hands with me because I've got a little chicken on them, but you'll drink a glass of water that comes out of this filthy sink."

Lonnie laughed. "Who said I drink water? I don't drink water. Stuff don't taste right."

"Need to get you one of those water filters. Filters out all the chlorine and crap they put in it."

"It'd have to be some filter to make Nashville water taste good. Like sucking up a swimming pool."

The table with the scorched hole in it had been pushed into a corner. In the middle of the room on an old blanket sat some kind of disassembled motorcycle engine.

"You rebuilding the bike?"

Lonnie looked at me real serious, then sat in a chair and planted his feet against the wall. "You didn't come here to talk about engines and feed Shadow. First time I've seen you in a week. What kind of trouble you got yourself into?"

I pulled a chair around backward, spread my legs, and sat. I rested my chin on the back of the chair. "It's like this, Lonnie," I said, and I began telling him everything that had happened since the day of Conrad's funeral. I started with Bubba, worked my way through James Hughes and the medical students, LeAnn Gwynn, Jane Collingswood, Albert Zitin, and anybody else I could think of who even remotely might have wanted to kill Conrad Fletcher. And I ended with pulling into Rachel's driveway the night before and finding Walt Quinlan's car parked behind her house and all the lights off except in the bedroom.

Lonnie whistled. "You got yourself in a hell of a mess,

boy. Damn lawyers'll stab you in the back every time.''
Lonnie'd never met Walter Quinlan; they didn't exactly run
in the same circles. But he knew who he was.

"You want to know what I think?" he asked.

"Sure."

"I think she killed him."

"Rachel?"

"Yeah. A man gets killed, first thing you do is look at the
wife."

I sat for a second, thousand-yard stare pasted on my face.
"Don't think I haven't thought of it," I said finally. "But it
doesn't make any sense. Besides, she's got an airtight alibi."

"Airtight alibi, my ass. Ain't no such thing. And what
you mean, it don't make sense? She told you they weren't
getting along."

"So? You don't kill someone because they're not nice to
you. No, she might have divorced him, would have divorced
him. But not killed him. You don't kill doctors; you divorce
them and take everything they've got. That hurts them a lot
worse than killing them."

"And they had a lot worth having?"

"You ought to see this place, Lonnie. Straight out of the
country club crowd. And I don't know what kind of money
he made, but it had to be serious."

"You're looking at appearances again, man. You got to
look behind that, beneath it, around it."

"I know. That's why I came here today."

"Yeah?" he asked, confused. "What've I got to do with
it?"

"You still got your laptop?"

Lonnie smiled. "Is Elvis still making records?"

"Let's go."

Lonnie stood, led the way down the hall to the back bedroom of the trailer. This was Lonnie's private office, with all
his electronic surveillance gear, computers, nightscopes,
cameras, wiretappers, super-secret stuff that you didn't want
to get caught with in a routine traffic stop. Only this time,
we were going legitimate.

Lonnie unlatched the cover on the laptop computer, folded it back to reveal a screen and built-in printer. The laptop was a dedicated computer rented from the credit bureau. You didn't have to program it. You just turned it on and it booted itself up.

"You got a Social?"

"No, I don't know what his Social Security number was. Can we just run an inquiry?"

"Sure." Lonnie typed in a command to dial up the credit bureau.

"Would the computer already have Conrad listed as deceased?"

"Maybe. I'm not sure. Sometimes it takes ten days, maybe a couple weeks. Depends partly on whether Rachel's notified them yet."

My stomach churned as the screen began displaying a message, then a menu of options. This was as sleazy as anything I'd ever done in my life. I felt like I was betraying Rachel, a breach of trust so serious that even if I never told her, it would lay inside me for the rest of my life like a sleeping virus strain.

The worst part was that I couldn't figure out whether I was doing this because it was part of my job, or if I wanted to know out of some sick compulsion.

"Got a middle name or initial?"

"No," I said. I stood behind Lonnie as he sat there, typing in commands, looking over his shoulder at the silver and blue LCD screen.

Lonnie typed in a string of letters, followed by *Fletcher*, *Conrad*. He hit the RETURN button, and we sat there for what seemed like a long while.

"Maybe this don't work on Sunday," I said.

"No, the offices are closed. But the computer's on twenty-four-hours-a-day, seven days a week. Except when it crashes or shuts down for maintenance."

The screen lit up in a burst of characters. There were four Conrad Fletchers, each with a different middle initial and address.

"That's him," I said. "The third one."

Lonnie moved the cursor up to the line and pressed RE-TURN. "It'll take a minute or so to print out. Want some coffee?"

"Your coffee?" I asked.

"Yeah, who the hell you think's coffee?"

"No thanks. I'll pass."

The thermal printer started buzzing and spewing out paper a line at a time. I paced the office while Lonnie went for his coffee cup. I was afraid to look at the report as it came out of the back of the computer. I could still not do this. All I had to do was tear it up and throw it away, and I'd still be able to stand myself in the mirror.

The computer beeped, indicating the report had been sent. Then the printer buzzed as it rolled out the rest of the sheet. Lonnie came into the office with a dirty mug full of coffee.

"Well," he said, setting the cup down on the desk, then reaching behind the computer to tear the paper, "let's see what we got here."

I stood back as he ripped the paper out of the computer. He held it under the desk light and looked it over. His eyes flicked back and forth across the paper.

"Well?" I asked.

Lonnie cocked his head toward me, still bent over the desk.

"Sweet Mother of Jesus," he muttered.

Chapter 27 _____

This pain shot up the back of my neck, radiating out through my skull like heat waves. "What is it?" I asked.

He handed me the curled sheet of paper. It had a grayish shiny cast to it, almost as if it had been wet. Credit bureau reports are complicated creatures; you have to know the codes or they're largely indecipherable. When I started skip tracing for Lonnie, he gave me a handout that explained it all, but I hadn't looked at it in a couple of weeks.

A row of asterisks ran across the top of the report, broken only by the letters REF A64 centered in the line. Below that was a line that read: NM—FLETCHER, CONRAD, J., DR., and below that, the address, and Conrad's Social Security number.

The first chunk of the report was personal information: his age, the date he established credit, spouse's name, spouse's maiden name, her Social Security number, and their former addresses, going back at least five years. Below that, Conrad's employer, position, and salary were reported.

"Jeez, he did okay for himself, didn't he?" Conrad made just over $250,000 last year.

"Keep reading," Lonnie said. He could digest the data a lot faster than I could. He could go through a two-page report and pick out the important material in about thirty seconds.

I read on. There was a section on Public Records, which was empty. At least he hadn't filed bankruptcy, and there were no current judgments against him. The next section started after another row of asterisks, then a series of col-

umns headed: FIRM; CURRENT STATUS; RPTD-OPND; LIMIT P—
D; HICR TERM; BAL; and 24-MONTH HISTORY.

"Aw, man, look at this," I said, as the statement's impact
hit me like another shot to the gut from Bubba.

"These guys were in hock up the ya-ya," Lonnie said.
"See, their house had two mortgages. They're one month
behind on the primary and three months behind on the sec-
ondary."

"Look, both their cars are leased," I said.

"And see up here in this section," Lonnie said, pointing.
"They had a Mercedes repossessed last year."

"Oh, hell, is that what that code means?"

"Yeah, it wasn't one of mine, though. I didn't pop it. I'd
remember a car like that."

I suddenly felt dizzy. "Man, I got to sit down. You mind?"

"Sure." He pulled the chair away from the desk for me.

There it was, the Great American Success Story. No wonder there was tension in their marriage. It's tough making
medium six figures a year when you're supporting a high six
figures lifestyle.

"Look," I said, "two MasterCards, three VISAs, American Express Gold, Optima, Diner's Club, Carte Blanche."

"All maxxed out or over their credit limits," Lonnie commented, standing over my shoulder. "Look, they're three
months behind on that VISA, two on the other ones."

"Where did it all go?" I asked, exasperated.

"Beats me. Maybe up their noses."

"No, you toot up that kind of dough, people are going to
notice. Man, I think it's just fancy living. Vacations, cars,
clothes, restaurants."

"Look, that's another mortgage, I'll bet. Bank of Cooke-
ville—that's up by Center Hill Lake. Sixty-five grand out-
standing. Man, it's almost got to be a summer home or
something. See, next column over. They're four months behind on that one. I don't know why the bank hasn't already
foreclosed."

I stared down at the paper, seeing the letters and the numbers, but too much in shock to make much sense out of it.

"Check it out, man," Lonnie continued, "Saks Fifth Avenue, Neiman-Marcus, Dillards, Castner's, Lord & Taylor. Damn, man, what'd these two do? Fly up to New York every weekend to shop?"

"Down here at the bottom," I said, pointing. "Look, a charge off."

"Twenty-five hundred to Dominion Bank. And here, look. His student loan is even late. Now that's some serious shit, man. You deadbeat a student loan, they go after you hard. They'll pull your freaking income tax refund nowadays."

"If he had one. The one thing I don't see is an IRS lien."

"It wouldn't necessarily be there. I usually don't see personal liens on these reports until after the IRS has come in and seized everything you own."

"Then they list it afterward on your credit report?"

"Yeah. Keeps you from replacing all your stuff with something else. I tell you, fella, these two were on the edge of it."

"Edge of what?"

"Collapse, man. Collapse."

I scanned down to the end of the report, each printed line another nail in the financial coffin. How can anyone let themselves get in this kind of shape?" I wondered.

"We can get out the calculator," Lonnie said, "but my guess is that between the credit limits, the mortgages, and the judgments, they owe somewhere around three-quarters of a big one."

"No, don't. I don't want to know." I let the paper fall out of my hand onto the floor, then wearily put my head down on the desk next to the computer. Lonnie leaned against the door frame, cradling the cup of coffee in his hands.

"Man, I know it's tough," he said. "But you gotta get straight about this. You're either going to have your head in the right place, or your ass in the wrong one."

I raised up and rubbed my burning eyes. "How could this happen? They were so bright, so successful."

"Hey, you think they're different from anybody else? I don't want to get too political on you here, buddy, but it's the legacy of the Reagan years. You got your billionaire stockbrokers in New York that went down the toilet when the bubble burst. What makes you think a doctor could get away with it? Fletcher was a pauper compared to Ivan Boesky."

"I know, man. You're right."

"Of course, I'm right. And I tell you one other thing, bucko. She whacked him. As sure as I'm standing here wearing boxer shorts under my jeans, Rachel Fletcher killed her husband."

I leaned back and stared at him as if he were an escaped lunatic. "You're off there, Lonnie. It don't make sense."

"What the motherfather you talking about? Makes perfect sense."

"No, Lonnie. It'd made perfect sense if he didn't owe a nickel. But Conrad was in hock up to his eyebrows. What could Rachel inherit? I mean, what's the benefit to her? A week ago, she had a husband who was pulling in two-hundred-grand a year. Now all she's got is a house the mortgage company's going to take within a matter of days, two leased cars she can't afford, and a purse full of plastic a clerk in East Bee*hay*soos wouldn't take."

Outside, a rolling, burbling rumble came from the sky. I pivoted and looked through the thin gauzy curtain over the window. In the distance, a flash of lightning tickled the horizon, followed a few moments later by a hard thunderclap. Rain began falling, at first only light drizzles. Then, in a matter of seconds, the roof of the trailer rattled like BBs falling on sheet metal.

"If anything," I said over the din of the rain, "Conrad's death leaves her in worse shape than before. Now she hasn't even got the income they had."

"You're forgetting one thing, Ace."

"What's that?"

"Life insurance."

"Oh, right," I said, suddenly angry with him. "Like I'm just going to walk over to Rachel's and say 'okay, babe, where's the key to your lock box?' I'm sure he had insurance, although God knows how he paid for it. I know his university policy won't come anywhere near paying off those debts. There was probably barely enough to bury him.''

Lonnie stood still for a second, his face blank, expressionless. Finally, he said: "There's one way to find out, my man. But this is one you really got to keep quiet about."

"What're you talking about?"

"Insurance companies are like anybody else. They don't want to do anything stupid. They got certain standards for certain occupations. You're a freaking ditch digger carrying five mil worth of insurance on yourself, the insurance company's going to want to know why you value yourself so highly. The scam used to be you buy a bunch of policies spread out over several companies.

"Not anymore," he continued. "Now they got a computer. When you buy an insurance policy, the insurance companies run your Social through a database and see how many policies you've got with other companies."

"Get out of here. . . ."

"I'm serious, man. You wouldn't believe what you can find out. You got a modem, a phone number, a password. You go to a new doctor with a bad back, he's going to run your name through the MIB, see if you've ever been involved in a malpractice suit. You got a track record for suing doctors, he's going to tell you to hit the road, Jack. Go see a witch doctor."

"Great," I said. "We don't have to worry about the government being Big Brother. The corporations'll do it for us."

"You got that right, bro. Only thing is, there's always somebody out there who can infiltrate. You make it accessible to one person, you've made it open for everybody. Just takes a little ingenuity."

"And let me guess," I said. "You're a very ingenious person."

"So I've been told," Lonnie answered, smiling. He set his coffee cup down on a table, came over to the desk, and shooed me out of his seat. He took the chair and flipped on the PC next to the laptop. A green glow filled the screen, followed by the computer's self-test.

Then a menu appeared. Lonnie chose the option labeled COMMUNICATIONS. He hit a few more keys, then the speaker in the computer gave out a dial tone, followed by a series of beeps as the computer dialed.

Seconds later, we were logged on. I don't know where Lonnie got a valid password, but he had one. He worked his way through a couple of layers of menus, then set his cursor on a line labeled CUST INQU.

Then he picked up the credit bureau report and typed in Conrad's Social Security number. The cursor blinked, the green pulsating dot like a heart monitor.

"How long does it take?"

"Shouldn't be too long. Be cool."

"Can't man. No chill to cop on this one."

The dot went solid green. Then the computer spit out line after line of numbers and letters.

"Need a calculator?" Lonnie asked.

The amounts were even, large and even. "I think I can handle it."

"That one there is his university-supplied policy," Lonnie said. "See, it matches his salary."

"Then there are two association policies. The rest must be private."

"Yeah, looks like. Hmmmm, interesting. It seems the good Dr. Fletcher was carrying about—"

"Two million," I said.

"Which leaves, after paying off the debts—"

"Maybe a million, three. Would you kill somebody for that, man?" I asked.

Lonnie leaned back in the chair, looked at me in amazement. "Only my mother, man, only my mother . . ."

I fell against the wall and slid down to the floor. Damn, could it really be? An overwhelming fatigue enveloped like a sudden onset of flu. I saw Rachel in my mind, her face floating out in front of me, her body, her hair. I smelled her in the air, heard her deep inside my brain. She was part of me, and while I hadn't exactly figured out how big a part yet, I knew it was going to be something important.

"No, Lonnie. It can't be."

"You told me she's a nurse, right? She'd know what to get, how much to shoot into him, right?"

"But that still doesn't answer how it happened."

"What're you talking about?"

"Why did Conrad Fletcher simply lie there and let her shoot him full of the stuff?"

"You never said anything about him laying there."

I looked at him intently. The expression on his face was blank. Apparently he really didn't know what I was talking about.

"I told you. Remember? I found him lying back on a bed. No sign of a struggle, no marks on him. They didn't even find anything in the autopsy."

Lonnie shook his head. "No, man, you never told me that. All you said was he got shot up with some kind of synthetic curare. I figured he was knocked down, tied up. Hell, I don't know."

I pushed against the wall and stood back up, my hands out in front almost in supplication.

"No, see, that's the mystery here. How did it happen? How come he didn't fight? I asked Marsha Helms if it could have been a TASER or a stun device, and she said every one she'd ever seen left a mark where the darts hit you."

Lonnie laughed, more of a snort, really. "Then she hasn't been keeping up with the literature, my man."

I went cold. "What are you talking about?"

"Follow me, bud."

He hopped out of the chair, back out into the hall, and down to the living room of the trailer. He pulled open a wooden desk drawer, dug around in a pile of stuff, then found what he was looking for.

"Latest generation, man. State of the art. Close support self-defense weapon. Small, hand held, you can't fire it at anybody. You have to be close enough to jam it into them. It's just a capacitor circuit, actually. Like the ignition coil on a car. Takes a nine-volt alkaline battery and turns it into a 65,000 volt charge. No darts. Doesn't leave a mark on you.

No permanent damage. It just short circuits every nerve in your body, and you drop like a rock.''

He held up the device in the palm of his hand, a small black plastic box with four metal prongs poking out of the end. Lonnie pushed the button; there was a crackling noise in the air. An inch-long blue spark danced between two of the contacts. Right out of *Frankenstein*.

''Completely legal, and only fifty bucks at your local gun dealer's. Disables a mugger for about five minutes. Gives you time to get away, call the cops. Maybe get a tire iron out of your trunk and tap dance on the sucker's head.''

He tossed the black box toward me. ''It'd also give you time to press the plunger on a syringe,'' he added.

I caught the stun gun, held it in my hand. The edges of the plastic rectangular box were molded to provide a good grip, the button right under my thumb. It was comfortable, at home in a hand. I held it up and took a long, close look at it.

Damn thing looked just like a beeper.

Chapter 28 _____

Outside, the rain came down in sheets, the layers of water pounding so hard the sky was completely obscured. I splattered through the mud, fumbled with the chain link fence gate, and was thoroughly soaked when I got back to my car.

Lonnie was right, of course. It was all there. Maybe had been from the start. I just refused to see it, which made me feel like an even bigger yutz. I still didn't want to believe it. How could that petite, blond, middle-American, Betty Crocker-cute woman take another human life? How did she get the alibi? It didn't make sense, or if it did, then all the basic fundamental illusions we depend upon to get through from one day to the next are just useless drivel.

Or maybe her alibi was good. Maybe it was a contract killing. People killed for cheap these days, or so my deep background sources used to tell me at the paper. Didn't make any difference. If Rachel paid somebody to ice him, it's the same as if she did it herself.

I had to sit in the Ford for a couple of minutes to get myself together. The defroster on the car had long since gone to meet its maker; whenever the humidity gets within a few degrees of the dew point, fog settles in over the inside glass so thick it's like flying by instrument. I started the car, turned on the defroster full blast out of hope and habit, and sat there while the car warmed up. It was no good though; the only way those windows were going to be clear was for me to wipe them that way. Even then, visibility was so bad I was afraid to pull out into the street for fear of being T-boned.

It didn't matter, anyway. I wasn't going anywhere, literally

or metaphorically. I found myself alternately angry and de-
pressed, believing and disbelieving. Somebody I once loved,
maybe still loved, was a murderer. And I had to figure out
what to do with that.

That, then, was the most frightening part; the notion that
I could sit here and even consider letting her slide. Had I
gotten that desperate, that cynical, that I'd know who did a
murder and let them get away with it? If Rachel got away
with the murder, she was going to be rich. But she and Walter
had something going now. Was I going to be a part of her
life, her rich, sheltered, safe life?

This prospect made me feel even lower. Not only was I
considering keeping my mouth shut about a murder, but if I
did talk, it would be at least partly because I wouldn't get
any benefit from it.

Sometimes I don't feel like a very nice person anymore.
We grow up with these little, safe notions about the lives we
want to lead, the people we want to love, the work we want
to do, and how we'll be rewarded for our hard work. Then
we get out there in twentieth-century urban America and it's
Dodge City all over again. The spoils go to the ones with the
best aim, the quickest draw, the biggest guns. It tends to
make one want to be as big a bastard as the rest of the world.

"Quit thinking, damn it," I said out loud. "Stop this ridiculous pontificating. The world's the world, that's all, and
there's no use in pouting because it isn't what you think it
should be."

What I had to do was figure out how I was going to handle
this. Any way I looked at it, all the options sucked.

In a blind leap of faith, I pulled out onto the roadway and
made the curve around to Gallatin Road, then out into the
heavy traffic. Up ahead, the brake lights of a large, mid-
Sixties Chevy suddenly glowed cherry-red, then oscillated
back and forth across the road as the car hydroplaned. The
thunderstorm pelted us with rain so hard it was like staring
through a shower spray. I pumped the Ford's brakes carefully, feeling for that moment when the wheels lost contact
with the road and you became simply a passenger in a two-

ton chunk of out-of-control metal. The Chevy ahead of me slid into the oncoming lane of traffic, slammed into a rock wall, and came to a floating stop in six inches of water, blocking both lanes of traffic. I slowed the car to stop, but there was a semi behind me, the driver laying on his horn, letting me know that if I slowed any further I was going to wind up roadkill tartare.

Yeah, I thought, the world's a dangerous place. It seems more so now than it did when I was young. Or maybe I just notice it more.

I slowed to a fast walk and drifted easily into the left-hand turning lane. Once off Gallatin Road, I made it safely back to Mrs. Hawkins's driveway and into the backyard. My dry, safe apartment was only a few feet and a flight of stairs away.

One thing was for sure: I couldn't handle seeing Rachel. I wasn't ready to deal with it, and there was no way I was going to make chatty all evening, drink wine, have a good dinner, maybe wind up in bed with her again. I'd see Rachel, and soon, but only after I sorted some things out.

As quickly as it roared in, the storm was gone, leaving everything damp and lush. I stood on the landing outside my kitchen, that peculiar earthy smell that hangs around after a heavy rain filling me. I'd changed into a dry pair of jeans. The rickety metal stairway up the side of Mrs. Hawkins's house groaned a little; I wondered how long it would be before I came home from work one day and found myself stranded by a twisted heap of metal in the backyard.

I looked down at my watch: 3:30 in the afternoon. I was supposed to pick up Rachel at six. There was some new fern bar trendy chic restaurant in Green Hills she wanted to try. I'd have been happy to run her through Mrs. Lee's and let her see how the other half eats.

I felt sour, out of sorts. I either needed to resolve this whole mess or start taking a fiber supplement. If I'm not going to dinner, I thought grumpily, then I damn well better call her and beg off for the evening.

I dialed her number and waited through six rings before she picked up. She must have had the answering machine off. Maybe she had to tear herself out of Walter's arms. God, I'm a bitch.

"Hello."

"Rachel?"

"Harry, how are you?"

Her voice sounded different. Maybe it was because in my mind, hers was now the voice of a murderer.

"I'm fine, Rachel. But listen, I'm going to have to skip out on dinner tonight. I've had some things come up at the office that have to be taken care of tonight."

"On a Sunday night?"

"Yeah," I said, lying as convincingly as I knew how. "It's another client of mine. Sometimes he calls me up with some strange requests. I can't really talk about it, and it's not a big deal or anything. I'll just need to reschedule with you."

"Okay, you want to give me a call tomorrow?"

"Yeah, that'll work. Okay with you?"

"Sure. Harry, are you sure there's nothing wrong?"

My heart thumped in my chest. I swallowed a gulp of air, then let it out evenly as I spoke. "Yeah, everything's fine, Rach. I'll miss seeing you tonight. I'll make it up to you, though."

"All right, Harry," she said, hesitating like she wasn't sure whether to believe me. If I were her, I wouldn't. "Call me tomorrow, okay?"

"Yeah, I will. Listen, you take care now."

"I will. You, too."

"Bye, now."

Yeah, I thought, take care. I wish she'd done that before, back before she got herself into something that was bigger than all of us.

I didn't have much appetite, but I figured a trip to the store would at least get me away from the shrinking walls of my apartment. I picked up some salad makings, a six-pack of beer, a few other munchies, then returned to my apartment in a fog that was at least as thick as what was on my windshield earlier.

I turned on the television, looking for something totally

mindless. Television being television, I found it with no trouble at all. But while my eyes watched "America's Funniest Heart Attack Videos," or some such crap, my mind was subliminally running around in circles.

I still wasn't sure, still couldn't believe it. Could, in fact, still create a half-dozen ways in which she didn't do it. Husbands die with lots of insurance every day; doesn't mean the wife did it. Rachel was a nurse; that didn't mean she was the one who shot Conrad full of protocurarine. She wasn't the only person in the world who knew how to read a *PDR*, or how to fill a syringe.

I bounced around from one extreme to the other, one moment my heart racing because she was innocent, the next sinking because she was guilty. I ate my salad without tasting it, drank a couple of beers, picked up books to read and couldn't stay focused, looked for a decent old movie on television, found only trash. Mind pudding.

Ten o'clock rolled around. I locked up, turned off the lights, stripped down to my shorts, and crawled in bed with another beer. Three beers on a Sunday night; Christ, this whole business was driving me to drink. The news came on. More disasters. Muggings, rapes, armed robberies—the whole litany of savage horrors in an allegedly civilized world. I was beginning to think I needed to buy a gun, especially in my line of work. Maybe get one of those electronic zappers. I wondered if that was what she hit me over the head with the night of Conrad's—

Wait, I thought, shooting up in bed like a bird dog on point. That's it. My head. I held the answers right beneath the butterfly strips on my head, only I'd been too stupid to see it. But maybe not. I had to be sure. If I were right, that cinched it. But if I were wrong . . .

There was only one way to find out. And that wasn't going to be pleasant. I flicked on the nightstand light, grabbed the white pages, flipped through to the *S*s. I ran my finger down the column, hoping like the devil he wouldn't have an unlisted number. I could see where he'd want to keep his num-her a secret. After all, cops probably get some pretty weird phone calls.

"Spellman," I said out loud, reading down the list. Then I came to it. He was listed as *H*, with no address. Just a number.

"All right, Howard! Who loves ya', baby?" I said, dialing the number. A few seconds later, a sleepy woman's voice answered.

"Mrs. Spellman?"

"Yes?" She yawned as the end of the word rolled off her tongue.

"May I speak to Lieutenant Spellman, please."

"He's asleep right now. Is it important? Who is this?"

"Ma'am, I hate to bother you. But this is important. This is Harry Denton. I'm a private investigator. He knows who I am."

Her voice changed from sleepy to irritated. "Can't it wait until the morning?"

It could wait until the morning, but I couldn't. "Mrs. Spellman, it's real important. And it'll only take a minute. Please?"

"Oh, all right." There was a shuffle of blanket as she handed the phone over to Spellman.

"Yeah?" his gruff voice answered.

"Lieutenant Spellman, this is Harry Denton."

A long sigh came over the phone. "Damn it, what do you want?"

"I hate to bother you so late."

"Then how come you're doing it?"

"Just one quick question, then I'll let you go back to sleep. The night of Fletcher's murder, when you interviewed other people in the hospital, his friends, notified his family, all that good stuff, did you tell anybody I got hit in the head?"

"Aw, damn it, Denton, you woke me up to ask me that?"

"Yeah."

There was a long pause, and I could hear something that almost sounded like growling over the phone. "I been investigating murders nearly twenty years, Denton. I got better sense than that.''

"So you didn't tell anybody?''

"The only people who knew you got hit in the head were the people who saw you in the hospital and treated you.''

"And you didn't tell anybody the next day?''

"No, nobody. What's this about, Denton? You holding out on me?''

"Thanks, Lieutenant,'' I said blankly. "I'll let you go back to sleep now.''

I hung up and sat there in bed, staring at the silent, flickering images on the television.

Now I knew.

Chapter 29

I didn't have to wake up the next morning; you can't wake up when you've never been asleep. I've had some long nights before, but this was the longest night I'd ever spent. Even when things were at their worst with Lanie, when we lay next to each other, silent and sleepless, it was nothing like this. There was a kind of unreality about it, as if I'd gotten myself cast in a remake of some film noir classic. Only this was very real, and the difference between what this felt like and reality was the same as the difference between a gunfight on television and a gunfight in your neighborhood.

I washed down the last of a tasteless biscuit with cold coffee, then started toward the door. The kitchen clock read 7:35, too early for me to be up as a rule. But these were days without rules. I put my hand on the doorknob, then stopped. I couldn't do this alone. I needed help. Rachel would need help. It's time we all came clean with each other.

I walked back into my bedroom and called Walter's office.

"I'm sorry," the receptionist said. "He's not in yet." I was surprised anyone was in yet, but after all, the sharks feed early.

"Can I leave him a message? It's urgent. In fact, it's an emergency."

"Go ahead. I'll see he gets the message." Her voice was concerned, serious.

I gave her Rachel's address. "Tell him to meet me there as soon as he can. It's very important."

"Can I tell him what it's about?"

I couldn't leave that in a message. "Just tell him to be there."

The drive over to Rachel's left me brittle, like the time Lanie wanted me to meet her for lunch. I knew she was going to divorce me; I knew that was what she was going to tell me. But I went to lunch anyway. It was like that today.

I turned onto Golf Club Lane and drove quickly to Rachel's driveway. I imagined Walter's BMW pulling out just as I pulled in; the thought made me laugh out loud.

The Ford chugged up the driveway, squealed to a stop behind Conrad's Jag. I wondered if she'd keep the Jaguar, now that she had all that money. I rang the bell a few times, with no response. But the cars were there. Odd, I thought.

I walked around the side of the house, down the driveway a few feet, and stood in the sun. The storm front had long since moved through. It was a beautiful, sunlit day. The sky was deep blue; even the air temporarily clean.

Rachel shot into view, running at a good solid clip from up the street to my left. She disappeared behind a line of hedges, then came back into sight running the street in front of the house. She moved quickly, with an ease and grace that gave me an ache in my chest. Rachel really was beautiful, on the outside anyway.

She turned into the driveway and slowed as she saw me. Her arms dropped to her side, and she loped up next to me, glistening with sweat and breathing hard.

"Harry," she panted. "What—"

"Hi, Rachel," I said. "How're you doing?"

"Tired. Out of breath. Glad to see you, though. C'mon inside."

She walked past me, head down, shaking her arms and shoulders to stay loose. She pulled her keys out of her fanny pack, turned off the burglar alarm, and opened the kitchen door. Inside, the remnants of a breakfast eaten solo remained on the table.

"Let me run upstairs and get a towel," she said, pulling off the fanny pack and laying it on the table. "Be right back."

She left the kitchen and went down the hall. I heard her

footsteps on the stairs. The fanny pack was lying there; I reached over, unzipped it, spread it open wide.

Inside the dark pouch, I could see what looked like a black plastic box. I pulled it out. A button on the side, four metal contacts on the end. Just like Lonnie showed me.

I shoved the stun gun back inside the pouch, zipped it shut. Damn, I thought.

Footsteps padded down the stairs, then through the hall. She stepped into the kitchen, hair combed straight back, face rinsed, towel around her neck.

"Good run?"

"Yeah, almost an hour. Great way to start the day. You want coffee or something?"

"Sure." I stepped around the counter to get out of her way.

"You look like you've been up all night, darling. Been on a stakeout?"

"Something like that." It hurt to have her call me darling.

She opened a bag of gourmet coffee. I recognized the store's gold sticker. They imported it special, mixed the blend themselves, ground it right in front of you. Real class.

"Harry," she said, pouring water into the coffee maker, "how come you're here?"

My heart made a big thump inside my chest. I shut my eyes, tried to get centered, get ready.

"Rachel, we have to talk," I said.

She turned to me, fidgeted with a couple of coffee mugs, sugar, milk pitcher. "About what?"

"I found out how Conrad was killed." She stopped cold, her eyes meeting mine for a split second, then turning away again.

"We know how Conrad was killed, don't we?"

"That's not what I meant. I meant how he came to be killed."

"Really? Who killed my husband?" she asked. "If you know who killed him, you should tell me." Her voice was soft, almost far away. But a deep red color rose in her cheeks.

"The way I see it, whoever killed Conrad was paid to do

it. A contract job. Paid by somebody who knew their way around the hospital, knew pharmaceuticals. Somebody with medical training. Somebody who could get into a hospital, steal what was needed, then make sure the hired killer did it right.''

She laughed, a short, nervous snicker. ''Well, that narrows it down. Only about a thousand suspects.''

''It does, Rachel. It narrows it down a lot.''

''So who was it?''

''The only person I can find who not only had the knowledge and the opportunity, but the motive. Homicide 101, Rachel. I should have figured it out sooner. The first thing you ask is 'Who benefits?' ''

She looked up from the counter. The color that rose so quickly in her face had drained away just as fast, leaving her skin a perfect, almost translucent alabaster.

''There's only one person who benefits,'' I whispered. ''You.''

Nothing showed in her face, no reaction, no flicker of reflex or fear. Her eyes were steady, calm.

''Harry, you've been watching too much television.''

''It would have been easy for you to steal the protocurarine. It wasn't a class narcotic, would have been accessible for somebody who fit in at the hospital.''

''Harry,'' she laughed, ''I didn't even work there.''

''But you spent time there. Your husband worked there. You put him through med school. You're a nurse. You knew how the system worked. There are hundreds of nurses in that facility every day. You put on the uniform, blend right in with them. You just went where you wanted. Who was going to stop you?''

''You're crazy,'' she said quietly after a long moment.

''I even know how he was put down without a mark on him. I know about the stun gun,'' I said. I reached over, unzipped the pack, turned it upside down and poured all her belongings onto the kitchen table.

Her eyes darkened. ''No marks,'' I continued. ''No permanent damage. When he was lying on the bed helpless, the killer shot him full right through his pants leg."

"Harry, I –"

"Did you imagine you heard his breathing after that?" I demanded. "Could you hear his death rattle inside you? I did, Rachel. I felt him die under me."

Her eyes reddened, filled with tears. "I don't know why you're doing this to me."

"Am I wrong, Rachel? If I am, show me how."

"You are wrong! Why would I want him killed? I loved him!" she yelled.

"I know about the money, Rachel. I know how far in debt you were. I know how close to collapse you were." I paused a moment, steadying myself against the back of a chair. "And I know about the insurance. You're a wealthy woman, Rachel. If you get away with it."

She stared at me silently, her face a blank. We stood there like that for what seemed like a long time.

"How much did it cost you, Rachel? Where'd you find the guy? I'm glad, for some reason, that you couldn't do it yourself."

"I didn't kill him, Harry. And I didn't pay to have him killed."

"How long," I asked, "have you been seeing Walter Quinlan?"

For the first time, I saw real fear in her face. She seemed to sway on her feet, as if her knees were about to give way.

"I don't feel well," she said. "I need to sit down."

I stood aside, pulled out a chair for her. She came around the counter, slumped in the chair with her arms on the table. I crossed around to the other side of the table and sat opposite her. The stun gun lay between us. She looked at it, then quickly at me.

"Dogs, Harry. I run. I've been attacked by dogs."

"And you saw what it could do, didn't you?"

"You're twisting things," she cried. "These are horrible accusations!"

"Does Walter know about this, about how you had Conrad killed?"

"I didn't kill him!"

"Tell me, Rachel," I said. It was time to play my last card. "The morning after Conrad was murdered, I came over to see you. Remember?"

"Yes."

"You ran up to me in the kitchen, when Mrs. Goddard was here and the police were in the den. And the first thing you said was that you'd heard I got hit. You said that before you even saw the back of my head."

"Well, yes, I know, I—"

"How did you know I got hit, Rachel?"

"Well," she stammered, "I—I, the police told me. The police told me when they questioned me."

"No, Rachel. The cops wouldn't tell you anything like that. And they didn't. I checked. The only way you could know I got hit on the back of the head was if you were there, or if somebody who was there told you about it."

She had this shocked look on her face, as if I'd grabbed the stun gun and jammed it into her. She stared through me, about a mile off, her mouth cracked barely open.

"Jesus," she whispered.

"Rachel," I said, my arms on the table toward her. I reached over, took one of her hands in mine. "I want to help you. We can help you. This doesn't have to be the end of everything."

"You don't know what you're saying," she said, her voice faint. "I asked you to let it go. Why didn't you let it go, Harry?"

"Rachel, I called Walter. He's a good lawyer, the best. He'll help you. I'll help you. We both care about you."

Her eyes shot open. She jerked her hand away from me. "You did what?"

"He's on his way here, Rachel. He'll want to help you."

She jumped up from the chair. "You fool," she screamed. "You idiot!"

I stood up, confused. "What the hell are you talking about? I only want to help you."

She stepped quickly up to me, got right in my face, yelling so loud spit flew. "Oh, you've helped all right! You damned fool, you've ruined everything!"

"Rachel," I said, as soothingly as I could, "please . . ."

Her eyes welled up; tears began to run down her cheeks. "Why couldn't you just leave it alone," she sobbed. "Why didn't you do what I asked?"

She hid her face in the palms of her hands. Her shoulders heaved. Something in me melted; I couldn't help it. I took two steps and wrapped my arms around her, pulling her tightly to me. Her breath came in ragged gulps, her body shaking as if she were freezing to death.

The kitchen door opened, and Walter Quinlan stepped in. He was wearing a starched white shirt, gray suit, and carried an expensive leather briefcase. His hair was swept back neatly. He was lawyer to the core of his soul. Good thing, too. Rachel would need the best.

"Walter," I said. "Hey, man, thanks for coming."

Rachel stiffened; the shaking stopped, every muscle in her slim body seemed to lock up. She pushed away from me, turned toward him and stared.

"Well, well, well," Walter said. "Harry and Rachel. How nice to see you guys again. Hope I didn't interrupt anything."

"Walt, this isn't some kind of relationship confrontation," I said. "We've got some serious problems here."

He smiled, but it was more of a contemptuous sneer than anything funny. "Oh, yeah, I'd say we got problems all right. Enormous problems."

Rachel turned to me, fear in her eyes. "Harry, I—" she hesitated. "I'm so sorry."

Walter set his briefcase down on the counter. He fiddled with the catches, the lid of the case rising toward us.

"You don't understand," Rachel said. "I didn't pay anyone to kill Conrad." Her voice was barely a whisper, the color completely gone from her face. There were dark circles under her eyes, as if a fatigue beyond measure had settled on her.

"I didn't have to." She turned, stared at Walter.

"Oh, for chrissakes, Rachel, you really need help," I said, shocked. "You can't really believe anybody's going to believe that. Walter's an attorn—"

I turned. As Walter shut the lid of the briefcase with his left hand, I saw in his right hand a pistol.

And again, in one of those senseless, idiotic sparks that run rampant through human brain cells in the middle of catastrophe, I thought: *Hmmm, looks to be about a 9 millimeter. Nope, I ain't gonna mess with that.*

I stared at him. My jaw cracked open this time.

"Does this mean no more racquetball?"

Walter smiled. "You always were an asshole, Harry."

This ain't real, I thought. This isn't happening.

His smile disappeared. "This wasn't my fault, Harry. She talked me into it."

"You, Walter?" I was still dazed by it all. It was the one option I hadn't considered.

"It was her idea, damn it! She put it together."

I looked at Rachel. She stared at Walter with an expression I'd never seen before. An expression of pure, distilled fear.

"We'd been having an affair for about a year," he continued. "She was going to divorce him after I made partner. Big bucks in being partner."

"Then you didn't make partner," I said.

He moved his eyes from her to me. "Yeah, that's right, Harry. I didn't make partner. Rachel and Conrad were falling apart, the marriage dead. In debt up to their eyeballs. The money almost gone. I'm in deep, too, man. Don't you see? This was the way out. For both of us."

He motioned with the gun, his hand shaken by a quick tremor. "Both of you, sit down. Now."

I looked at Rachel. Her eyes bulged in terror. She backed into a chair, then sat without taking her eyes off him. I came around the other side of the table, sat as well.

The pistol looked small in his hand, the way it must have

looked to Mr. Kennedy. It was the last thing Mr. Kennedy saw in this life; I didn't want to have the same experience.

"Why'd you do Mr. Kennedy?"

"Who?"

"The black guy in the Lincoln, the one who worked for Bubba Hayes."

"Hell, I'd forgotten his name. I knew he was following you. I didn't know what he knew. But then he started following me as well. Not all the time, but enough to make me think he knew more than I wanted him to. Then I caught him parked out in front of Rachel's house one night when I was coming out. I knew he had to go."

I shook my head slowly. He hadn't even remembered the man's name. "Jesus, Walt. Did you have to kill him?"

"He was getting too close, damn it!" he yelled, his hair falling down on his forehead. "He brought it on himself!"

He reached up, loosened his tie with his one free hand, the pistol pointed at us the whole time. He was sweating now, perspiration dripping down his face. All I could think of was that I didn't want to die sitting at some goddamn kitchen table.

"Why me?" I asked. "Why'd you bring me into it?"

Walt grinned, but it was a painful grin, his lips pulled back like a dog baring his teeth. "That was Rachel's idea, too. When I told her you'd lost your job at the paper and had become a detective, we both got a good laugh out of it."

Pained, I looked over at Rachel. She turned my way, but couldn't bear to look at me.

"You were our backup," Walter said. "We figured the cops would never suspect Rachel if she had the alibi and also hired a P.I. We never figured you'd be smart enough to figure this out. Kinda broke a few patterns on us, buddy."

I looked at Walter, his face glistening, tight, and I realized at that moment how much he hated me. For whatever reason and from whatever source, Walter Quinlan hated me. I'd never seen it; even now, didn't understand it.

"I didn't break any patterns, Walt. I didn't figure anything out. I just thought I had. Actually, I've been blind to a lot."

"I'm sorry, Harry," Rachel said.

I looked at her. Her face had a look of resignation, as if she no longer had the energy to be afraid, or to even care.

"Me, too," I said quietly.

"Isn't this touching?" Walter sneered.

"What happens now?" I asked.

"Well, we can't leave things the way they are, can we?" His voice was cold, the voice of a stone killer. "No, we can't do that at all. Let me see . . . Harry finds out you killed Connie. Confronts you with it. Maybe he's blackmailing you. Yes, I like that. And so will the newspapers. You kill him. Then, in a fit of hysteria or guilt, you take your own life.

"Star-crossed lovers to the end. Oh, yes, the papers will love it."

Rachel gasped. "No, Walter—"

"He's right, Rachel. It has to be this way, doesn't it? It's the only way."

He smiled at me again, a little softer now. "I'm glad you understand. Stand up, you two. We need to go back to the bedroom."

He motioned with the gun. I stood up, glancing out of the corner of my eye at the mess spilled out onto the kitchen table from Rachel's fanny pack. Lying in the pile of tissues, gum, keys, and a couple of wads of paper, was the stun gun.

If I could just get to it.

I tried not to stare at it, hoping with every breath that he wouldn't see it. If I could only get to it . . .

I slid my arm over the table as I stood up, scooping the stun gun up into my right coat sleeve. All I had to do now was get close to him. My chest felt heavy, my heart thumping away helplessly.

Rachel sat there, frozen. The lines in her face were suddenly deeper, her eyes popping.

"You're serious," she whispered.

"Stand up," he ordered. "Now."

Then I heard it. Far away, at first, but louder by the second.

"What's that?" I asked.

"What's what?" he demanded.

"That. Listen."

We stood silent for just a moment. "What is it?" Rachel asked, looking at me. Maybe it was luck, maybe it was co-incidence. Maybe it was deus-ex-freaking-machina. Whatever, I was going to play it for all it was worth.

"Sirens," I said. "Hear?"

The unmistakable high-pitched whooping grew even louder.

"You call the cops, Walter?" I asked, mustering as much calm as I could.

"Shut up, damn you! Move, upstairs!"

"It won't work, Walter. They're coming. I don't know who did it, but they're coming."

"My God," Rachel said.

"Move!" Walter yelled. He came around the counter, was barely a foot away from me. I turned, my back to him, Rachel just beyond me facing the hallway. I uncupped my hand; the stun gun slid into my palm. I took a step, then dropped and spun, my hand on the button. I jumped for him.

Something hit the back of my head and exploded in searing heat and pain. Thought: oh, hell, so this is what a bullet feels like. Only it wasn't a bullet. It was the butt of the gun.

I felt the stun gun go into his gut, my finger mashing the button so hard it hurt. He screamed, jerked. I felt his arm slam down on my shoulder.

Then next to my left ear, the gun went off. It was a bellowing, sharp, excruciating crack, followed only by the echoing silence of a battered eardrum. I felt him go limp on me, then fall.

I was dizzy, nauseous, lying on top of Walter the same way I'd fallen on top of Conrad. I hyperventilated, my heart in my chest, my breath shallow, short, rapid gasps. I reached up and took the pistol out of his hand.

The sirens blared outside, but they seemed softer now that I was only hearing them out of one ear. Tires screeched from just beyond the living room behind us.

I struggled to get up, but I was dazed, the nerves in my legs a light year away from my brain. I couldn't move very fast. Nothing worked. There was a ringing in my head.

I tried to speak, but nothing came out.

I rolled off him, the gun in my hand. I turned. Rachel was on the floor, her back against the wall, staring at me.

A red splotch slowly widened in the middle of her shirt.

Time hung like that for what seemed an eternity, the adrenaline flooding my body breaking everything into microseconds. I tried to yell again, dropped the pistol, scooted over to her.

Her eyes were glassy, fading fast.

I took her hand. It was turning cold. She opened her mouth. I pulled her to me, my arms around her shoulder. I pulled my left hand away from behind her. It was covered in blood.

There was a long red smear on the wall.

Behind me, there was the crash of a door splintering, then the pounding of booted feet. I felt somebody behind me, then arms all over me, pulling me away from her. I fought, yelled. Nothing happened.

Rachel fell back against the wall, a gentle crimson foam filling her mouth.

Chapter 30

Somebody put one of those blue chemical ice packs on my head, over the bandage the paramedics had stuck on, then lifted my right hand to hold it in place.

"Everything you've told us jibes with what we already figured," Howard Spellman said. We were in the living room, facing each other across the coffee table as I sat on the couch. "We had credit reports, the insurance policies. We knew she had the motive. We just hadn't put it all together yet."

"I'm afraid that I just stumbled onto it," I said. "If she hadn't said something about my head getting bashed in, I'd never have figured it out."

"Well, you ever tell anybody I told you this, and I'll break both your arms," he said, "but that crack about your not being able to find your ass with both hands and an instruction manual. . . ."

"Yeah?" I twisted my head to meet his eyes. The ice pack slipped painfully.

"That was uncalled for."

Lieutenant Howard Spellman was being halfway nice to me. Go figure. "No problem. Forget it. By the way," I said, scooting around to face him, "how'd you guys get here, anyway?"

"Damndest thing," he answered. "We had a call on the police band. Officer down at this address. The uniforms that pulled up heard the shot from in here. You're lucky they didn't blow you away."

"Yeah, I've always been lucky that way."

"Is that all you want in your statement?" he asked.

"That's it, Lieutenant. That's everything."

"I'll have this typed up. You come downtown later, review it, sign it. Okay?"

"Sure, I'll come right down."

"Not immediately," a feminine voice said. I looked up. Marsha Helms was at the end of the couch. "I think he's going to need stitches this time."

"Great," I said. "Another trip to the emergency room."

Spellman stood up, walked back into the kitchen. Marsha and I were alone in Rachel's living room now.

"You're lucky, you know that?" she asked, matter-of-factly. "The Glock was loaded with Glasers. Hollow core round with shot suspended in liquid Teflon. Ninety-seven percent kill rate. The round doesn't kill you, the liquid Teflon poisons you."

I looked up at her. Her hair was pulled back professionally, cleanly, her shoulders square, her dress severe. She was a pro, doing her job. She arrived right after the police tore down the door, had done the forensics and filled out the death certificate with a coldness that was simultaneously attractive and repulsive.

"I think I've said this before, but you're amazing."

"So I've been told. Anyway, worked out better for the victim. She was history before she hit the floor. Went quick, no suffering. The slug—"

"Marsh, darling. I don't want to hear it."

She sat on the couch next to me. "So now it's Marsh darling."

I stared at her. "Yeah. That okay?"

She reached over, laid her hand on my forearm. Her touch was soft, sweet. "How deep were you in?"

"Deep enough," I said. "But not enough to drown."

I heard a ringing, but unlike the ringing that had been in my head, this sounded real. Then it stopped. A moment later, Spellman peeked around the door.

"Anybody know you're here?"

"No, why?"

"Well, Mr. Hot Shot Private Eye, you got a phone call."

I laid the ice pack on the coffee table. Confused, I stood up slowly, crossed the room to a cordless phone on a bookshelf. I picked it up, pulled out the antenna, flicked it on.

"Yeah?"

"It was the lawyer, wasn't it?" The line was full of static, like a car phone.

"Lonnie," I said. "How'd you know?"

"Hope you don't mind my keeping an eye on you. I figured somebody better watch your scrawny ass. You didn't seem to be doing a very good job at it."

"So it was you who—"

"Hey, you want a cop, you either yell 'Officer Down' or you go to a doughnut shop."

"You're something else, buddy."

"Just keep it quiet, okay? Civilians aren't supposed to have police radios in their pickups."

"You got it, man. Anything you say. And yes, it was the lawyer."

"He the one that bought it? I heard over the radio you had one down."

"No, he shot her."

"Rough duty, man. You going to be okay?"

I looked over at Marsha. She was sitting on the couch still, looking at me intently. "Yeah, I'll be fine. Just need a little time."

"That's one thing you've got," he said. "Call me later." There was a scratchy click as he hung up.

I hung up on my end, then looked out the front window across the wide expanse of lawn, the gathered neighbors, the driveway crowded with squad cars and paramedic vans. Beyond them, on the street, a single black pickup with tinted windows drove slowly by toward Hillsboro Road.

I felt heavy, like lead. Exhausted beyond feeling.

Marsha came up behind me, put her hand on my shoulder. "C'mon, we better get you over to General. Get you sewed up. I'll give you a ride. You shouldn't be driving."

Something inside me wanted to break, but I didn't have

the energy. Numb everywhere. I walked past her, out into the hall and into the kitchen. The pictures had been taken, the sketches drawn, the preliminaries near conclusion. Rachel was on a gurney now, zipped into a bright orange body bag. Two hefty paramedics picked up the gurney and maneuvered it slowly out of the kitchen. I followed with Marsha behind me. She rubbed the tips of her fingers up and down the small of my back.

We walked out into the driveway just as a uniformed Metro shut the door to his cruiser with Walter in back. He was staring straight ahead, stone cold.

"Sad, isn't it?" Marsha said.

"Yeah."

"Look at it this way, though," she said brightly. "You've solved your first big case."

I looked at her. Talk about skewed perspective. "Yeah," I said. "Nothing like getting what you want, is there?"

We walked down the driveway toward the black Porsche. The end was sticking out, and I almost laughed out loud at the DED FLKS plate.

"I'm not going to bleed all over your car, am I?"

She stopped, looked at the top of my head without having to stand on tiptoe.

"I've got some tissues in the car. It's only oozing now. You'll be okay."

"Say," I said, as we walked toward the car, "you ever take on live patients?"

She turned to me. "Gee, I don't know. It's been awhile. Maybe I'm out of practice."

"I'm awful sore," I said. "I could use a little TLC."

"Well, I had a course in physical therapy back in med school. Let me do a little reviewing. Then we can talk about it later."

"Maybe over dinner," I suggested. "Real soon."

"Yeah," she said, walking straight ahead without looking at me. "I'd like that."

"One thing, though."

"Yeah?"

"I don't know about this rigor mortis stuff."

She stopped, looked at me funny, questioning.

"You know," I said, "the all-over . . ."

Marsha went blank for a moment, then a gorgeous grin spread across her face, and I felt alive again. She broke out laughing. Heads around us turned.

"Well, we'll just have to see what we can do about that."

"Dr. Helms," I said, holding the driver's door of the Porsche open for her, "I'm in your hands."

TORCH TOWN BOOGIE

by Steven Womack

NOMINATED FOR THE SHAMUS AWARD

A magnificent mansion in the funky part of
town is torched, and though it looks like a
typical arson case, this time someone has
been murdered. The bludgeoned victim
was a well-known psychotherapist and the
fiancé of Harry's ex-wife, Lanie. Lanie's
fingered as the suspect thanks to her
beloved's generous will in her favor. So
Harry must match wits with the firebug
before Lanie's life goes up in flames.

From Edgar Award winner

Steven Womack

come the further adventures

of Nashville private eye

Harry James Denton in

WAY PAST
DEAD

Denton has his hands full tracking down
the killer of a sexy singer-songwriter. Then
Dr. Marsha Helms, his girlfriend, is taken
hostage by the Pentecostal Evangelical
Enochians, a radical fringe cult. The mean
streets of Music City, U.S.A. are about to
explode in Harry James Denton's face.

Coming soon to your local bookstore.

Published by Ballantine Books.

CHAIN OF FOOLS

by Steven Womack

Harry James Denton is no fool. But his search for a rich runaway teen, Stacey Jameson, takes him to the seamy and very wild side of Nashville. "Nobody's chain lays straight," a friend tells Harry. But Stacey's is especially twisted, with links that lead back to a family filled with secrets. Even a hardboiled P.I. like Harry isn't prepared for what awaits him in the depths of hard-core hell, where only he can save a lost girl before she destroys herself—or lets a ruthless murderer do it for her.